Long Road Home

T0351974

ALSO BY MARIE MEYER

The Turning Point
Can't Go Back
Across the Distance
Live Out Loud

Long Road Home

MARIE MEYER

New York   Boston

Copyright © 2017 by Marie Meyer
Excerpt of *Across the Distance* copyright © 2015 by Marie Meyer
Cover design by Elizabeth Turner
Cover copyright © 2017 by Hachette Book Group, Inc.
Hachette Book Group supports the right to free expression and the value of copyright. The purpose of copyright is to encourage writers and artists to produce the creative works that enrich our culture.

The scanning, uploading, and distribution of this book without permission is a theft of the author's intellectual property. If you would like permission to use material from the book (other than for review purposes), please contact permissions@hbgusa.com. Thank you for your support of the author's rights.

Forever Yours
Hachette Book Group
1290 Avenue of the Americas
New York, NY 10104
forever-romance.com
twitter.com/foreverromance

First ebook and print on demand edition: March 2017

Forever Yours is an imprint of Grand Central Publishing. The Forever Yours name and logo are trademarks of Hachette Book Group, Inc.

The publisher is not responsible for websites (or their content) that are not owned by the publisher.

The Hachette Speakers Bureau provides a wide range of authors for speaking events. To find out more, go to www.hachettespeakersbureau.com or call (866) 376-6591.

ISBN 978-1-4555-4272-7 (ebook edition)
ISBN 978-1-4555-4276-5 (print on demand edition)

For mothers. For daughters. You're stronger than you know. Embrace your strength.

Long Road Home

CHAPTER ONE

REN

I swing my hip into the door, my hands overtaken by the giant garment bag containing the maid-of-honor dress my best friend chose for me. A bell sounds as I exit the bridal shop. Stepping onto the sidewalk, the warm breeze of an early June morning ruffles the plastic slung over my forearm. I speed-walk to my car, having exactly twenty-eight minutes to get to work. I am so late. There's no way in hell a final fitting should have taken forty minutes. I love Dylen, but being her maid of honor is beginning to fuck with my life.

Digging my keys from my purse, I slide my thumb over the unlock button, and my car's headlights wink in response. I yank the door open and snap the seat forward. Groping the interior wall of the car, my fingers brush over the plastic hook, and I tug it down, simultaneously losing the grip on my keys. They fall with a *thunk* onto the sidewalk.

"Shit! I don't have time for this!" I cram the dress into the car, prop the hanger on the hook, and take a step backward.

Bending over, I scoop the keys off the concrete just in time to hear a catcall. *Really?*

Standing, I whirl around. Two men in well-tailored suits, a few paces up the sidewalk, look over their shoulders and grin at me.

"Looking good, nursey. Loving the SpongeBob scrubs," the shorter one says—probably the same one that let out the disgusting whistle. "I'd like to visit your Bikini Bottom." The taller guy laughs and congratulates his buddy with a jab to the shoulder.

What morons.

Shaking my head, I give them the one-finger salute and round the car. "Oh, that's original," I shout, climbing into my car. If I wasn't already so late, I would have thought of a better comeback, but then again, they aren't worth my time. "Dicks," I growl under my breath. With my mood in the toilet, I start the car and ease out of the parking space.

Traffic is light through town, and thankfully, the interstate isn't backed up—an advantage to being late, I guess.

With the road wide open, I press my foot onto the accelerator and don't let up. The speedometer inches its way toward seventy and doesn't stop.

Cranking the volume on the radio, I let the sweet, sad lyrics of Tim McGraw and Taylor Swift's newest collaboration rid me of my lingering irritation at the male gender, and I fly down the freeway.

I tap out the beat of the song on the steering wheel, and with the next line on the tip of my tongue, I swallow the words as my eyes are drawn to the rearview mirror.

Red and blue flashing lights.

I glance at my speedometer and back off the gas pedal. I'm not going *that* fast. My heart drops into the acidic pit of my stomach. "You've got to be fucking kidding me," I groan, guiding my car to the shoulder. *Maybe if I just get out of the way, he'll go around me?*

No such luck.

The cruiser slows to a halt several feet behind my car. *Could this day get any worse?* I did not have time for this. I close my eyes, take a few deep breaths, and try to slow my racing pulse. Eight years of being a licensed driver with a spotless record are about to go down the drain.

With a sigh, I turn off the radio, and reach for my glove box. I withdraw my registration, and then go for my purse, tugging my license from my wallet, anything to speed along the process. However, glancing in my rearview, I can tell the police officer has designs to make this take as long as possible. What the hell is he doing? Why is he just sitting in his cruiser?

For three long minutes, I sit and stare at the road, watching car after car happily speed toward their destination, before I hear a tap on my passenger-side window.

Startled by his sudden appearance, my heart jumps into my throat. "Oh, goodness!" I choke, my hands flying to my chest.

Shaking, I press the button and the window lowers.

"Good day, ma'am." He nods, removing his sunglasses.

Hello, Green Eyes.

He's young. My age at least. And hot. Doughnuts aren't one of his staple foods. *Maybe being pulled over isn't so bad after all.* "Hi," I stutter. How I stumble on a one-syllable word, I don't know, but I did nonetheless.

"In a hurry?" he asks in a deep, authoritative voice.

"I'm sorry, Officer, I didn't think I was—"

"I clocked you at seventy-six," he says, cutting me off. He stares unblinkingly, like he's daring me to argue with his assessment.

"That's only eleven miles over," I say, pleading my case.

"Exactly, 'over' being the applicative word. The speed limit isn't a suggestion, miss." He cocks his head and brings his hand up, fingers wagging impatiently. "License and registration."

I pass the items over, and he clutches them between his giant thumb and forefinger.

He stands up to his full height, and I have to slouch in my seat to see him out the window. He squints his eyes in the sunlight, reading the information on my vehicle registration card. While he looks over my identification, my eyes fall to his nametag: C. Sinclair. I wonder what the "C" stands for. Am I allowed to ask? I try different names... *Chris Sinclair? Cameron? Calvin?*

My lips pull up at the corners. The only Calvin I know of is the one in the *Calvin and Hobbes* comics I read as a kid. This guy doesn't look like a Calvin to me.

Officer Sinclair taps my license on the window frame and bends low to peer into my car. I shoot up in my seat, trying to conceal the smile on my face. I wouldn't want him to think I thought this situation was funny. That might get me into more trouble. And there was no way I can tell him I was checking him out. Judging by his no-nonsense attitude, he would have no tolerance for that. "I'll be right back, Ms. Daniels," he grumbles, sounding irritated.

I watch him walk back to his car, his ass looking fine in my rearview. He may be Officer No Nonsense, but he is fun to look at.

Damn, look at his arms! I'd like to pin him to my Pinterest "arm porn" board. I can't help it, I gawk, unapologetically. Jesus, their circumference is larger than my head's. He's so freaking hot.

I pull my eyes from the rearview and scoop my phone off the passenger seat and type out a text to the charge nurse, letting her know why I'm so late.

My eyes flick from the rearview mirror to my dashboard clock. *What is he doing?* It's not like I have any outstanding warrants, or anything. I've never had so much as a parking ticket. Yet, he sits in his cruiser, typing away on his dashboard computer.

Five minutes later, he reappears at my window. "Okay, Ms. Daniels, we're about finished." With a flick of his wrist, he tosses back the cover of a small, thick book and begins scratching his pen across the paper. "I need a signature right here." He taps the paper with the pen, where he wants me to sign. Flipping the pad around, he holds it through the window.

Leaning over the passenger seat, I take the pen and scribble my name next to the "X" he's drawn. "There," I say, handing his pen back.

Without a word, he snatches it and rips the yellow paper off the top of the pad. "Slow down, Ms. Daniels." He holds the ticket between his big fingers, waiting for me to take it.

I mourn the death of my perfect driving record. Scowling, I pluck the ticket from his hand and look up at him.

He pierces me with his green eyes, but still no congenial smile. No hint of humor in his demeanor. Zero bedside manner; it's a good thing he isn't a doctor. But, he's got the badass cop thing going for him.

"Thanks," I whisper, embarrassed that I got caught breaking the law.

Officer Sinclair steps away from my car but doesn't make a move to return to his cruiser. I put up the window, toss the ticket and my forms of identification onto the passenger seat, and then put the car in drive.

Remembering excerpts from *Rules of the Road*, I turn off my hazards and signal, waiting for the opportune moment to merge back onto the interstate. Each move I make, I feel Officer Sinclair's scrutinizing gaze, watching me...evaluating me. *Why is he just standing there? Back to your car, mister, nothing to see here. I'm a law-abiding citizen.*

Once I'm on the road, picking up speed—but careful not to exceed sixty-five—I sneak a peek in my rearview. He has his door open and is climbing inside.

I fumble with the settings on the cruise control and take my foot off the accelerator. At least this way, I won't run the risk of my heavy foot getting me into trouble again.

In my haste to get away from Officer Sinclair, I neglected to look at the ticket. How much do I owe the lovely state of Missouri for my disobedience?

Picking up the small, unassuming paper from the seat, I scan my eyes over the scribbled writing, looking for a dollar sign. Then I see it: $108.00.

One hundred and eight dollars? For eleven miles over? That's highway robbery. Literally! *Shit!* After shelling out a hundred and fifty bucks for my maid-of-honor dress, and footing the bill for Dylen's bachelorette party tonight, I'm flat broke. Looks like I'll be checking into a Starbucks rehabilitation program and breaking out the Folgers.

Great. The perfect beginning to a twelve-hour shift.

CHAPTER TWO

Cayden

Leaving the station, I pull my phone from my back pocket and fire off a text to Bull. *Still heading to the Whiskey House?*

It's been almost a year since I've meet up with the guys from my former squad. It'll be nice to see those jackasses. I can't believe they're deploying in a month, and I won't be with them this time.

Shaking my head in disbelief, I unlock my Ford F-150, toss my gym bag across the seat, and slide behind the wheel. Pulling the door closed, my phone beeps. I glance down at the incoming message. *Hells yeah. See ya in a few.*

I could use a bourbon. Every person I pulled over today was a prick. The day I get promoted to SWAT cannot come soon enough. Nothing pisses me off more than when people try to argue their way out of ticket they've earned, and today was no exception, save one. There was that woman I pulled over.

What was her name? I put the key in the ignition and turn over the engine. The truck rumbles to life as my brain picks through names that aren't quite right. *Remmy? Renee?* I shake my head. No, that's not it.

Renata?

"Renata." I try the name out on my tongue. Yeah. That's right.

I remember now. Those dark eyes of hers…damn sexy. I haven't been able to get her face out of my head since she crossed my path this morning.

It's not like I wanted to give her a ticket, but I have to set a precedent at the station: that I'm not willing to compromise the law for any reason. I want that damn promotion.

Too bad though, it would have been nice to send her off with a warning. Thank God she didn't get the waterworks going, I wouldn't have been able to go through with it. Yet, a part of me enjoyed giving her that ticket. Getting her riled up, under her skin. I could tell she was pissed…the flush in her cheeks, the sass in her voice…shit, she was hot.

A block from my apartment, my phone beeps again. I steal a quick glance at the passenger seat, searching the illuminated screen to see who's texting me. When my eyes catch sight of *Mom* my heart kicks into second gear. She had another round of chemo today. Something's wrong.

I press my foot down on the accelerator, ignoring the speed limit. I refuse to text and drive, so speeding is the lesser of two evils. I need to get home…I need to make sure she's all right.

My phone beeps again, knowing that I ignored it the first time.

Pulling into my driveway faster than I intend, my tires screech. I kill the engine, grab my phone off the seat, and punch in my passcode, opening Mom's message. *Call me please. Urgent.*

Thinking the worst, I find her name in my contacts and wait for the call to connect.

Ring….ring…ring…

"Come on, Mom. Pick up." I tap out a nervous beat on the steering wheel as I listen to more ringing.

I wait another thirty seconds and her voicemail kicks on.

I cease tapping and ball my hand into a fist, slamming it down in frustration. "Dammit, Mom! Answer the phone."

Wasting no time, I redial.

Ring…ring…ring…ring…

"Hello?" she croaks.

"Mom"—relief floods my body at the sound of her voice—"what's wrong?"

"Cayden," she whispers. I can sense a similar relief in her voice, now that she's gotten ahold of me.

"You okay?"

"Cayden," she repeats, breathing heavily. I know she's trying to muster the strength to finish her sentence, so I give her time, careful not to interrupt. Chemo treatments kick her ass. "I'm sorry, hon'. I need…help…tonight," she wheezes.

I squeeze my fist tighter, hating the cancer that's fucking with her life. Two years ago, it took my dad away from us, and now it's doing a damn fine job of sending my mom down the same path.

I refuse to lose another parent to cancer. I won't let her give up. "I'll be there right away."

"I'm sorry, Cayden."

It breaks my heart hearing her sound so weak. My mom is the strongest woman I know. She ran marathons, competed in decathlons, hiked some of the most difficult mountains; she's always taken care of herself. She doesn't deserve what's happening to her.

"Mom, you don't need to apologize. I told you that I would help you fight this." I've never backed down from a war. I promised my dad that I would take care of his Katy. Mom is the reason I'm not leading my squad back into the desert. She needs me here, helping her wage the battle for her life. Fucking cancer will not win this war...not against Katherine Sinclair.

She coughs. "Thank you, Cayden."

"I'm on my way, Mom. Get some rest."

"Okay. Thanks."

The line goes quiet. I drop my head against the headrest and stare up at the truck's ceiling, letting out a long breath. I need to call Bull.

Shit.

I lift my head off the back of the seat and fumble with my phone, pulling up his name. Again, I listen to it ring.

"Big Daddy! Where the hell are you, man?" Bull answers over the background noise of the Whiskey House.

"Hey, Bull. Sorry, I'm not gonna make it."

"Man, the ass you're blowing us off for better be good," he says, laughing. I can hear Vince and Taz in the background, too.

"Nah, nothing like that. It's my mom, she had a round of chemo today and it's kicking her ass. She needs some help."

"Sorry, big guy. I didn't mean..." He trails off. I can hear the apology in his tone.

"Forget about it. No worries. When do you guys leave for the sandbox?"

"The twentieth." The serious, all-business Marine replaces the joking, good-natured Bull.

"I will make it point to see you guys before you leave, you have my word." I run a hand over my fresh military cut, the stubble scratching against my palm.

"I know, man. Now, go take care of your mom, she needs you."

"Thanks. Tell Vin and Taz I'm sorry."

"Will do."

I silently pound my fist against the steering wheel. "Later, man."

"Yeah, see ya."

Pulling the phone away from my ear, I disconnect the call, and bury the disappointment of not seeing my boys tonight. I've got to stay focused on Mom, she's my priority now.

I grab my bag, swing open the door, and climb down. I make quick work of unlocking my house and jog down the hall to my bedroom.

Unpacking my gym back, I pull out my holster and unlatch my revolver, pulling the lockbox from my bottom drawer. I don't take any chances when it comes to my firearm; when it's not with me, it's locked away. Working in the city, I've seen one too many accidental shootings. Most of them involving kids. Those are the worst calls.

Placing the sealed box back into the drawer, I pull out a pair of mesh basketball shorts and a Green Bay Packers T-shirt. I strip out of my gym clothes, slide on the shorts and T-shirt, slip on a pair of athletic sandals, and grab my wallet and keys from my pants pocket before I'm heading back down the stairs and out the door.

* * *

I knock on Mom's door and give her two or three seconds to answer before I'm fingering through the keys on my key ring. Unlocking the door, I push it open. "Mom?" I call. The house is quiet and dark. I step inside and close the door, saying her name again, louder this time. "Mom."

"Cayden?"

My name, weak and garbled, floats from somewhere upstairs.

Hitting the stairs, I go in search of her. Usually, after a chemo day she likes resting on couch in the living room, but tonight, she must have moved back to her room.

I give a few taps on the door and push it open. Following the muffled groans into the master bathroom, Mom's kneeling beside the toilet. I rush to her, scooping her sparse, shoulder length salt-and-pepper hair into a ponytail at the nape of her neck. "Aw, Mom, why didn't Lacey stay with you until I got here?"

Lacey Andrews, Mom's neighbor and best friend. When I can't take Mom to her chemo appointments, Lacey steps up. Having been neighbors for so many years, they've been through a lot together, from raising kids to losing their husbands around the same time. I know it's killing Lacey seeing Mom like this, but her friendship, and the fact that she's willing to help out when I can't, keeps Mom fighting. Mom, more than anything, doesn't want to let Lacey or me down. That's why she puts up such a good fight.

"Lace had to get home; Parker was coming over with the baby."

I twist her hair at the nape of her neck, so that it will stay put while I go in search of a washcloth. As I stand, a large clump of Mom's hair remains in my hand. Cancer, a weapon of mass destruction. And there's fuck all I can do against this enemy. "How long ago did she leave?" I ask, wrapping Mom's hair in a tissue and tossing it into the waste can.

"Not too long," she answers weakly.

Pulling open the closet beside the vanity, I grab a washcloth and run it under the cold water. Once it's thoroughly soaked, I ring it out and crouch down beside her, dabbing, wiping away beads of sweat on her forehead and cheeks. She leans into the washcloth, the hint of a smile at her lips. "Thank you," she mutters.

"Any time." I smile back and toss the washcloth into the sink, hook-shot style. "Here"—I put my arms at her waist—"let's get you into bed."

With a labored grunt, she braces herself against my arms and lifts her tired body off the bathroom floor.

"Why don't you let me carry you?" I bend my knees, ready to sweep her into my arms, but she shakes her head.

"No, Cayd. I can walk."

I roll my eyes. She's always been so damned independent. It took both me and Lacey to convince Mom that she *would* need help once chemo started—she was positive she'd be able to drive herself to and from appointments.

Mom shuffles toward the bed, and I keep my hands at her waist, giving her something strong to cling to. Reaching for the comforter on her antique four-poster, she pulls back the cover and climbs between the sheets.

Out of breath from the short walk from the bathroom to her bed, she ekes out a feeble, "Thanks, hon." Even at her lowest, my mom has a class that sets her apart from all other women.

I nod and pull the covers up to her chin. The humongous bed swallows her. For the first time, I can see the toll cancer is taking on her body. The hell chemo is putting her through. She's sallow, her skin is pale, thin, almost see-through. The sparkle in her eyes has been replaced by dark shadows. It's the worst fucking thing in the world watching someone you love being consumed by something so evil and unforgiving.

I let out the breath I'm holding and run a hand over my buzzed head. "What can I get you? Do you need anything?"

She looks up at me, and I can't read the expression on her face. Sadness? "I know you're busy, but I need some help tonight."

Laying my hand on her bony shoulder, I nod my head. "You need me to stay, I'm here. You're not fighting this alone."

"Thanks, hon." She gives me a weak smile and closes her eyes, letting her head loll to the side.

"I'll be downstairs if you need me." I pat her shoulder and turn toward the door.

"Cayden?"

Turning, I say, "Yeah?"

"Are you going to Blake's wedding tomorrow?" If I know my mother, she's beating herself up because she can't.

Blake Thompson was like another son to my parents. He and I grew up together, our parents the best of friends. For years, Mom used to babysit him. But when Blake and I got to high school, our interests took us in different directions. I was on the football and basketball teams, Blake was on the debate team and student council, so our paths didn't cross often. We had our own sets of friends. But whenever our families got together, Blake and I would pick up our friendship right where we left off.

Now, he's a big-shot lawyer—those years on the debate team paying off—and he's marrying his college sweetheart.

"Yeah, I wouldn't miss it."

"Oh, good. I wish I could be there."

I walk back to her side and lay a reassuring hand on her arm. "He'll understand."

The corner of Mom's mouth pulls up in a legit smile this time. "Are you taking anyone special?"

Of course. That would be the question that puts a smile on her face. I almost hate that my answer will make it disappear. Almost. *Mom, an eternal romantic at heart.*

"Sorry to break it to you, but I'm going solo."

She sits up and rests her back on the headboard. "You mean, you couldn't find one nice girl to take as your date?"

Where is this burst of energy coming from? Energy enough to scold me for not dating. *That's a mother for you.*

I shrug. "I'm fine. Honestly, I don't have time for any of that stuff. I've got to dedicate every ounce of my time to work if I want that SWAT promotion."

"Don't lose yourself in work, Cayd. One day, you'll look up

and you'll be all alone. Life isn't just about moving up the work-force ladder. Some things are more important, like family."

"Yeah, I know. And I'm sure I'll find someone, one day. But not right now." As the words come out of my mouth, the girl from earlier today, Renata, floods back into my thoughts. It's been a while since a woman has gotten under my skin. Her dark chocolate eyes aren't easy to forget. Just my short inter-action with her, I could tell she has spirit. I wouldn't mind getting to know her. Too bad that won't happen.

"Don't wait too long." There's a warning in her voice, but how is that fair? Everything I'm putting on hold is for her…and my career. Besides, my job's too dangerous. I couldn't get involved with someone and have her heart broken if something happened to me.

"I'm good, Mom. All I want right now is for you to get well. Once that happens, then I'll kick my search for Mrs. Sinclair into high gear. Deal?"

She shakes her head and sighs. "I just don't want to see you alone. You're not a spring chicken anymore."

"And when did twenty-five become decrepit?"

"Lacey's youngest daughter is only twenty," she tempts. "She's really pretty, too."

Mom the matchmaker. I bend down and kiss her cheek, knowing that I'm not going to win this argument, so I might as well concede and take the loss. "'Night, Mom."

She puts her hand on my cheek. "'Night, baby."

Walking from her room, I brush my hand over the light switch and close the door.

Downstairs, I grab a blanket from the front closet and

stretch out on the couch, flipping on the TV. Lacing my fingers behind my head, I close my eyes and listen to Jimmy Fallon write thank-you notes.

As I drift off to sleep, images of Renata once again invade my consciousness, and I know I'm in for some good dreams.

CHAPTER THREE

REN

"Do you have the veil?" I shout as I lock the door.

"Got it!" Lexie calls from the end of the hall. "Oh, wait! Dylen forgot her earrings."

Spinning on my heel, I carefully lay the plastic garment bag with Dylen's dress across my forearm and fumble with my keys, unlocking the door.

Kicking it open with my foot, I bound through the living room, down the hall, and into the guest bedroom. "Where are they?" Scanning the room, I notice the diamond studs lying on the dresser. Skirting the bed, I scoop them into my hand and dash out of the room. "If she forgot anything else, she'll have to deal," I mumble, grabbing the dress on my way out.

I kick off my heels, pick them up, and shuffle down the hall hoping my hair and makeup aren't in shambles.

Outside, Dylen, Lexie, and Shae are already in the limo. Climbing in beside them, I see they've wasted no time in passing out the champagne flutes. "Time for some bubbly!" Shae says, fiddling with the top.

With the neck of the bottle pointing in Dylen's direction, Lexie reaches over and moves Shae's hand, leaving the bottle pointing to the front of the limo. Lexie winks at Shae. "Just in case. We can't arrive at the church with an unconscious bride."

"Right," Shae agrees, twisting the wire cage and freeing it from the cork. Shae keeps a tight grip on the bottle, her thumb over the cork as she pulls the wire away. Twisting and pulling down on the bottle, there's a soft *pop*, and the cork is out.

"You opened that like a pro, Shae. I would have had it spewing all over the floor," Dylen says, holding her glass out.

Pouring some champagne into Dylen's flute, Shae winks. "You can learn to do anything on YouTube."

Passing the bottle around, we fill our glasses. "To Dylen and Blake!" Lexie says. "May you have a long, happy life together."

"Oh, blah, blah, Lexie." I stick out my tongue. "We need a better toast than that." I raise my arm higher, hoping the car doesn't hit a bump and make me spill. "To amazing sex and a lifetime of orgasms."

"Oh, yeah!" my friends cheer in unison.

"I'm drinking to all of it," Dylen says, pressing the glass to her smiling lips.

* * *

I button the last pearl on the back of Dylen's dress and glance at her in the mirror. I've never seen a more gorgeous bride. "Dylen, I..." Words stick in my throat. She's been my best friend for six years. I wouldn't have gotten through college without her. And now, she's getting married. Deep down, I know she'll still be around, but everything feels so... different...like we're not kids anymore.

We stare at our reflections in the mirror, the enormity of what Dylen is about to do, hitting us like a speeding train. Dylen reaches over her shoulder, and I grab her hand. "Thanks, Ren, for always being there for me."

I glance at the ceiling, trying desperately to keep my tears from spilling over the rims of my eyelids and ruining my makeup. "Stop it! You're making me cry." I blow out a breath and step away from her, fanning my face with my hands.

I feel Dylen's hand on my shoulder. "I mean it, Ren. When my sister died, it was you that got me through."

I gather my wits, holding my tears at bay, and turn to look at her. "We got each other through that awful year." With Dylen losing her younger sister three years ago, and me having gone through my own hell—being drugged and raped at a party—we clung to each other for strength.

"But," I shout, plastering on the biggest smile I can muster. "I refuse to dwell on the sad times, especially today. Tayler loved you and she would be so, so happy for you today. She's here with you in spirit, Dyl."

This time, Dylen looks up, sniffling. "I know."

"Now, for some important business," I say with mock seriousness.

"What?" Dylen looks confused, a shadow of concern darkening her eyes.

"Something old, something new, something borrowed, and something blue." I count them off on my hands.

Dylen nods, licking her lips. "Got 'em."

"You do?" Now it's my turn to be confused. "What do you have?"

Smiling, she points to her earrings. "These were Tayler's. They're not heirloom old, but I'm counting them anyway."

"They're perfect."

"My dress is new. I borrowed this bracelet from my mom"—Dylen holds her wrist out, showing me the tiny circle of pearls—"and my blue." She touches her right side, the place where her bluebird of happiness is inked…the same place where I have a similar one.

For the two of us, the last three years have been an uphill battle, albeit for different reasons, but the idea of getting tattoos was meant to give us strength, remind us that there is happiness and beauty in the world. I once read that the bluebird symbolized the sun in ancient Chinese culture.

Since the day Dylen and I got our tattoos, I've drawn strength from the small bird on my side, knowing that I am strong, that one horrendous moment in my life doesn't define me.

I pull Dylen into another hug. Her arms are around my shoulders, squeezing me like I'm her lifeline, but really, she's mine. *What am I going to do without her?*

Tears pool in my eyes and one manages to escape. I don't want to let go of Dylen, so I sacrifice my makeup to hold on to my friend for a few more precious seconds.

Dylen sniffles and relaxes her grip, pulling away. She's crying too. "Uhhh." She stares up at the ceiling, fanning her eyes. "I can't cry yet," she says, giggling.

"Come on, Blake's waiting for his bride."

"Hey, Dyl, you planning on walking down the aisle anytime today?" Shae peeks her head around the dressing room door. "The wedding coordinator says it's time."

With a quirk of her eyebrow, she gives me a conspiratorial wink. "Let's get married."

I laugh. "Umm…I love you, Dyl, but you're not my type. You should marry the great guy waiting for you upstairs."

"Right." She nods. "Let's go."

Trailing behind Dylen, I hold the train of her dress as she climbs the stairs, entering the back of the church.

"Ladies"—a supermodel-tall blonde claps her hands—"let's line up. You're up next." She holds Lexie's elbow, guiding her to the place she wants us to gather. "Now Shae, yes…and Ren. Great job, girls," she cheers, like we're five and lining up for recess. She lays her hand on Lexie's shoulder and speaks very slowly, "Now, wait for my signal before you take off down the aisle."

I turn my head and glare at Dylen. *Is this woman for real?* I mouth.

Dylen grimaces, her teeth pressed together resembling the emoji with big, white teeth. *My mom hired her,* she mouths in return, then shrugs.

When Dylen was ten, her parent's split. Her mom moved in with the much younger guy she'd been sleeping with, while her dad moved back to his hometown in Brittany, France. For years Dylen and Tayler would spend the school year stateside with their mom and their summers in France, with their dad.

Never wanting to be outdone, Dylen's mom and dad have always been in competition with one another—who could give the girls the best things. When Tayler died, it only got worse. I guess Wedding Coordinator Barbie is Dylen's mom's latest contribution to the "I'm better than your dad" war.

I shake my head and wink, tossing Dylen an air kiss.

"Aaaaannnnd," Wedding Coordinator Barbie sings. "Go!" With a linebacker worthy nudge to the shoulder, Shae is propelled forward down the aisle, "Trumpet Voluntary" blasting from the pipe organ.

Wedding Coordinator Barbie turns to me. "Ren, you're next!"

I walk up to the church doors.

"And…go!" Barbie shouts, giving me a push.

Geez! This lady needs to lay off the 5-Hour Energy.

The organist does some finger calisthenics over the keys, the music swells and I take my place next to Shae at the altar.

The familiar strain of Mendelssohn's "Wedding March" fills the church. Dylen and her father wait at the doors for Barbie's go-ahead, and they're off. Dylen is glowing. I've never seen her smile so vibrant. Her eyes never stray from Blake.

My heart swells for Dylen, bursting with love and joy, but it's heavy, too—weighed down by awful nightmares of the past. I want very much to give my heart to someone, to fall in love and have my own happily ever after. But that would be asking too much of another person: to carry around my cumbersome heart.

CHAPTER FOUR

CAYDEN

I shoot the banana peel into the trashcan, sinking the shot like a pro. It's been too long since I've played basketball. I miss when the guys and I would get a game going on our R&R days in the sandbox. As I wipe the counters down, my mind drifts to Bull, Vince, and Taz. They're headed back.

"Shit," I mumble. "I should be going with them." I shake my head, disgusted that I can't be in two places at once. It kills me knowing that my boys are headed back to that hellhole without me and my mom is stuck here, in her own personal hell. For once, this is a situation I can't fix...a situation with no right answer, and it pisses me off.

Pivoting on my heel, I give the tray a final glance, straighten the silverware, and pick it up. There's nothing I can do for the guys, but I can make damn certain Mom has all her favorite foods: French toast with butter pecan syrup, cheesy grits, and a banana. Hopefully, this will get her to eat something, gather up some strength.

I climb the stairs, careful not to spill the açaí berry juice on the tray—I read somewhere that açaí berries are great for cancer patients. Not sure if it's true, but what harm is there? They've got to be healthy. I'm at her door in three strides. I listen for a second, praying nothing happened during the night.

Inside, the muffled sounds of the TV break through the silence, but nothing else. I knock lightly. I need to make sure she's all right, but I don't want to disturb her if she's still asleep.

"Cayden?" Her voice is weak. Is she still nauseous, or just tired?

Balancing the tray on one hand, I push the door open. "Morning, Mom." I walk into her room and am once again blown away by her tiny body swallowed up in the queen-size bed. She's lost so much weight since her treatment began—colorless skin stretched over a tiny skeleton. I truly know what the term "skin and bones" means and it breaks my heart.

"How are you feeling?" I cross the room and sit down on the edge of the bed.

Mom pulls up and rests her back against the headboard. "Better today." She smiles and pats my hand. "What is this?"

"Breakfast." I wink. "Got to get you back to fighting weight."

"Thanks, hon."

I shift the tray from my lap to hers. "I'm going to be heading out in a few. Blake's wedding."

With the knife and fork in her hand, she cuts through the French toast and snags a small bite, pulling it off the fork with her front teeth. "Oh," she sighs, her mouth full. "Maybe I should go."

"Uh-uh." I shake my head. "No way. You're staying right here. I'll give him your love; he'll understand."

Mom chews slowly and pushes her food around the plate with the fork. I can almost see the wheels turning in her head and I know what question's coming next.

"Really, you're not taking anyone? I can give Lacey a call, I'm sure Allyson would go with you," she presses one last time. "Weddings are so romantic, Cayden. I'd like grandchildren one day, you know. You shouldn't go alone."

"And that's my cue to leave." I pat Mom's leg and stand. "I'll have my phone on me. Call if you need something."

"Go"—she waves, shaking her head in disgust—"I'll be fine, dreaming about the pitter-patter of my grandbabies' feet."

I stand and point at her. "That's evil, Mom."

"It's all I can do; guilt trips don't require physical exertion." She winks.

I shake my head. She is ridiculous. "I mean it, if you need anything, call me."

She points her bony index finger at me. "Got it."

Bending, I plant a kiss on her cheek. Her skin is cold against my lips and paper-thin. Cancer's a coldhearted bitch. I stand. "'Bye. I'll check in later."

"Have fun. Tell Blake how happy I am for him and Dylen, and that I love him. Dance with all the pretty brides-maids."

"You just don't stop," I say with a chuckle. With one last

wink in Mom's direction, I walk out of her room, wondering why I agreed to go to this wedding in the first place. I hate putting on a suit. And what the hell is Mom thinking, dance with all the bridesmaids? I can't dance.

* * *

I swing the F-150 into the nearest parking space and kill the engine. With a quick glance at my watch, I have two minutes before Blake's shindig gets underway. I pull the door open and my feet hit the pavement. Taking the stairs in front of the church three at a time, I reach the heavy red doors and yank them open.

I'm greeted by a couple of bridesmaids in pink dresses and put on the brakes, careful not to run them over on my way into the sanctuary. "Ladies, pardon me." I dip my head in apology.

The taller one nods in return and the beginnings of a smile pull the corners of her lips upward. "It's okay, sugar." She unapologetically sends her gaze trailing over my body. "I'll let you make it up to me with a dance at the reception." She winks.

She's gorgeous, despite the awful pink dress she's wearing, and she's my type—dark hair, tall, and fit, with just the right amount of curves. An image of Renata Daniels sparks my memory from yesterday. Damn, now *that* woman was my type. Those come-hither dark eyes...*Jesus.* I shake my head, trying to get Renata out of my system.

"You bet...sugar." I return her endearment and her wink,

then continue my way into the church, listening to the giggles of the two women behind me.

I find a seat near the back and as soon as my ass hits the pew, the music starts. At least a hundred people turn in my direction, their eyes fixed on the aisle. One at a time, ushers escort Blake and Dylen's family members to their seats at the front. Mrs. Thompson notices me and waves as she walks down the aisle.

The music changes and the bridesmaids line up at the door. My dance partner is second in line. She's tall enough to see over her friend standing in front of her, and I watch as she scans the crowd. When she catches my eye, her smile turns from happy to sultry in a matter of seconds. Tonight might not be so bad after all.

One after the other, the pink ladies step-touch down the aisle, taking up their marks at the altar. The music shifts again, this time, to a tune I recognize, Pachelbel's *Canon in D*—a song Mom loves to play at Christmastime.

I turn my head and look to the back of the church again. Standing in the doorway, ready to walk down the aisle is a tall, slender woman, the shiny material of her pale pink–ivory dress outline the contours of her stunning body. I know her.

I pull in a deep breath, floored. The maid of honor is Renata Daniels?

Fuck me.

She glides past my pew, down the aisle, a smile that could set the world on fire brightening her face.

I cannot believe she's here…and a really close friend of Blake's bride, no doubt. It is a small fucking world.

This wedding just got a whole hell of a lot more interesting. And I hate to disappoint the other bridesmaid I already promised a dance with, but there's no way I'm letting Renata speed away from me this time.

I can't keep my eyes off her. I barely register the "Wedding March" blasting from the organ and everyone rising to their feet. I'm reluctant to take my eyes off Renata fearing she'll disappear or just end up being a figment of my imagination.

I stand, tossing a quick look at Dylen and her father making their way down the aisle. She's a lovely bride, Blake's a lucky man, but Dylen is not who I'm interested in. I turn my head back to the front and lock my gaze on Renata.

I don't have the best view of her from the back of the church, but I can make out the shape of her full bow-shaped lips. They're painted a deep shade of pink, like a rose. I'm not a fan of lipstick, but in this case, the added color helps bring out her features.

Dylen makes it to the front, standing to the right of Renata. "Who gives this woman to this man?" the reverend says.

"Her mother and I," Dylen's father replies with a thick French accent.

The reverend nods and Dylen's dad steps back, giving Dylen room to stand at Blake's side.

The ceremony continues but I'm oblivious to what's going on. I watch the way the light casts shadows on Renata's dress when she moves her hips, shifting her weight from one foot to the other. My hands twitch at the thought of running my hands over the smooth fabric of her dress, along the contours of her slim waist and outer thighs. She's tall enough to complement my six feet two inches.

With her tiny waist in my hands it wouldn't take much to pull her to me and kiss that lipstick right off.

My thoughts don't stop at kissing and soon I'm leaning forward in my seat, trying to hide an inappropriate church erection.

Great, Cayden. You're in church, man. Church. Knock it off.

The last time I got a hard-on in church, I was fourteen and Kelly Fleming was sitting in the pew in front of me. Kelly Fleming had a nice ass. Not as nice as Renata's though. Damn, that material is magic.

Shit! Stop thinking. Just STOP!

I close my eyes and try to focus on work stuff. My SWAT interview coming up next week. How much I want that position.

A loud shuffling pulls my thoughts away from work and I open my eyes to see everyone standing. With my situation under control, I stand and take a deep breath. *What the hell is my problem? I'm worse than a horny teenager with a stash of* Penthouse *magazines under the bed.*

"I now pronounce you husband and wife," the reverend says. Blake and Dylen turn and face the congregation. "It is my pleasure to present to you, Mr. and Mrs. Blake and Dylen Thompson."

The organ joins the applause and Blake puts his hand on Dylen's cheek. She leans into his touch, giving him her full attention. Bending to meet her lips, Blake kisses her.

It's been a long time since I've been with a woman and

damn, would I love to do the same thing to the maid of honor.

* * *

Unfastening the top few buttons of my shirt, I take a long pull on my beer. "Shit, it's hot in here."

"No kidding." My old high school friend Gabe puts a finger inside the collar of his shirt and pulls, trying to loosen the fabric. "Did they forget to turn the air on?"

I shrug and take another drink, looking around the room. Blake's reception is like a high-school class reunion, except that most of the people here didn't run in my circles. Friendly acquaintances at best. But Gabe, he crossed the academic–jock line, formidable debater and skilled football player. Brains and brawn. The ladies loved him.

"The wedding party's limo just pulled up." A very pregnant woman comes to stand beside Gabe and puts her arm around his waist.

Gabe drapes his arm around the woman's shoulders, hugging her to his side. "Cayden, this is my wife, Elise. Elise, Cayden."

I put my beer in my left hand and run my right hand down the side of my pants to dry the condensation from the bottle before I extend my hand in greeting. "Nice to meet you, Elise." I give her a smile as we shake hands, then look at Gabe. "I didn't know you got married."

"Two happy years, man." He turns to Elise and gives her a quick kiss. "Our first little one is due next month." He runs a hand over the swell of her belly.

While I was overseas, it seems all of my old friends decided it was time to get married and start families. Where did the time go? I feel very out of touch with the people I grew up with. I've always wanted to find a woman that would put up with me, marry her, and have a bunch of kids—I never liked being an only child—but, I thought that would all come later, when I was older…more grown up. When did getting married and having kids happen at twenty-something? When did that become the "grown-up" age?

"Congratulations, you guys. Great news. Do you know what you're having?" I ask.

"A boy."

"A girl." Gabe and Elise answer together and then laugh.

"We both have our suspicions, but no," Elise explains. "We decided to wait and be surprised."

"Well, he or she is lucky to have you two as parents."

"Is there a Mrs. Sinclair?" Gabe raises an eyebrow.

I pick up my beer and put it to my lips, taking the last swallow and shaking my head. I set the bottle down with a loud thump. "No. My tour in Afghanistan didn't leave me much time to date."

Gabe waved away is comment. "Oh, I'm sorry, man. That came out the wrong way. I didn't mean anything—"

"Honestly, Gabe"—I cut him off—"I've been so caught up in advancing my career, I put my love life on hold. And I'm taking care of my mom, she's not well. Now's not the right time." I shake my head.

"I'm sorry your mom is sick," Elise chimes in. We don't know each other, but it's nice of her to show concern.

"Thanks, Elise."

"Ladies and gentlemen," the DJ's deep voice booms through the speakers. "Put your hands together for the wedding party."

Dance hall music blasts and the crowd begins clapping to the heavy beat. A rush of excitement goes through me as I wait for the DJ to call Renata's name. I hope she's not here with anyone. *Do you really think that's possible? Did you see the way she looked?* Even my conscience thinks she's hot, and definitely not single. I'm so screwed.

After five minutes, the DJ has gone through most of the wedding party. The best man and the maid of honor are all that's left, besides Blake and Dylen.

An upbeat rock version of "Zip-a-Dee-Doo-Dah" floods the room and the doors open. "Give it up for Ren Daniels and David Thurston!"

Ren. She must go by Ren. My heart pounds in my chest just like it did yesterday when I pulled her over. I can't put into words how stunning she truly is. Watching her dance, my mouth goes dry. I pick up my beer bottle from the table and bring it to my lips. *Shit, it's empty.*

I set it back down, but don't take my eyes from Ren. David, Blake's best man, twirls her on the dance floor, and I can hear her melodic laugh even above the loud music. She looks happy. Are she and David a thing? Fuck, I hope not, because I have got to get to know this woman.

Leaning toward Gabe, I cup my hand around my mouth and ask, "Know anything about her?" I nod in Ren's direction. "The maid of honor?"

Gabe shakes his head. "Not really, just that she and Dylen were college roommates."

"She here with anyone?" I'm dying to know.

"Don't know, man." Gabe looks at me and shrugs. "You should find out though; she's hot."

Elise hears Gabe's comment and knocks her fist lightly into his shoulder. "Watch it, bud."

Gabe puts his hands up in surrender. "Not as hot as you, Leesy." Lowering his arms, he wraps them around her, folding his hands on her stomach. Gabe kisses her cheek, she smiles, and the two of them sway together to the music.

Maybe I do have my priorities fucked up. Seeing how happy Gabe and Elise and Blake and Dylen are, maybe I should have listened to my parents and put more effort into finding someone and settling down.

But then I think about everything I've been through. Bombs echo in my head. All the death and destruction I saw in Afghanistan—those nightmares still plague me. Asking another person to share those scars would be asking too much. And my job, the potential danger that comes with each call or traffic stop. Who knows when my number will be up? I *can't* get involved with someone right now. What kind of life would that be for my girlfriend, or wife? There's always the distinct possibility that I won't come home. I put my life on the line each day because I enjoy helping people, keeping people safe. Can I ask someone I love to live with the fear that I could be injured or killed? I want a family, but are my career ambitions asking too much of someone?

And Mom. She needs my undivided attention. I don't need

a relationship getting in the way of what is important—making sure Mom keeps fighting.

I watch Ren, smiling, dancing, and having a good time. Selfishly, I want nothing more than to get to know her, despite all the risks.

CHAPTER FIVE

REN

"Oliver and I are going to dance," Lexie says, grabbing hold of her boyfriend's hand. "You gonna be okay?" she asks. She's the last of my friends to hit the dance floor.

I wave a dismissive hand and toss back the last of my champagne. "Go, I'm good." I yank the bottle from the ice bucket and give it a once over. I could save myself the work of pouring multiple glasses and just drink out of the bottle? Nah, got to keep it classy for Dylen's sake.

Lexie frowns. "I feel bad. Are you sure?"

I look to Oliver. "Will you get your girl out on the dance floor?"

He smiles and nods, pulling Lexie along. I waggle my fingers at them as they disappear into the crowd and chug glass number three. I pour another and enjoy the numbing heat that spreads over my cheeks. I've craved this feeling all day long.

What is it about weddings that makes being single feel like a contagious disease? People stare at me funny, and I can read their thoughts, *What's wrong with her? Why couldn't she get a date?*

Getting a date isn't the hard part, putting my trust in a man is where I break down. Tears sting my eyes and I reach for the champagne bottle again. *Fuck, I hate weddings.*

Holding my glass as steadily as possible I tip more bubbly into the flute. I can feel the music thump in my temples. The glittering lights bounce off the disco ball at the center of the dance floor, making me dizzy. I put the nearly finished bottle back on the table and close my eyes for a second, hoping the vertigo will pass.

After taking several deep breaths, I open my eyes and the swirling, dancing specks of light have disappeared behind a giant shadow. I look up and see a guy standing in front of me.

He's tall and has the broadest shoulders I've ever seen. He's already ditched his tie and unbuttoned his collar, but that only makes the white dress shirt and tailored suit pants look all the more sexy—very *GQ*. Bringing my gaze up to his face, there's something familiar about him.

With his lips curled up at the corners, he extends his hand. "I'm Cayden."

Through the haze of champagne, I shake his hand. "Ren."

"Would you like to dance, Ren?"

His voice…a memory tickles the back of my brain. I've heard it before. Who is he?

Anxiety washes over me. I hate it when I can't remember shit. Bad things happen when I can't remember things.

Bad things happen when you drink, Ren. Knock it off.

Yes. I need to stop while I can still feel my face.

My hand is still in his and he tightens his grip, gives me gentle tug, bringing me to my feet. I wobble like one of those toddler toys with round bottoms and no feet, unsure if it's the champagne or just him trying to sweep me off my feet.

He puts his free hand on my shoulder to steady me. "Whoa. You okay?"

Standing, I'm only a handful of inches shorter than him. I can see his face clearly. A strong square jawline shadowed with fine dark whiskers. He was probably clean shaven this morning. He wears a nice five o'clock shadow. My fingers itch to touch it; feel the prickle beneath my fingertips. His eyes reflect the shimmering disco lights, but it's too dark to make out their color. He smiles softly, looking truly concerned for my well-being.

"I'm good," I whisper, as the fog clears from my brain. Yesterday's events come speeding to the front of my thoughts. The lights in my rearview. The officer peering through my passenger window. The bright green eyes of Officer C. Sinclair staring back at me.

"Your name starts with a 'C,'" I say, finding my voice.

He nods. "Yes ma'am, last time I checked."

Yep. That voice. It's him. The cop that gave me a ticket yesterday.

I stare, not sure if I'm supposed to be friendly and accept his invitation or be upset with him for costing me a hundred and eight dollars. The thin strap of my dress slides down my shoulder. Cayden lets go of my elbow and catches it, pushing it back into place. His fingertips skim along flushed skin, and I shiver.

It's not cold—the damn air conditioner hasn't worked all night. Flashes of his muscular arms, straining against the sleeves of his blue trooper uniform, jog through my mind. I want to be mad at him, but he's just too damn sexy to stay angry at. I give him a quick smile. "You gave me a speed—"

"Speeding ticket," he interrupts. Cocking his head, he grimaces and bites his bottom lip. "Sorry about that."

"Sorry?" I hadn't been expecting an apology, but if he's offering, I'll take it.

"I'm sort of up for a promotion and I need to prove to the higher-ups that I'm the best at what I do. I"—he puts his hand to his chest—"didn't want to issue you the citation, but the law kind of said I had to."

"I see." I like this groveling Cayden, as opposed to stickler-for-the-law Cayden.

"Look, I'm sorry about the ticket. Can we start over?" He puts his hand out for me to shake, again. "Hi, I'm Cayden Sinclair, friend of Blake's. Doing the wedding thing solo. Really need a dance partner."

My eyes lock on his. Of course I'm going to accept his offer—I'd be stupid not to—but I'm getting a kick out of watching him sweat, awaiting my answer.

I put my hand in his and nod. "Ren Daniels, friend of the bride's. Doing the solo thing too, and yes, I would love to dance." I bite back a smile.

With his hand securely wrapped around mine, he leads me to the dance floor. God, it's been forever since I've danced with a guy. I feel like an awkward fourteen-year-old.

Thankfully the song changes from a fast song to a slow song, I selfishly want to know what it's like to have his muscular arms around me.

Cayden smiles at me and hesitates. "Now that I've lead you out here under false pretenses, I should tell you…" He pauses, glancing around the crowded dance floor. Leaning in close, he puts his mouth to my ear: "I can't dance."

His warm breath drifts over my skin and all of my nerve endings come to life. Goose bumps rise on my arms. Stepping back he gives me a goofy grin and shrugs.

I swing our clasped hands to the rhythm of the music, unable to keep my snark in check. "If you can't dance, Officer, then why did you ask me?"

"Because it's absolutely criminal that the most gorgeous woman at this wedding is sitting over there all by herself." He lifts his chin in the direction of the wedding party's table. "It's my job to stop crime."

Like the bubbles rising in the champagne, laughter bubbles up from my core, bursting from my mouth. "Oh my gosh! Your pickup lines are *the worst.*"

"Are you laughing at me, Renata?" he says, smirking.

"I'm sorry." I stifle a giggle. I feel bad, I shouldn't laugh. But's he's so hot…and his voice…and the champagne…and his sexy arms…and…*I'm in trouble.*

"Don't apologize. I'd give you lines all night if it meant I'd get to hear your cute-as-hell laugh." His thumb traces along the back of my hand making my belly clench. "And if I'm being honest, I haven't been able to stop thinking about you since yesterday."

Whoa. Wait. What? He hasn't been able to stop thinking about me? Okay, heart, slow down.

"You see, it's fate. You have to dance with me."

He shrugs again, charm in spades…and when he moves, his shoulders flex in the most captivating way, like artwork come to life. Artwork I want to touch.

"Well then, let me give you a lesson, Officer Sinclair." I position his hand at my shoulder and take his other hand in mine. "I'll lead."

"I knew you were a woman in control."

I am now…but it took me a long time to get here, Officer.

I put my right hand in his and my left on his shoulder. His hand against the bare skin of my shoulder blade radiates heat, searing me with his touch. My cheeks burn, and I'm thankful I can blame my heavy blush on the champagne.

Holy hell! I thought he was hot when he pulled me over yesterday, but in real life he is scorching. And he smells so damn good, like walking in a woodsy pine forest with subtle notes of lavender in the air.

Cayden firms his grip on my hand and pulls me out of my thoughts. With slight pressure in our clasped hands, I lead him to the right. Our eyes are locked on one another: a deep, penetrating stare.

Every now and then, the shimmer of the disco ball catches his peridot eyes, putting me in a trance. I've never seen eyes like his.

"You're quite the dancer, Officer Sinclair," I tease, changing directions, leading us in a graceful step-touch.

"Cayden. Please," he corrects. "I'm just me tonight. Not looking to pull anyone over." He winks. "And thank you, I have the *best* teacher."

"Catch her next season on *Dancing with the Stars*." I stand up straighter and toss my head, feigning an air of cockiness.

A spray of blue and red lights fall on his face and I notice a scar that runs from the hairline at his temple to just below his right eye—a thick jagged line. My fingers tingle with the urge to touch it. Ever since I was a child, I've had a fascination with scars and the stories they tell. You can learn a lot about someone by the scars they bear. But, in my opinion, it's the traumas that don't leave physical reminders that are the most scarring.

"Let's see," he says, and I snap my gaze back to his. "I know your height, weight, that you're an organ donor, and your birth date. Tell me something I don't know, Renata."

I square up my shoulders, bristling at my full name. Why my mother thought giving me her maiden name was a good idea, I'll never know. "Only my mother calls me Renata, and it's usually because I've said a dirty word in her presence." I can hear Mom's indignant voice in the back of my head, an exaggerated whine on the second syllable—*Ren-AHH-ta.*

"Naughty girl." He raises an eyebrow and the corner of his lips pull up in a sinful smirk. "I'll stick with Ren, then."

Please do. When it rolls off his tongue, it's like his voice is gift wrapped in the most lush, rich velvet.

My heart thumps against my chest, double the rhythm of the song we're dancing to.

"So, if I wanted to spin you, or dip you, Ren, how would I go about doing that?"

"I'm not sure you're skills are up to that level yet."

He drops his stubbled jaw to my ear. "Are you doubting my game, sweetheart?"

Tingles head southward, my lady parts coming to life. *Ohh.*

I breathe, caught off guard. My feet do their best to keep me upright and I tighten my grasp on his hand like it's the last chocolate bar in the world and I'm PMSing.

"I bet you have serious game," I mutter under my breath, imagining his bedroom game.

"Let's give it a try."

"What?" I squeak, surprised.

He extends his hand, guides me in a slow twirl, and tugs me back in, only this time he puts his hands at my waist, draws me close, and takes the lead. There is nowhere for my arms to go…except around his neck.

Oh. Realization dawns. *Give the spin a try.* For a second, I thought I'd said something about his bedroom skills out loud, and he wanted to give that a go.

"How was that?" Our faces inches apart now, he looks down at me, a confident smile on his face. "Still doubting my skills?"

No. Not ever.

With our close proximity, it's hard to concentrate on words. The fine stubble on his jaw and his arresting green eyes have stolen the words right out of my mouth.

The music swells and he pulls me even closer, dipping me slightly.

I am lost in the feel of his solid body enveloping mine, and I can't fight the fantasy that comes to mind…his *naked* body pressed close. Does he have any other scars…more chapters to his book? I want to read more.

I shake my head, trying to give my brain a kick start. "You're a fast learner."

"Only when I have a hot teacher." He winks. "School me, Ren. Give me the rundown on you."

"I help deliver babies," I blurt out, brain still malfunctioning. Well, I just managed to suck all the sexy out of this moment. *Way to go, Ren.*

Cayden's grin never leaves his face, though. "Babies?" Our bodies as one, not missing a beat.

"Yeah," I sigh, wishing I hadn't opened this can of worms. From past experience, the thought of babies and the gory details of my job don't make for pleasant "You're really hot and I want to get to know you better" conversation.

"I'm a labor and delivery nurse."

He squints his eyes. Fine creases gather at the outer corners. "Ever deliver one?" By the tone of his voice, he actually sounds interested. *Huh.*

I nod. "A few times, when the doctor didn't make it to the hospital in time. But, most often, I just assist."

"Me too." His voice dips low and there's a glint in his eye.

"You've delivered a baby?"

He nods. "There was a traffic accident. I was the first officer on the scene. The couple involved in the crash was on their way to the hospital when the driver lost control of his vehicle. When I got there, the woman was in active labor. There was no time to wait for the ambulance, the baby was already crowning."

My mouth hangs open, caught on his every word. "Was everyone all right?"

Cayden nods. "Bringing that baby into the world was an incredible experience."

Is this guy for real? I've never met a guy that wasn't completely grossed out and turned off by the thought of babies and childbirth.

His gaze burns, but I can't look away. "Yeah, it really is," I mumble.

Cayden slides his hands up the smooth silk of my dress, and along my arms. Stepping back a fraction of an inch, he repositions our arms. I'm Baby to his Johnny Castle. Patrick Swayze's voice coaches me: *Lock your frame. Lock it.*

With a flourish, Cayden dips again and my legs turn to wet noodles.

He draws me back up and our bellies are flush. With each sway, my boobs rub against his chest, sending lightning bolts of pleasure right between my legs. My breath comes quicker and my shoulders heave. If he lets go, I fear I might collapse in a heap of *Holy shit this hot!*

And then, Justin Timberlake floods the dance hall, bringing sexy back.

* * *

"Who is that delicious piece of military man you've been dancing with all night, *chouchou*?" Dylen raises an eyebrow and steps out of her dress.

I smile at my nickname: *chouchou*. She has called me that term of endearment since our freshman year of college; says it's a term of endearment in France, meaning "pet." I've always loved the way it rolls off her tongue, so perfectly accented.

Sighing, I bend over and pick up her insanely expensive

French couture wedding gown off the sticky reception hall bathroom floor.

"Well?" She turns on me, propping her hands on her hips.

"Cayden Sinclair. He's a friend of Blake's. Do you know him? Is he in the military? I know he's a cop."

Dylen's thoughtful for a moment, trying to recall whether or not she's met Cayden at some point in her and Blake's long relationship—they've been together for five years.

"I may have met him before, who knows. But, no, I don't know him. He's not one of Blake's close friends. The haircut and all, he looks like the military type."

I shrug, hanging Dylen's dress on a hanger. "Cayden said he and Blake grew up together." I hand Dylen her getaway outfit—a white, athletic warm-up suit that has "bride" printed down the side of one pant leg, and her new last name spelled out on the back of the shirt. It's Dylen to a tee; she's a CrossFit queen and hates dresses. I'm actually surprised she didn't get married in the tracksuit.

Slipping the shirt over her head, she says, "I'll ask Blake for you, do some vetting." Her head pops through the neck hole. "He's all kinds of yummy, though. *Très délicieux!*" She wags her eyebrows and licks her lips.

"Oh my God, are you three?" I swat at her.

"Not three, but wasted? Yeah. And horny as hell." She nods. "I haven't been this drunk in a long time. I'm ready to go find Blake, blow this shindig, and have sex…with my husband!" She giggles and almost falls over as she puts one leg into her pants. Catching herself on the basin, she regains her balance. "Husband…that sounds so weird! I have a friggin' husband, Ren!"

"Am I going to help deliver my godchild in nine months?" A twinge of jealousy pulls at my heartstrings. In the last few years, I've come to terms with the fact that I may never have children—I thank my rapist for that—but the thought of Dylen getting to experience the joy of motherhood, if not right now, at some point, still hurts. I've overcome so much pain after the rape, and not knowing my attacker made it all the more difficult, but the knowledge of being robbed of having children because of him, hurts more than anything.

Dylen wrinkles her nose in disgust. "Hell no. I'm on the pill, and I happen to know I am not ovulating right now." She picks her phone up off the counter and waves it around. "I've been tracking for this very reason, just to be sure."

"Those apps aren't one hundred percent accur—"

"Shoosh. Shoosh. Shoosh." Dylen shakes her head and presses her index finger to my lips. "Shhhhhh. No, no. Don't want to hear it. Don't burst my innocent little bubble."

I give her two thumbs-up. "Have fun!" I mumble, her finger still on my lips.

"That's the Ren I know!" Removing her finger from my face, she claps her hand down onto my shoulder and yanks me into a tight hug. "Thank you for today."

"You bet, *sœur*. You're like a sister to me. I'd do anything for you."

"I know, *chouchou*."

Tears get stuck in my throat. My best friend is *married*. It hits me hard. I'm truly alone. She has Blake now, she doesn't need me in the same way any more…and it's time to let her go. "Come on now. Your husband's waiting."

Dylen squeals in my ear, "Husband!" She pulls back and bounces on her heels. Marriage suits my hyperactive friend. "Let's go." She grabs my hand and yanks me through the door.

Across the room, I see Cayden talking to a little white-haired lady. She reaches up and pats his cheek and he bends down and gives her a hug.

"Listen up!" the DJ shouts into his microphone. "Dylen and Blake are about to embark upon their first outing as a married couple." The crowd cheers and claps. "Let's give them a proper send-off, shall we? I need everyone out on the dance floor."

I look to Dylen and she shrugs. "Probably one of Wedding Coordinator Barbie's ideas."

As we walk to the center of the reception hall, the screech of chairs floods the room. Dylen and Blake's family and friends move onto the floor and wait for more instructions.

"Mr. and Mrs. Thompson, I need you to stand in the center of the dance floor. Guests, make a circle around the happy couple," the DJ instructs.

Dylen squeezes my hand and lets go, skipping to the center of the circle. She throws her arms around Blake and he draws her close, kissing her as the rest of us spread out around them.

The DJ makes his way onto the dance floor, microphone in hand. "Dylen and Blake are going to make their way around the circle and say their goodbyes."

Justin Bieber is piped through the speakers and the crowd claps as Dylen and Blake dole out hugs and thank-yous. I scan the circle for Cayden, but can't find him. *Where did he go?* Maybe he bailed, so we wouldn't be forced to deal with an awkward goodbye. Snippets of our conversations from the evening flip through my mind. *Had I made an ass of myself?* My Magic 8 Ball response: *It is certain.*

"Good Lord."

Startled, I whirl to my left. Cayden is right behind me, leaning into the circle, his face nearly resting on my shoulder.

"I thought Aunt Sunny would never let me go. Here, slide over." He puts his hands on my waist, shifting me to the right, butting into the tight circle.

Tilting my head upward just a little, I touch his cheek, tracing hot pink lips. "Aunt Sunny?"

He rolls his lovely green eyes. "I believe she thinks I'm still seven."

"Was there cheek pinching involved?" I smirk, pulling my hand away.

Cayden rubs his right hand over the lipstick, smearing it as he winces. "It still hurts."

I laugh. A genuine, honest-to-goodness laugh. Cayden has made me laugh more times tonight than I have in the last three months, especially since my brother's motorcycle accident. "Poor baby," I coo.

He leans in, stopping a finger's breadth from my lips. We're so close we share the same oxygen. "Got the number of a good nurse?"

Uhhh…dead. I'm dead. Heaven bound.

We've depleted our shared oxygen supply. The overabundance of carbon dioxide has affected my thought processes. *There he goes with those cheesy pickup lines. And I'm all swoony. Damn you, ovaries!* If that line had come out of any other guy's mouth, I would have given him my single-digit number, as in the middle finger variety.

"My number?" is all I'm capable of choking out.

He cocks an eyebrow. "Are you a *good* nurse?"

"*Chouchou!*"

At the sound of my nickname, reality smacks into me like a freight train. An overly excited, hyperactive freight train named Dylen. She hugs me, my arms pinned at my sides. I can't breathe. I can't move. Hell, I can't even talk, my head is buried between her C cups. I'm tall, but Dylen is friggin' Gwendoline Christie. Trapped in her hug, I'm the perfect height to receive the grand tour of her lady lumps. Dylen always did have great boobs, but this is ridiculous.

"Um, Dyl," I mumble. "Dyl?"

She squeezes me tighter for a split second and then lets go. "Oh, Ren, thank you! I love you. I'll call you when I get back from Islamorada."

"I can't wait to hear all about it. Love you, Dyl. Have a great time." I give her one quick hug and kiss her cheek.

Before she steps away she whispers in my ear, "He's more than yummy. You better be getting some fucking dessert tonight."

Then with a deft pivot, she's standing in front of Cayden, drawing him into an awkward hug.

I open my arms, welcoming Blake. "Take care of her." I pat his back.

"Always." He nods and looks at Dylen, who is already bouncing over to the next couple in the circle. Blake loves that girl, it's written all over his face. The softness of his stare, the light in his smile, if love could be drawn, captured on paper, Blake would be the poster child.

"Blake, my man," Cayden says, holding out his hand. "Congrats." Blake slaps his palm to Cayden's and they pull each other into one of those back-slapping guy hugs.

Once Cayden says his goodbye to Blake he turns to me, all silliness gone from his face. "How are getting home tonight?"

Hmm. I hadn't thought that far in advance. I really don't know. I came in a limo…that's no longer here. My brain flips through the names of my family—Mom, Dad, Jillian—any of them would gladly come pick me up. "I should probably call someone."

Looping his hand around my upper arm, he leads me out of the goodbye circle. "I'd be happy to give you a ride."

Do I want him to give me a ride? Yes. In more ways than one.

Jesus, Ren! The reserved little angel on my shoulder blushes a deep crimson.

I know, right? I'm surprising even myself. But, the thought of sex and actually doing the deed is as deep as the Mariana Trench. The pressure is too great, and I'd collapse under the weight. I couldn't do it.

"It's okay. I've got family who can come."

"Nonsense. I'm here, I don't mind. Let me take you home."

Gah! I really do want to go with him. But, it isn't smart. Cayden Sinclair is a stranger. I don't do well, alone, with strangers. It freaks me out.

But he's a cop. One of the good guys. I bet he's really, really good. The sultry devil on my other shoulder weighs in. *You know you want to.*

I bite my lip. "Are you sure you don't mind?"

His shoulders relax and he grins. "Not at all."

"I just need to get my purse." I point over my shoulder, to the head table.

"Great. I'll walk with you."

I glance at him as we slip through the dwindling wedding-goers. Dylen and Blake have left, so there isn't much of a reason to hang around. The usual apprehension I feel when I'm faced with a situation that puts me and a guy alone together, doesn't manifest. The gut-twisting uneasiness hasn't reared its ugly head. All night I've felt safe in Cayden's arms. I'd be an idiot if I let this chance pass me by. *Isn't this what you've pined for, Ren? A strong handsome man that makes you feel wanted and safe? What are you waiting for?*

Indeed. What am I waiting for?

I snag my purse from under the table and look at Cayden. *Him. I've been waiting for him.*

CHAPTER SIX

CAYDEN

She lives downtown? I've witnessed some horrible shit in this city. No way is it safe for a woman to live here, alone. Tension gathers in my shoulders, dreading the fact that I have to leave her somewhere a criminal could all too easily cause her harm.

Opening the door of my truck, I help her down. "Thank you, again," she says. "It was really nice of you to bring me home."

I shut the door and the clang vibrates off the dirty concrete. "You're welcome. It was my pleasure."

Ren bites her lower lip, something I've noticed she does when she's nervous. "Goodnight, Cayden."

Damn, I do not want to watch her leave. "'Night, Ren."

She turns and steps up on the little stoop outside her building's security doors. When her hands touch the handle, it hits me that I don't have her number.

"Ren!" I call.

She turns.

I hop onto the stoop next to her, unsure of what to say, but needing to say so much. Anything to keep her at my side a few minutes more. "I almost didn't go tonight. But, I'm glad I did." I scoop her hand in mine. "I haven't been able to get you out of my mind since I met you yesterday. *Please*, please, don't make me do the creepy thing and look your number up in the system, down at the station. I want to say I got it the old-fashioned way: by badgering the beautiful woman for her number until she gave it up."

"Oh," she lilts. "I wasn't aware that was how it worked. Somehow, I don't think you've ever had to do much badgering."

"Then don't be the first, sweetheart."

"Got your phone?" she asks, tugging on that lower lip with her teeth again.

I lick mine, fantasizing about pulling her lip between *my* teeth. Yanking my phone free of the belt-clip holder, I hand it over.

Her fingers fly over the screen as she adds her contact info. When she finishes, she hands it back and smiles. "Oh, and for the record, Officer: earlier, you asked if I was a good nurse"—she steps up on her tiptoes, puts her lips to my ear—"I'm a *great* nurse." She winks, turns on her heel, and disappears through the security door.

Umm… I think I'm going to need a great nurse. My heart just quit beating.

* * *

I pull my laces tight and stand, kicking my left foot backward, pulling my ankle upward to stretch out my quadriceps. I hold the stretch for a handful of seconds and let go, repeating the motion on the other side.

Dropping my foot, I hit the pavement, accelerating to a steady jog. The sun beats down and the air is already thicker than MRE oatmeal. I'm glad to get my run in early.

The morning's quiet, despite the chatty birds. Last night is on replay in my head. Ren's lips, her infectious laugh, the way she swung her hips as she walked into her building… kill me now. I hated that she went into that dark apartment, alone.

Sweat rolls down my temples and I welcome the familiar burn in my lungs. I pump my arms and legs faster, pushing myself. My SWAT physical fitness test is next week and there's no way in hell I'm backing down now.

Not a good idea to get involved with someone right now, Sinclair. I need to stay focused. And then there's Mom. My life is such a shit storm right now. What am I doing thinking I can handle a fledgling relationship on top of everything else? Not to mention the danger that comes with my job. I can't ask Ren to deal with that kind of stress.

My brain dials up the feel of Ren in my arms. The silkiness of her skin when I slid the strap of her dress up her shoulder, her slender waist, and how my big hands fit so perfectly around it, the feel of her thumb caressing the back of my hand as I held her manicured fingers in mine.

Yep, its official, my body and my brain are damn traitors.

Pulling in a deep breath through my nose, I try to get Ren

out of my head and concentrate on finishing my third mile strong. *Focus, Sinclair. You've got a lot riding on this.*

But, no matter how much I try to push Ren Daniels aside, the thought of her number stored in my phone back at home is my biggest motivation for running harder, faster, because the second I hit the door, I'm calling her. I don't know what spell she put me under last night, but I've got to see her today.

I dig deep and finish my third mile, twenty-eight minutes flat. Breathing hard, I shove my key in the door and push it open with a little too much force and it smacks against the wall.

"Oh, shit!" I reach for the knob and yank it back, running my hand over the wall, inspecting it for damage. I do not have enough time to add home repair to my plate.

Making my way to the kitchen, I drop my keys on the counter and pull open the fridge. I grab a bottle of water and drain it while I muster the nerve to call Ren.

Her breath blowing across my ear, *I'm a great nurse.*

Confidence bolstered. That didn't take long.

Shooting the empty into the small recycling bin beside the trashcan, I jog down the hallway. In my room, I scoop the phone off my dresser and find Ren's number stored under the name *Speed Racer*. She's got a sense of humor, too. Chuckling, I tap the nickname and wait for the call to connect.

Two rings. No answer.

Three…

My heartbeat kicks up, despite having just finished running three miles.

"Hello?" a breathy, sleep-laden voice answers.

"Hi, Ren? It's Cayden, from the wedding last night?"

Silence.

She's not saying anything. Why isn't she saying anything? I notice the time on the bedside clock; it's before eight. I just woke her up. "Shit, I'm sorry, Ren. I didn't mean to wake you." She has me so off my game. I can lead a troop of Marines through hostile territory, but when it comes to calling a beautiful woman, I am completely useless.

"No, no! It's okay," she responds quickly, sounding more startled than awake. "Hi, yes, Cayden, how are you?"

Pissed at myself for being a complete idiot. "Great. Hey, you busy today?" *Already fucked this up, might as well dig yourself a deeper grave, Sinclair.*

"Today? Umm…"

She's looking for a way to let me down gently. *Affirmative.*

"Uh, no. The only plans I have are laundry and an all-day date with Netflix."

No plans. She's not busy. Dammit, I didn't think this through very well. What the hell should I ask her to do? Dinner and a movie? No, that's too cliché. I want our first date to be different…memorable. She needs something special.

I scan my bedroom hoping something will jump out at me, then I see my hiking gear on the closet floor.

Hiking. Of course. We could do some caching. I haven't been caching in months and it's always more fun with someone.

"Ever been caching?"

"Um, no?" she drawls. "I mean, I've been check *cashing* before. It's fun and all, but I've never required the help of another person."

A laugh rumbles in my chest. "No, caching, as in 'geo-caching.' When you locate hidden objects using a GPS."

"Oh, then no. I have never heard of that kind of caching." Her voice brightens. Glad she doesn't think I'm a complete moron. "So, how 'bout it, up for some hiking and geocaching today?"

She doesn't answer right away. All I hear is the hum of the air conditioner kicking on. My stomach twists in knots. Shit, I've always thought this was the worst part of asking a girl out, waiting for the answer. If the answer is yes, you know you've got a chance. If she says no, you feel like a goddamn loser all day. I'm too old for this; I hate feeling like I'm sixteen and asking a girl to the prom.

"Sounds fun," she says. "I can be ready by nine."

I exhale, running a hand over my head. "Perfect. I'll pick you up then."

Hanging up, I send a quick text to Mom. *How are you feeling this morning? Need me to stop by?*

My phone vibrates with an immediate response. *Fine. Lacey's here. Enjoy your day off.*

God bless Lacey. I'm glad she gives Mom someone to talk to; it's got to be hard talking to your son about your battle with breast cancer. Not that I mind when she does confide in me, but having Lacey around is a godsend for Mom. *Call me if you need anything. I mean it.* I text back and toss my phone on the bed and hit the shower.

Knowing Mom is taken care of today is a weight off my shoulders. Guilt won't eat away at me. Although, it does take a small bite because of Bull, Taz, and Vin. I didn't leave the

Corps so I could chase after women. My boys are going back to that fucking place and I'm taking a beautiful woman on a date. What the hell's wrong with me?

Mom is supposed to be my first priority, getting involved with someone is the absolute worst idea. I've got work and Mom to concentrate on; there's no room in my life for a woman.

Ren isn't just some woman, though. My brain is miles ahead of the game.

I peel my sweat-soaked shirt over my head and walk to the bathroom, turning on the shower. As I adjust the temp to near scalding, clouds of steam rise from the faucet. I can hear Ren's voice, exuberant and sweet. She sounded genuinely excited that I had called, despite waking her up.

I drop my shorts and boxers and step into the hot stream. The jets spray over my sore muscles and I relax. Just one date. Maybe we won't hit it off and I can get her out of my head.

But my head offers other thoughts, *Yeah right, Sinclair. You lost this war when you pulled her over on Friday.*

* * *

I pull up to Ren's apartment building downtown and kill the engine. Stepping out of my truck I stare up at the old warehouse, which had been converted into one of those ultra-swanky loft apartments. It's not quite as menacing in the daylight. Less Gotham City, more St. Louis. Still, I've always been more of a country guy. I'll take lots of land, fresh air, and the sounds of nature over sirens, smog, and thirteen hundred square feet of living space any day.

A car comes peeling around the corner and the driver lays on the horn. Glancing over my shoulder, I slam my door closed and press my body close to my truck in the nick of time. I get a good look at the driver who flicks me off as he speeds away. Dick. He nearly ran me over and almost made my door his hood ornament.

I squint, trying to read his plates, but he's down the street faster than Vin Diesel. I shake my head and round my truck, stepping up onto the sidewalk. Asshole. I may have not been able to catch his plates, but I hope there's a cop up the street waiting to nail his ass.

At the entrance to Ren's building, I pull open one of the glass double doors and locate Ren's last name on the nameplates. Pushing the button to the left of her name, I wait. A crackling, electronic buzz sounds, followed by Ren's garbled voice, "Hello?"

"Hi, Ren. It's Cayden Sinclair." I let go of the button to hear her response.

"Yay, come on up. I'm on the third floor, apartment three fourteen."

The door clicks.

Yanking it open, I find the elevator bay to the right and press the up arrow.

When the elevator doors open on Ren's floor, I follow the signs to her apartment. It's like living in a hotel, complete with a faint chlorine scent.

Metallic gold numbers are nailed to her front door: 314. I knock and my nerves kick into overdrive. This is more stressful than being called into the captain's office on a day when he hasn't had his morning coffee. What if she regrets accepting my invitation? What if hiking and caching aren't her thing? What if she hates it? What if she thinks I'm a complete tool? Oh, shit, why didn't I just go the dinner-and-movie route?

The door pulls back and Ren is standing on the other side. The sides of her dark brown hair are pulled back leaving bangs covering her forehead. All the heavy makeup from yesterday is gone. Her skin is fair and pink, a natural blush highlighting her cheekbones. And her dark eyes…God, her eyes…they're so big. A man could get lost her eyes, and I very much want to be that man. Ren Daniels is stunning.

"Good morning," she says. If you could hear a smile, Ren's voice is what it would sound like—sweet, and warm, a light breeze sweeping over freshly mown grass on a spring day with birds chattering nearby.

You're a goner, Sinclair, my inner voice notes. *Yes. Yes I am.*

"Good morning, Ren," I reply, at a loss for more words.

She glances downward. I follow her gaze. She wiggles her toes inside her mismatched socks. "Come on in. I just need to put my shoes on." Ren steps aside and ushers me inside.

"Thanks." As I pass her, I catch a subtle tropical scent mixed with the hint of baby powder, very feminine and utterly intoxicating. *Goddamn, this woman is too much.*

Ren shuts the door and walks over to the bar stool, scooping a lime-green Nike running shoe off the hardwood floor. She plops down and fits her foot into the shoe, deftly tying it and moving onto the next.

"Sorry, I'm running late." She stands, shoes tied, hands on her hips.

Now it's her body I can't keep my eyes off of. The hot pink straps of a sports bra are visible beneath her blue tank top and her skintight black shorts hug her hips and backside in the most delicious way. "No problem." *I'm in no hurry, sweetheart. We can stay here all day long.*

I've never been the kind of guy to objectify women, but damn, I want to pin her to the wall and touch every curve her little outfit is showing off. *Shit. How am I going to get through this date with my sanity?* She's already driving me crazy.

The bright pink lettering on her shirt catches my eye: *Nurses make it better.*

Oh, sweetheart, your shirt does not lie.

Ren grabs her keys off the counter and turns, our gazes locking together. "So, what's this geo thing we're doing today?" She walks in my direction, toward the door.

I'm well aware that the only words I've uttered since showing up at her door have been three syllables or less. *Pull yourself together, Sinclair.* "Um"—I blink, trying to get my *brain* involved in this conversation—"Uh...I thought we'd head down to the Meramec River, there are some good hiking trails there. We can scope out what caches are around, too."

"Caches? You said they're hidden objects?"

I nod and follow her to the door, catching a whiff of coconut this time. I hate that I'm going to have to hand her a can of Deep Woods Off!—it's a crime to cover up that divine scent—but bugs will devour her like a ripe peach, smelling the way she does.

"Yep. Millions of them, hidden all over the world. We'll start small and see what we can find by the river."

We step into the hallway and Ren locks her apartment, stuffing her keys into a small backpack and slinging it over her shoulder. "Cool. I've never been treasure hunting before! We're like pirates looking for booty!"

A deep carnal laugh erupts from inside my body. *All the booty I want is right here.* My hands twitch, begging to run along the curves of her ass. Those shorts…*damn.* This caching expedition is going to be fucking impossible with the hard-on I'm going to have all day.

Ren puts her hands on her waist, jutting out her curvy hip. *Fuck me. This chick is walking, breathing sex.*

I keep my dirty thoughts locked down. "As I recall, sweetheart, you laughed at me last night. Turnabout's fair play." I wink.

"So it is." She scrutinizes, trying to figure me out. "What's so funny?"

A beam of sunlight shines through the high windows in the corridor and falls on her face making her espresso colored eyes sparkle. Excitement is written all over her face.

"You can't say 'booty,' wearing those shorts, and not expect my mind to…wander."

"Oh." The twinkle in her eyes fades.

Abort! Abort! Too soon, Sinclair. Fix this.

Embarrassed, I cough out an apology, "Sorry. I—"

The shadow dissipates and the mischievous sparkle returns to her eyes, but she's biting her lip again. "No, it's okay," she says, laughing nervously, tugging the back of her shirt a little lower.

God, I'm such a shit. I hate that my words made her feel

self-conscious. Time to clear the air, change the subject. "When I was younger, my parents and I went caching all the time. You never know what you'll find."

"Well, what are we waiting for then, you promised me some treasure." She grins, reticent body language abating.

I get to spend the entire day with this girl; a thrill singes my veins. Last night, when we danced, she didn't shy away from me, hopefully I didn't ruin things with my big mouth, because I'm craving her touch like a starving man craves breadcrumbs.

I tempt fate and reach for her hand, lacing my fingers between hers.

When she gives our entwined hands a gentle swing, I know today is going to be fan-fucking-tastic.

* * *

I open the door for Ren, help her down, then fold her seat forward and grab my hiking gear from the back. I've got a couple GPS devices, bottles of water, bug spray, power bars, first-aid kit, flashlight, batteries, multipurpose tool, and matches. I went for the smaller backpack knowing we wouldn't be doing any major hiking today. I'll go easy on her, I want there to be a second date.

Before shouldering the pack, I unzip it and pull out a can of bug spray. Remembering the subtle wafts of Ren's tropical perfume and baby powder scent back at her apartment, I toss her the can. "You're going to need this. Being this close to the river, the area is a breeding ground for mosquitoes."

Ren catches the can and pops the lid off. "Thanks." She

sighs and extends her left arm, making several passes. A heavy mist coats her skin and she repeats the process over her other arm, her long, slender legs, neck, and then turns the can and showers her clothes and hair.

I chuckle at her excessiveness. "Hopefully it's just the bugs you're trying to keep away."

A sheepish smile tugs at the corner of her bow-shaped mouth. She wrinkles her nose and my heart skips a beat. "I hate to admit this, but I'm terrified of bugs. And…" She hesitates. "I'm not really the outdoorsy type."

I step closer and wrap my hands around her fingers that are still clinging to the can of Off! like it's a cross, warding away vampires. "Stay close, I'll keep you safe," I say, slowly lifting the can free from her grip.

She no longer smells of citrus, but like she bathed in DEET. She may repel every six- and eight-legged critter in a hundred-mile radius, but I'm more attracted to her than ever. Off!, bug repellant and aphrodisiac. I know it's too soon to kiss her, but damn if I don't want to.

She lets out a breath. "Lucky for me."

"Mind if I use this?" I hold up the can between us.

I don't take my eyes off her, while I give my arms and legs a quick spray. "Glad you saved me some." I wink and stuff the can back in my bag.

"Oh, I bet you have another can in there somewhere, Boy Scout."

She isn't wrong, I do have more, but I can't help but tease her.

"Boy Scout? Try Marine."

"You're a Marine and a cop?"

"Yes, ma'am, enlisted right out of high school. Not active duty anymore, though. Just the cop gig."

She looks me up and down, not hiding the fact that she's checking me out, and I don't mind being her eye candy.

"Why aren't you still with the Marines?"

I look down and rummage through my backpack for the GPS device. I'd hoped Mom's story would have come up later. I don't want to mire all our positive sexual tension in depressing crap.

I draw the GPS out of the bag and look back at Ren. "My family's gone through some shit in the last two years. My dad passed away while I was in Afghanistan, then my mom was diagnosed with an aggressive form of breast cancer. With Dad gone, she needed me, so when my time was up, I didn't reenlist."

"Cayden, I'm so sorry." She reaches for me, touching my shoulder.

Yeah, the last couple years have sucked; I've been holding the best poker hand for the worst jackpot. But, hearing my name caressed by Ren's voice has me ready to fold, to let her be strong for me.

Tapping the GPS against the palm of my hand, I give her a half smile. "Thanks. What's important now is staying strong for my mom." I power up the nav, something to do while I get my head back in the game. Can't lose focus. Got to stay strong.

She lowers her hand and presses her lips into a thin smile. More questions cloud her face, but thankfully she holds them in. When it comes to losing Dad, and Mom being sick, I don't like to talk about it.

"Ready to hit the trails?" I hold up the GPS.

Her smile widens. "I do believe you promised me some *booty*."

I raise an eyebrow, smirking, glad she's relaxing a bit. "And I never break a promise, sweetheart."

I dial up the coordinates of a nearby cache and grab her hand. "We're going this way."

The trail starts off friendly, but soon I'm forced to give up her hand when the terrain gets rough. The well-worn dirt path ends in a tangle of overgrown weeds. "Well, I think it's safe to say that this cache is safe from muggles."

"Muggles? Now that's a word I know," she says, coming to a stop at my side. "What do muggles have to do with treasure hunting?"

Pushing the brush aside, I motion for Ren to pass through. "Well, the term is borrowed from those Harry Potter books, but in geocaching, muggles are what seasoned cachers call those who aren't cachers." Ren hikes through the clearing I made for her. The path is tight and when she walks past me, her shoulders brush against my chest. *Shit. Even her shoulders turn me on. This girl will be the death of me.*

"Yesterday, you were a muggle. Today, you're not." At this, she flashes me a wide, toothy grin.

"That is so cool! And I thought I was doomed to live the rest of my days as a muggle."

Safely past the overgrown foliage, she takes my hand in hers, setting them swinging. "Maybe now, since I'm no longer a muggle, I can master the Wingardium Leviosa charm. I've always wanted to fly." Looking at me, she wags her eyebrows. "Are you a Harry Potter fan? What house are you?" She stops abruptly, whirling on me. "No wait, let me guess."

I lean back against a tree and cross my arms, enjoying the moment, reveling in how damn cute she is, and how much she's going to freak out when I tell her I've never read *Harry Potter*, or seen the movies. Reading just wasn't my thing in school and back when the movies were popular, I was all about doing the exact opposite.

"Given your professions, the whole protecting-and-serving gig, I'd say you're a Gryffindor." A breeze ruffles her wavy hair and she swipes at her bangs.

I shrug and drop the backpack and GPS on the ground, smiling wryly.

Ren's big, dark eyes get even bigger. "That's it? A shrug? Am I right?" She takes three steps, inching up the small incline to where I'm standing.

"I'll have to take your word for it. I don't know what a Gryffindor is, or a Wingdingum Lovesa."

Ren's eyebrows dart up and her eyes pop wide. "WHAAAT!" she roars. A bird, startled by her outburst, swoops from the tree overhead and a shower of leaves rains down on us. Ren claps a hand over her mouth and giggles, stepping right in front of me. If it weren't for the playful smirk on her face, I would have thought she was seriously angered by my admission. *Fuck, I want to kiss her.*

Quieter this time, she adds, "You did not just say you don't know what a Gryffindor is, did you? And it's Wingardium Levi-*o*-sa," she enunciates.

I lean down, our faces just inches apart. "I hope this isn't the deal breaker, because I really want to kiss you right now." I pick a leaf from her hair and tap it against her nose.

For a moment, I think she might be considering her escape options. Maybe it is beyond the realm of possibility to be attracted to someone who is not a Harry Potter fan. I can't get a read on her. She stares, blinking a few times, and I'm distracted by the way her lashes curl, brushing along the delicate skin beneath her eyes. Every time I look at her, I find something new and fascinating, something that makes me realize she's more special than every other girl in my past.

It may be too soon to kiss her, I know we only met last night, but I can't help it. I rest my palm against her cheek. She's soft and warm and when she leans into my touch, I don't need any more of an invitation. Inches become millimeters and then my lips are on hers.

Our mouths find a slow, hesitant rhythm, dancing just along the surface, getting acquainted. She's shy and tentative, guarded.

I bring my other hand to her face, cradling her head between my palms, letting my body language speak to her... *You're safe with me. I'll protect you.* With the slightest pressure in my fingertips, I draw her closer.

Keeping it slow, I open my mouth and trace my tongue along the seam of her lips, memorizing each curve, tasting the subtle flavor of her fruity lip balm... pressing, hoping she wants more.

Ren sighs; melting into me, and her tongue meets mine.

Lightning rips through my veins, white hot, and my self-control is incinerated. I slide my fingers into her hair, and sweep my tongue into her mouth. I can't stop there. My arms are around her, engulfing her body with mine.

Her hands go to my face, anchoring me to her. The tips of her fingers trace over the scar at my temple. The usual apprehension doesn't come. I welcome her touch, the wildfire that's sweeping through my body.

In one quick motion, I spin her around and guide her backward until she thumps against the tree I was just leaning on. I plant my hands on each side of her head and press our bodies together.

"Oh—" she murmurs, exhaling.

Her breath becomes mine.

I take her bottom lip between my teeth and nip before plunging my tongue deeper into her mouth, unable to fight the groan that rumbles in my chest. Kissing her destroys all my self-discipline. I can't get enough.

"Mmm," she hums, pressing her hands against my chest. "Cayden..." She pushes more forcefully.

And that's my cue to stop.

I drop my hands and step back. Falling into the depths of her eyes, my shoulders heave. "Are you okay? Did I hurt you?"

She shakes her head, pulling in a lungful of air. "No, not at all."

Even though she's smiling, there's an unsure, almost skittish quality to her features. *Great, Sinclair, you're batting a thousand. Way to scare her. Again.*

"I'm sorry," I breathe out. "I got a little carried away."

"You're not the only one," she sighs, putting her hand on my arm. "Don't apologize, you did nothing wrong. I haven't been kissed like that in a long time. It was nice." The anxiety that clouded her face a second ago subsides, replaced by the easygoing playfulness that she's exuded all day long.

"Are you sure?" Worry stabs my gut. I don't want to screw things up with her. I know it's selfish—there are so many reasons why I shouldn't pursue a relationship right now—but she makes me want more than just a career, more than being alone at night. I don't know Ren yet, but the promise of getting to know her negates all my reservations.

Ribbons of sunlight fall over her face as it filters down through the trees. It takes all my restraint not to run my fingers over her cheekbones. I'm already addicted to touching her, craving the high her contact brings. "Positive," she reassures.

Nodding, I take her hand and she gives them an easy swing.

"Okay." Lifting my belongings off the ground, I make a point to save this location as a waypoint in my GPS. My dad was a hopeless romantic when it came to my mom, and I learned from the best. I save the coordinates of our first kiss, triangulated to this very point on earth, forever, because I don't ever want to forget.

CHAPTER SEVEN

REN

I grip the sides of the GPS and spin around. The arrow on the screen follows suit. "I don't know which way to go. It says this way." I point to a path overrun by a sticker bush with adamantium thorns that could easily be confused with Wolverine's claws. I look like the resident bad-boy of the X-men ravished me.

"I led us that way and there's nothing there." Frustration bleeds into my voice. I hope he doesn't think I'm not having fun, because I am; this is the best first date I have ever been on, Cayden hit the ball out of the park with this idea. And whoa, that kiss…that was Noah and Allie–level hot. I hadn't intended to slam on the brakes when things were getting good, but my self- protective mode kicked in, as it always does.

"Here, let me see." He holds out his hand for the device and I plop it down with a huff. Cayden turns slowly, letting the arrow get back on course. He points. "That way."

"We just came from that direction," I sigh. "I suck at this."

"Nah, you're doing great for your first time. Not all caches are hidden in such difficult terrain."

In three wide steps, Cayden leaps over the adamantium thornbush and scales the incline on the other side. *Show off.* Unlike me, he's in top physical condition (a condition I wouldn't mind having the pleasure of exploring someday). The thirty minutes I put in on my treadmill every now and then have not equipped me for leaping large bushes in a single bound.

"Ren, get a running start, jump over the bush, and reach for my hand. I'll pull you up," Cayden shouts from the top of the hill on the other side of the path.

He doesn't know it yet, but I give the best side-eye in the state, just ask my little brother. Every time Griffin asks to borrow my car, I get a little closer to side-eye perfection. "Yeah, why didn't I think of that?"

"You can do it," Cayden cheers. He's enjoying every minute of this.

I take five giant steps backward. One of two things is going to happen: I clear the bush and make it up the steep hill unscathed, or I end up with thorns up my ass and Cayden has to pluck them out. I can see the headlines now: *Nurse Attempts Death-Defying Leap Over Rare Adamantium Bush. Nurse's Ass Impaled by Wolverine Claw–Like Thorns. Would-be Boyfriend Forced to Perform Radical Thornectomy—There Won't Be a Second Date.*

With a deep breath, I take off down my crude runway, closing in on the bush. *One. Two. Three.* I clench my eyes shut, hold my breath, and jump.

Before my feet even hit the ground, a strong hand latches on to my left forearm and hauls me up in one swift motion. I exhale and feel muscled arms around my waist, gently lowering me to the ground. When I open my eyes, Cayden's beaming face is all I see.

"You made it." His voice rumbles low, and I feel the vibrations against my chest.

I'm glad he's holding me, because the bones in my legs just disintegrated. "Nice catch," I gasp, still out of breath from jumping that damn bush.

"I'll catch you any day." He winks, holding me tighter against his body.

Okay, bones in legs, gone. Lady parts, melted. Cayden Sinclair's superpower is reducing me to a quivering mass of goo. "Where do we go from here?" I ask, trying to compose myself.

"Oh, I've got some ideas." One of his eyebrows darts up.

I start to feel my legs again. Slapping his arm I pull back, but don't break out of his hold (I'm not that stupid). "I'm beginning to think the whole 'men think about sex every seven seconds' myth has some truth behind it," I tease, feeling more comfortable with him.

"Only if they're with the right woman. Then it's probably every five."

"Oh my God!" I take a step backward and laugh.

"Sorry, sweetheart. Now that I've kissed you, my mind is thoroughly in the gutter."

My breath hitches and my heart skips a beat. I really like him and he's so friggin' sexy, he's got *me* thinking about sex every five seconds. But, how far will he be willing to take our relationship when he finds out that I'm all he'll ever have—no kids, no family, just me.

It's so ridiculous to be thinking that far down the road, I mean, we only just met. But that's my life now. Every man I meet, I have to consider the fact that he's looking to settle down and have a family. The downside to dating in my mid-twenties. High school, college, guys didn't care about settling down. Now that I'm older, family is on my mind, so I know it has to be on his too, right? I can do the settling down part, no problem. As a matter of fact, I want to settle down. I'm over the dating scene. But, the family part is a little more difficult. I've had some time to come to terms with the fact that it's very unlikely that I'll ever be able to conceive a child, but is it right to give a guy false hope and keep quiet? Yet, if I bring up the subject of children now, on our first date, I'll have him running for the hills.

I tear my gaze away from his and locate the GPS. Time to change the subject. No more sexy talk…at least for five seconds. Bending over, I pick the device off the ground. "I meant, where does *this* thing say we should go?"

Cayden walks behind me and rests his chin on my shoulder, bringing his arm around me to point to the arrow on the screen. "We're here." He taps the screen, drawing a line to the right. "And the cache is here. About four paces east."

I angle my head in his direction. "Is that far?"

"Nah, roughly ten feet, give or take."

"Well, come on then. You promised me a treasure." I reach backward and find his hand. Latching on, I pull him along, pretending I can read the GPS…and picturing what it would feel like to have his hands on other parts of my body.

* * *

I come to a stop when the arrow is resting directly on the location of the treasure. "Wait. It's supposed to be right here. What does it look like?" I glance around half expecting to see a gleaming beam of sunlight shining down from heaven on a wooden treasure chest just waiting for Cayden and I to discover it. And I'm slightly disappointed that all I get is a heavily forested area and ground covered in soggy dead leaves.

"I could tell you what the cache looks like, but that's kind of like cheating. Half the fun is searching the area until you find it."

"You're a stickler for the rules, aren't you? Giving me the full caching experience?"

"You bet." He winks. "Nothing but the best for you, sweetheart." There's a note of seriousness in his voice, like he'd stop the world from rotating if I asked him.

"What time is it?"

Cayden cocks his head, giving me a puzzled look. "About noon, why?"

"I just wanted to see how long it has taken me to track this thing down. I must have set some world record for the longest treasure hunt, right?"

He waves away my sarcasm. "Nope, I don't know a cacher yet who's found the one stored on the International Space Station It's going to take a civilian a damn long time to locate that one."

I let out a long breath and squat low to the ground. Trying not to get to dirty, I carefully pick through the rotting leaves, brushing them to the side. I flip over a huge oak leaf and my heart jumps in my throat. "*Ahhhh!*" I jump back faster than a kid getting a flu shot. "Whoa! Yikes! That is a whole lot of yuck! I'm not going anywhere near that!" I point, still dancing around.

"What is it? What's wrong?" Cayden crouches beside the upturned leaf for a better look. Glancing over his shoulder, he laughs. "They're pill bugs, Ren."

"I don't care what they are, I'm not touching that. I *hate* bugs!"

Cayden brushes the nest of vile creatures away and waves me over.

I shake my head vehemently and fold my arms across my chest. "Uh-uh, mister. Ain't happening."

Coming to stand beside me, he offers me his hand. "Trust me." His words are baby soft. "I got rid of them. I promise." Slipping his fingers against my palm, he gives a gentle tug, and my arms come undone. Reluctantly, I let him lead me over to the *breeding ground*.

I bend down beside him, holding my weight in the balls of my feet, ready to spring away if I see any more critters.

"Here"—he guides my fingers to the dirt—"what do you feel?"

Cringing, I give my fingers a wiggle, feeling nothing but cold mud, thank God. Images of giant millipedes and scorpions come to mind. I know they're down here, swimming in the muck, waiting to snatch my fingers off the moment I bury them too deep. But then, my heart skips a beat when my fingers strike gold, or plastic rather.

"I think I found something." Pulling the cylindrical container out of the mud, I stand up, shaking away the sludge. It's a film canister. "Oh my goodness, is this it? Did I find it?" Giddiness takes over and I do a little victory dance. That GPS thingy wasn't lying; there really was something hidden here (I had my doubts).

Cayden laughs and it's like a warm ocean wave: strong and all consuming. I've always had a love affair with the ocean, the majestic pull that draws me close and won't let go, like the moon to the tide. That's Cayden's laughter. It rolls over me, engulfs me; I want to drown in it.

He wraps his arms around me and plants a kiss at my temple. "Congrats, you found you're first treasure. Hard fought, but you found it. Go on, open it."

"There isn't anything living inside, is there? None of those *things*?"

"The seal's pretty tight on those containers, that's why people use them. You're safe."

"I'm taking your word for it." I slip my thumb under the edge of the gray lid and pop it off. Turning the canister over, I shake the contents onto my hand: a rolled up piece of register tape, a miniature plastic tiger, a golf pencil, a pink bead, and a little silver charm shaped like a bird.

Cayden lets go of me and comes to stand at my side. He picks the register tape and pencil off my hand. "What is all of this?" I ask.

He holds up the paper, pulling it straight with his index finger and thumb. "This is the log. We're supposed to sign it."

"How many signatures are on there?" I sidle up next to him

to get a better look. This is fascinating. I know it's a long shot, but I sort of want there to be no signatures on the paper. I want this treasure to be mine and Cayden's, no one else's.

"About a dozen," he says, signing his name on the slip. My heart sinks a little as he passes me the paper and pencil.

I take it from him and do the same, writing my name and the date below his. "What's the point of this other stuff?"

"That's the fun part. If you have something to put into the cache, you can take one of those items."

I look down at my hand. I know exactly what item I want. This might not be our personal treasure chest, but how fitting that the first cache I find, it contains a bird. I love birds. Their ability to soar above everything, to get away, to be free and safe in the sky…there was a time in my life I wished I were a bird…weightless and unfettered…fearless.

I run my thumb over the shiny charm and look up at Cayden. "I guess I should have worn shorts with pockets." Patting the side of my hip, I quirk the corner of my lip up in a glum half smile and shrug. "I don't have anything to put inside."

Cayden holds up his index finger. "I'm glad you didn't wear shorts with pockets. I like those shorts, remember." His eyes flash and he spins on his heel. "Don't worry, I've got you covered." Kneeling down at his backpack, he rummages through it, pulling something out as he stands. "If you want to take something from the cache, you can replace it with something from this bag." He holds a gallon size Ziploc bag out to me, filled with miscellaneous trinkets.

I fold my hand around the small items from the film canister and drop them back inside. Reaching for Cayden's bag,

I take a quick inventory: dozens upon dozens of beads, coins, plastic animals, rocks, gemstones, fake bugs, the list goes on and on.

"What should I put in there?" I don't want to take something from his bag that might be sentimental.

"Anything you want."

Unzipping the bag, I piece through it. "Are you sure?"

"Ren, it's not like there's a diamond in there, or anything. I carry it along so I have something to trade when I find a cache."

I look up at him and the sun catches his eyes making his bright green irises even more verdant. Fine lines crease his forehead and his gaze is thoughtful. "Is something wrong?" I ask.

He shakes his head and the lines soften. "Not one thing." Again, he points to the bag. "So, what'll it be?"

I wonder what he's thinking, but shove the thought away. Whatever it was, he's moved on. Turning my attention back to the bag, I spy a shiny, two-tone coin at the bottom. Digging my fingers through the trinkets, I latch onto the coin and draw it out. "How about this?" I hold it up between us.

"Does it fit inside the canister?"

I set it to the opening, turn it a few times, and press. "Yep."

"Good. Now, which item are you keeping?"

I stick my finger into the container, move the coin to the side, and shake the smaller contents back onto my hand. Picking up the silver bird, I say, "This one."

"Good choice." Cayden nods. "Now, we have to hide the cache exactly where we found it."

"Right." I snap the lid back on and hand it over to Cayden. "I'll let you do the honors."

Laughing, he takes the film container from my hands. "You're damn cute, you know that?" Walking back to the tree, be leans over, digs out a small hole with his finger, and plants the canister back into the mud, shoving black, wet leaves on top. "Like we were never here."

With the bird safe in my closed fist, I stand, and brush my other hand off on my shorts. I'm dirty and I still feel like bugs are crawling all over me. Cayden joins me slipping his dirty hand beneath mine—the one holding the charm—and slowly peels my fingers back, revealing my treasure.

"The bird, huh?" he murmurs.

Neither of us is looking at the charm, our eyes fixed on each other. I nod infinitesimally. Cayden traces his thumb over my palm, lightly fingering the charm. His touch sends shivers down my spine and my legs almost forget they're meant to hold me up.

His hands don't stop, though. His fingertips skim along my forearm…my elbows…down my hips as he pulls my body flush with his. Desire blazes in his eyes like green flames.

Without a word, he dips his head and kisses me, no hesitation. His mouth is firm, yet tender, and I answer with the same yearning, leaning into him. I stand on my tiptoes, and wrap my arms around his broad shoulders.

Cayden's hands glide over my ass, and I moan against his lips. This time, I take things further, trusting him more and more. I pull his bottom lip into my mouth and bite, just hard enough to elicit a groan and feel his tongue plunge into my mouth. I like this side of me, a woman who knows what she wants…a woman in control.

Each time our bodies rock together, I can feel his desire, hard and wanting, brushing against my legs. An ache blooms at my core, demanding attention...his attention.

Cayden's fingers knead my backside, pushing me as close as we can possibly be in the middle of a state park. He drags his lips across the corner of my mouth, over my jaw. I lift my head to the side, giving him better access. I can't catch my breath. My body screams to be touched by him, but I recognize the onset of panic just at the edge, a warning for me to slow things down. *Too fast, Ren. Too fast.*

"Cayden," I moan. *God, he feels so good.* "Cayden, we need—"

My words are silenced with his mouth and my head spins. His tongue is insistent for a second more—a hot dance of give-and-take until we're both out of breathe, and he slows, opening his eyes. His lips steal a final kiss, and he breaks away.

How can he already read me? Sense when my anxiety kicks in? Know how far to push me, and when to back off?

Pressing his forehead to mine, he whispers against my lips, "Ren..."

"Hmm?" My shoulders heave. My body screams to finish what we started, but my brain is saying a quiet *thank you* for obeying the speed limit and throwing on the brakes.

After so many sessions with my therapist, I've learned to accept that intimacy will always be difficult. And it is, especially when trust hasn't been established. It's why dating is so hard for me, but Cayden is different, and I don't know why. Building trust with him seems as easy as breathing.

"There I go, getting carried away again," he says, laughing

under his breath. "I don't know a thing about Harry Potter, but I do know you've put a spell on me. You are definitely not a muggle."

The dark thoughts of my past disappear and a laugh buried deep in my core bubbles to the surface. "Cayden"—I choke on a giggle—"that is the worst pickup line I have ever heard." I drop my head onto his shoulder, still laughing.

His hands, big and strong, rub up and down over my back. "I could listen to you laugh like this all day long."

Lifting my head, I stare into his lovely green eyes. "That's nice to hear. But, your lack of Harry Potter knowledge is frightening, could be the deal breaker," I tease, knowing all to well *I* could be the deal breaker for him, in the end. But I keep quiet; it's way too soon to start talking long term. For now, I'll play it safe and see where this leads. "I know exactly what we're doing for our second date."

Cayden presses his lips together, trying hard to conceal the cocky smirk pulling up the corners. "A second date, huh? My pickup lines can't be too bad then."

"Well, considering this all started because you pulled me over. I have to say, Officer, you're pickups are very unconventional." I give him a wink and lean in for another kiss, softening at his touch.

CHAPTER EIGHT

CAYDEN

"So, what's this I hear about Big Daddy hooking up?" Vin teases. "'Bout fucking time you got laid."

I roll my eyes and knock back my bourbon. "How the hell did you hear about that?"

"Can't keep his trap shut." Vin tips his head in Taz's direction.

I give Taz a sour look. He shrugs, a smug grin on his face. I can't tell that asshat anything in confidence. "And it's not like that, Vin. We are not 'hooking up,' we've been on one date." And, Ren isn't that kind of woman.

"I'm happy for you, man." Taz clamps his hand on my shoulder. "At least this time, you aren't leaving. You can actually put the time in, commit. See where it goes."

"Yeah, but I'm not sure if the time is right. Mom's sick, SWAT is this close"—I hold my thumb and index finger an inch apart.

"B.D., you deserve to be happy, man. Cut yourself some

slack," Vin says. "I mean, come on, look at me and Emily. We've been married two years, I've been deployed seven months of those two years, and now she's pregnant, and I'm going back. I'm not going to get to see my kid be born. Don't bitch to me about timing. The time's never right, but if you want a life, a family, you can't keep waiting for the stars to align. Sometimes, you have to shove them into the fucking picture you want."

"That's poetic, man," Taz says, clinking his bottle's neck on Vin's.

Shit. Why am I such an insensitive bastard? I didn't even think about what Vin's going through right now. He's got to be scared out of his mind. "Vin, I'm sorry. I didn't mean—"

He puts his hand up, cutting me off. Lowering the beer bottle from his lips, he swallows. "Don't worry about it, man. I would hate for you to throw away something good, just because it wasn't convenient. In my experience, the best things in life come around when it's least convenient. That's how you know they're worth fighting for."

"What's her name?" Taz asks.

"Ren. She's coming over to my place for dinner tonight. A second date." Thinking back to our first date, three days ago, I can't help but smile.

"See, I know that look." He snaps his fingers and points at me. "You're a sappy mess and you've only had one date. I've been there, man. I've been there." Vin's trails off, lost in his own memories. "Now, we just need to find Taz and Bull women, and we'll all be happy."

"A poet and a romantic. Vin, I'm seeing a whole new side of

you," Taz says. "And I do not need a woman, thank you. I like my bachelor pad just the way it is. Speaking of which, B.D., would you mind checking in on my place while I'm gone? Feel free to stay over, use the grounds, whatever. I just want to make sure it's in good hands."

"Yeah, Taz, no problem." I wave my hand.

Reaching into his pocket, Taz pulls out his key ring. Twisting the key off, he says, "This is for the back door. I'll text you the code for the garage. If repairs or maintenance are needed while I'm gone, just keep a log and I'll reimburse you when I get back."

I've been in Taz's position. Mom and Dad were in charge of my place during my last tour. I'm glad I can pay it forward and help Taz out. "Consider it done, man. And Vin, I'll keep an eye out for Emily. If she needs anything, you have her call me. We're family. I may not be following you into battle this time, but I've got your six."

"Will do, Big Daddy."

"It sucks that Bull couldn't come out. You guys know if he needs anything?"

Vin and Taz shake their heads. "You know Bull. The closer it gets to go-time, he disappears from civilian life. One week out, he's gearing up for the mission."

A dose of reality sets in. The guys are leaving. And I'm not. We sit quietly for a moment, nursing our drinks, bombs going off in our heads and visions of all the shit we endured the last time we were out of country.

"Be safe over there, brothers." I raise my glass. "Ooh rah!"

Vin and Taz raise their bottles and join in, "Ooh rah!"

* * *

The doorbell rings and my pulse speeds up like I've just run a 5K. *What if Saturday was a fluke and we really aren't compatible?* Not seeing Ren for three days was just enough time for doubt to worm its way into my head.

I toss the dish towel on the counter and dial the slow cooker to low, heading to the door. When I asked Ren over for dinner the other night, she said she loved barbecue (can she get any more perfect?) and it just so happens that I make a mean pulled pork. I hope she feels the same way.

Drying my sweaty palms on my jeans, I twist the knob and tug. It's a warm summer night and I can smell rain in the air. Ren stands on the porch, a six-pack in one hand and a Harry Potter DVD in the other. She's even more beautiful than I remember.

"Sorry I'm late, babies always have their own schedule." She scrunches her nose into a sheepish apology. I noticed her do it a few times on Saturday and it still has the same effect on me: *breathtaking*.

"Hey, no worries. I can't very well get made at a newborn for delaying our date." I wave off her apology and open the door wider. "Come on in."

She crosses the threshold and a cloud of awkward tension swallows us like a sandstorm. I drum my fingers on the door and push it closed. Hug her? Kiss her? What to do? I know what I want, but what does she expect? Shit. I'm a goddamn mess. I've had women over to my home before, where the hell is my game? I'm a damn bumbling idiot around this girl.

Ren scans the room, then turns to me, her dark eyes relaxed. "Nice place." She nods approvingly. "You're a country music fan?"

Luke Bryan's twang filters from my sound system. "I'm a country boy transplanted in the big city."

"I can't wait for you to meet my brother," she says with a smirk.

"Oh yeah? Planning on keeping me around long enough to meet the family?"

"I think the outcome is likely"—she holds up the DVD between us—"as long as we rectify this situation."

Closing the space between us, I reach for the six-pack. *Fuck's sake, she smells amazing.* Sweet, flirty, and all woman. I wouldn't mind if a hint of that citrusy flowery smell lingered on my sheets in the morning.

Our fingers touch as I fit my hand into the makeshift handle, relieving the pressure from hers. "I think that can be arranged." Images of Ren curled up on my couch, the lights turned down, and my hands on her body flash through my head. *Harry Potter* just might be my new favorite movie.

I set the beer on the small table beside the door and move in. Ren stands still, her eyes wide with desire. I pluck the movie from her other hand, toss it onto the six-pack, and pull her to me. "I've missed you."

A light smattering of freckles dots her nose and cheeks and I can't resist the urge to touch them. Lightly, I trace my fingertip from the apple of her cheek to the bridge of her nose, drawing constellations across her face. "Like a map of stars," I murmur.

She sighs, her shoulders relax, and she gives me her weight

to bear. Gravity does the rest and our lips meet. She lights a damn fire beneath my skin. I claim her mouth, tasting, pulling, sliding, wanting. I'm like a starved man in a pastry shop. *Fuck dinner, I'm ready for dessert.*

My fingers inch beneath the hem of her shirt, until my palms are flush against her hot skin. I push my hands upward, enjoying the feel of her curves.

Ren tilts her head, giving me access to her perfect neck, and I kiss my way along the line of her jaw, tasting the skin just below her ear. "Ren," I moan, "what do you say we just skip to dessert?"

She sighs, running her hands over the hair at the back of my neck, then her stomach growls, loudly.

I laugh against her neck, watching goose bumps rise at my touch and she giggles, squirming. "Cayden…"

Damn, I love the way she says my name. "Hmm?" I nibble on her earlobe, working my way back to her mouth. It's been neglected for far too long.

I close my mouth around hers just as she sighs, her breath becoming mine. Her tongue plays a game of *touch…retreat…touch…retreat…touch….*

My hands roam higher on her rib cage, feeling the wire of her bra and the curve of her breast against my fingertips, but Sunday pops into my head, take things slow…don't push her.

My dick and brain are at odds, but it's my brain that takes over when I slide my hands down to her waist, slow our kiss, and pull back. "Well, hopefully that convinces you to keep me around.'"

"Hmm," she says dreamily. "I may need more convincing

later." The playful, sexy lilt to her voice is enough to make me want to present my evidence now. If I don't get us to the kitchen soon, my dick is going to pull rank and we're going to hold court in my bedroom.

"Are you hungry?" I ask, trying to change the subject, but it doesn't matter, everything that comes out of my mouth sounds like a double entendre, whether I meant it to or not. "For food," I add.

There's a gleam in her eye, accompanied by a smirk. "Famished."

Bending down, I touch my lips to hers, kiss her gently, and return her smile. "How about some dinner?"

At that, I hear her stomach answer before the words escape her lips. Ren's laughter peels through my living room. "Yes, please!"

I find her hand, grab the six-pack , shaking the DVD onto the table for later, and lead her to the kitchen.

"Cayden," she sings. "It smells amazing in here."

"Thanks. Everything's ready to go." I pull her chair out, "For you, ma'am." I sweep my hand, ushering her to the seat, and give a slight bow as she sits.

"Why, thank you, kind sir," she says, affecting a southern accent and batting her long lashes. Like Sunday, she wears very little makeup, if any at all. I love that. She doesn't need makeup; it would only hide the perfection she's got going on naturally.

I whirl around, pick up the slow cooker, and bring it to the table.

"Can I help?" she asks, lifting the lid on the crockpot. The scent of spices and smoked meat billows upward and a fragrant cloud fills the kitchen. Ren looks at me, blinking. "A gourmet cook?"

Setting the cornbread and grilled vegetables on the table, I scoff, "I hardly think grilling up some meat and letting it simmer in a crockpot counts as gourmet."

"Whatever, guy. This spread qualifies as food porn. It's Instagram worthy."

I shake my head, unable to keep the smile off my face. "Want a beer?"

"Yes, please. Besides indulging in a little too much champagne at Dylen's wedding, I'm not much of a drinker, but my brother said that's a good one."

I set two beers on the table, along with plates and utensils, and park my rear in the seat next to hers. "He isn't wrong. Can't go wrong with Schlafly. Go on, dig in."

We both dive into the pulled pork at the same time, filling our plates. I watch her pile her bun with a large portion of barbecue. It's nice to see a girl with a healthy appetite, not one of those "I only eat lettuce and drink water on a date" types. A woman who loves food as much as I do is a keeper in my book.

Picking up her sandwich, she takes a bite and moans, "Cayden—"

Hearing my name come out of her mouth like that sends all the blood in my body rushing south. My dick still hasn't given up trying to convince me that Ren and I should be in the bedroom. I shift in my seat, trying to accommodate the hard-on she just gave me.

I cough and take a long pull on my beer. Elements of the

SWAT physical training test run though my head as I try to compose myself: one-mile run, heavy, hot tactical gear, wall climb, vertical raises...

"Cayden?"

I feel a hand on my arm.

"Are you okay?" Ren asks.

I glance down, looking at her slender short-nailed fingers, then bring my eyes up to hers, I nod. "Oh, yeah. Great."

She smiles. "You disappeared for a second."

Yes. Yes I did... with you... in my bed. "Sorry." I flash a congenial grin.

"The food's amazing, Cayden. So much better than the bowl of cereal I had waiting for me at home."

"Cereal?" I raise an eyebrow.

"Let's just say, I didn't inherit my mother's knack for cooking."

That's okay, I'll cook for you any day, sweetheart. "Tell me about your family," I say, taking a bite of my sandwich.

"There's Mom and Dad and my little brother. The four of us. Oh, and my brother's girlfriend, I've known her since we were kids, she's like a sister."

"I take it you're close to your brother; you've mentioned him a couple times."

She chews for a second and nods, covering her mouth with her hand. "Mmm-hmm." Swallowing, she continues. "Very. A couple months ago, he was in a terrible motorcycle accident. We almost lost him. It was awful."

"He's okay now, though?" I ask, wanting to know everything about her; what she loves, what she hates, what kind of cereal is her favorite, what she dreams about when she falls asleep at night…will our children have her dark hair or my green eyes. I want to know her past, her present, and our future.

"Yeah, he's getting better every day."

"That's good to hear." I tip my beer in her direction and take a drink.

"How's your mom doing?" she asks.

"Hanging in there. Kicking cancer's ass."

Ren sets her elbows on the table and rests her chin on her folded hands, a tender smile touches her eyes. "I like that look."

I set my empty beer bottle down. "What look?"

"That one." She cocks her head in my direction. "The fire in your eyes that says you'll travel to hell and back for your mom. The fierce, protective set of your shoulders that says you would gladly fight this war for her. You love her with every fiber of your being, and it shows." She grabs her beer and holds it up. "You're a good guy, Cayden Sinclair."

I lean back in my chair, speechless, and in awe of the woman sitting next to me. *A good guy that's falling hard and fast for you, Ren Daniels.*

CHAPTER NINE

REN

"Lean forward a sec." Cayden puts his hand on my back and reaches over me, flipping the switch on the wall, turning out the lights.

The room is plunged into darkness, except for the glow of the lamplight on Privet Drive emanating from the television screen.

Cayden leans back, sinks down into the cushions and gets comfortable. He raises his arm and pats his chest, and invitation to snuggle up next to him.

Don't mind if I do! I slide in and lay my head on his rock-hard chest as he drops his arm around me. *Good Lord, does he smell good!* I have to fight the urge to plant my nose against his shirt and take a giant whiff. Faint scents of the grill still linger, along with a dark, woodsy smell. Very outdoorsy, which is so Cayden. Whatever cologne he uses, it's working for him.

"See," he says, running his hand up and down my arm, slow

and easy. "I knew there was a reason I waited to see these movies."

"Dylen and I had a Potter marathon about a month ago. Kind of a last hurrah before she got married," I say wistfully, wondering if we'll have any more weekends like that. Who says twenty-somethings aren't allowed to have sleepovers? *I miss my friend.* "We watched all eight movies over the course of a weekend, pigged out on pizza, peanut butter M&M's, and drank so much butterbeer, our stomachs hurt for three days. It was great."

"Butterbeer? That sounds disgusting."

Ahh! I love how his chest rumbles when he talks. It's so frigging sexy. I crane my neck to look at him. "Hey, don't knock it if you've never tried it."

"How does one come by the recipe for a drink that only exists in a work of fiction?" he asks.

I shake my head. "Pinterest. Duh."

Cayden flexes his biceps, in turn pinning me against him in a vise-like hug. Moving his hand to my side, he hums a breathy falsetto in my ear, "Pinterest. Duh." Mocking me, his fingers wiggle across my middle, firing a path of tickles over my sensitive abdomen.

I fall to pieces in laughter. "Cayden!" I shout. "Ahh!" I try to push his hands away, but he's relentless. "Uncle!" I cry. "Uncle!"

"Oh no, sweetheart, you don't get off that easy," he teases. "Sassing a police officer is a punishable offense, ma'am."

He sits up and I take the opportunity to squirm from under his deft fingers by falling back on to the couch. For a second,

I'm able to catch my breath. I watch him over the rise and fall of my chest and our eyes lock on to one another's. A lightning bolt of desire, fanned into a lust-fueled blaze, strikes our playful interaction.

Cayden shifts his weight, angling his body over mine. Pushing my knees apart with his, he hovers over me. "You have the most gorgeous laugh, Ren Daniels," he says, his voice low and husky. Sweeping my bangs out of my eyes, he runs his fingers through my hair.

Oh. My. God. Is this happening? Now? Am I ready? Do I want this? So many questions run through my head, but all I can focus on is the way my chest brushes against Cayden's when I inhale. Even through the material of my shirt and bra, my nipples harden.

If it's any consolation, I'm not the only one who's hard. I can feel Cayden's massive erection pressing against my inner thigh. A dull ache grows between my legs and heat spreads south. My body knows exactly what it wants, my head, not so much.

"Thank you." My lips form the words, but no sound accompanies them.

Cayden strokes his thumb along the side of my eye, easing the tension. I must wear my anxiety like a parka in summertime. And here I thought I was doing a good job at keeping my fears at bay.

It's been so long since that awful night three years ago—since that faceless guy stole a part of me. It's taken a long time to get where I am, lots of counseling and healing, but with each new relationship, I've come to realize that I'll always cling to that piece of uncertainty—never fully embrace intimacy—because I cannot find that severed piece of my soul.

"Ren"—my name falls from his lips like a blessing—"it's no secret that I'm attracted to you," he says, holding me with his eyes. "You are the most amazing, fascinating woman I've ever met."

My throat tightens. I don't want to cry. Not here. Not like this. He'll think I'm a damn basket case. I bite back tears, holding my breath.

"Whenever I get to close, or our kisses get out of hand, I don't know?" He shakes his head, turning his gaze downward. Moving his hand from my face, his fingers trace the hollow of my throat, fingering the charm I found in the cache on Saturday. He glances back up at me. "You look like a frightened bird." Pushing up, he grabs my hands, and I come up with him. "The last thing I ever want to do is scare you." His voice is serious and fervent. "I don't know what happened in your past. I hope to earn your trust, so you'll let me in one day. But I want you to know, *you* call the shots." He points. "We'll take things as slow or fast as you want. I'm just glad you're here. That you want to spend your time with me."

A small tear rolls down my cheek, betraying me. Cayden is quick to reach up, swiping it away with his thumb. "I never want to be the reason for your tears, but I want to be the one to catch them when they fall."

"Cayden—" No more words will fit through the constricted space of my throat, but his name is enough, and I smile.

Cayden presses his palm to my cheek. "There's your smile," he croons. "I don't ever want to be the reason it disappears."

I sit up on my knees and touch his face, feeling the jagged scar at his temple, the fine stubble of his cheek scratching against my hand. I can't talk, a cascade of tears threatens to pour from my eyes. But, I lean into him and wrap my mouth around his in a quiet kiss—a "thank you" for understanding what I can't articulate.

CHAPTER TEN

CAYDEN

After a day on patrol, five traffic violations, two domestic calls, and a grueling workout, I'm ready to hit the shower, pick up Ren, and spend a quiet night with her.

Peeling off my sweaty T-shirt, I massage my left shoulder. Fuck, is that sore. I really overdid it on the shoulder presses today.

"Yo, Sinclair!"

I freeze, mid massage. "Yeah?" I call back, recognizing my friend Rigg's voice.

Riggs sticks his head around the row of lockers. "Get your shirt on, man, Cap wants you in his office."

Captain? Why the hell does he want to see me? Being called into Captain's office is never a good thing. I can't think of anything I'd done wrong; I'm always so careful not to screw things up, with SWAT on the line, and all. I need that goddamn job.

I whip my shirt off the bench and shrug it back on. "You know what he wants?"

Rigg's bites back a shit-eating grin. "Hell if I know. What the fuck you do?"

I give him a sidelong glance and follow him out the door. "Did he say anything?"

He calls over his shoulder, "Yeah, 'Riggs, get Sinclair's ass in here.'"

Great.

Riggs and I stop outside Captain Fuller's office. Throwing a punch in my shoulder he says, "Good luck, man." He thumps his chest; right over his heart, "I'll remember the good times," he chokes up, swiping at a nonexistent tear.

I give him the finger. "Fuck off, Riggs."

Walking backward down the hall, he grins and returns my sentiment, twofold.

Shaking my head, I turn my attention back to Captain Fuller's door and knock.

"Come in," he barks from the other side.

I twist the knob, steel myself for the worst, and push my way in. *Oh, fuck. This is bad. What's with the "I just ate nails" grimace on Cap's face?* "You wanted to see me, sir?"

"Sit down, Sinclair." He motions to the chair in front of his desk.

Crossing the small office, I pull back one of the chairs and sit. Cap closes the file on his desk and stands, finally making eye contact with me. "SWAT, huh?"

My heart pounds like a jackhammer, but on the outside I keep my emotions on lock. "Yes, sir."

"You haven't been on the force for long, Sinclair. 'Bout a year and a half? A little soon to be throwing your name in the mix, don't you think?"

"Yes, sir. I agree. It is soon, but I've trained hard. I'm ready, sir."

Cap walks around his desk and sits on the corner, folding his arms across his chest. "SWAT members are usually chosen from a pool of candidates with more time under their belt."

Keep your shit together, Sinclair. Bile rises in my throat and the urge to plant my fist into my locker hits me like enemy fire.

"I've reviewed your application. You scored well on your written exam, physical training, and psych eval. Plus, your time in the Corps works in your favor, but I can't overlook the two-year rule the department has in place. I'm sorry, Sinclair, but I cannot pass your name onto Sergeant Duchesne at this time."

I bite down hard on the inside of my cheek. My blood runs hot, boiling with anger. I've worked so fucking hard for this opportunity only to be denied on fucking department proto-col, motherfucking red tape?

"I understand, sir." I stand and hold out my hand to him, keeping my cool. If the Corps taught me one thing, it was to keep my shit together when things go south, and right now, my career just took the express lane to fucking hell. "I appreci-ate the fact that you considered my application."

"It's just not the right time, Sinclair." He takes my hand, shaking it firmly. "If you're still interested in SWAT in six months, resubmit your application and well take another look. You'll have more time on the force at that point."

Interested? Resubmit? What the hell am I going to learn in six months that I don't know today? "Absolutely, sir. You will see my application again in six months."

Dropping my hand, he says, "I hope so. You're an asset to the force, Sinclair, you'll make a fine member of SWAT one day." Cap heads to the door and pulls it open. I'm officially dismissed. "See you, Monday, Sinclair."

Stepping out of Captain Fuller's office, I turn back to my commanding officer and kiss his ass again, "Thank you, Captain."

Cap nods and shuts the door.

Holding onto the rage a little longer, I walk back to the locker room, ready to pound the fucking shit out of my locker door.

* * *

Before my knuckles hit Ren's door, she pulls it open, and is in my arms. "So, any news?" she asks.

I close my eyes and my arms go around her faster than a round from an M40. Her coconut-scented shampoo conjures mental images of the two of us lounging on a deserted tropical island, waves crashing over our tanned, oiled bodies. After my shit day, the fact that my daydream is just in fact a dream, only adds to the dung heap. I can't tell her I didn't get the job. I can't let her know what a fuckup I am. She needs a strong man, someone that can provide for her, take care of her. Not a man that is passed over for a promotion on a technicality. My military résumé and exemplary department record should speak for its self, but none of that mattered.

Suck it up, Cayden. Six more months. Six more fucking months.

I shake my head. "Nothing yet." It kills me to lie to her, but I can't stomach seeing my failure reflected in her dark eyes.

She pulls back, holding me at arm's length, and my breath hitches. I get my first glimpse of her all dressed up and my sour mood disappears. She looks like the most decadent serving of strawberries and cream. The tops of her ivory breasts swell over the dipping neckline of her vibrant red dress, giving way to the short flare of her skirt and her long legs, which seem to go on for miles.

I brush the sides of her hair back, stealing the chance to run my fingers through her silky black waves. "I am so glad I pulled you over that day." Knowing I'd get to hold her at the end of this shit day quelled my anger.

"There are better ways to meet women, you know," she says, smiling reproachfully. "And technically, you didn't make a move until the next day."

"You have no idea what was going through my mind when I pulled you over." I lean in and kiss her, long and slow.

"Mmm," she hums against my mouth before drawing back. "I have a pretty good idea." She shimmies her hips against my crotch, seizing the attention of my dick. *Damn, the things I want to do to her.*

I sneak one more kiss, then glance at my watch. "You ready? We have dinner reservations at the Sidney Street Cafe."

"Oh, yeah. I just need to grab my purse." She runs back into her apartment and returns in a flash. As she locks the door, she says, "You do realize they don't serve barbecue and cornbread at Sidney Street, right?"

Spinning on her heel, she wheels around and grabs my

hand, giving it a playful swing. "I've been known to eat food that wasn't prepared on a pit or served at a Memorial Day picnic from time to time. But thanks for the heads-up."

Ren's heels click on the title floor as we make our way down the corridor. "Just looking out for you, big guy."

"Then I consider myself a lucky man if I've got you looking out for me."

"Not that superheroes need someone looking out for them, but I'm up for the job," she says with a wink.

"Superhero?" I scoff. *Definitely not that, sweetheart.* "Yeah, right."

"Well, let's see; you served our country as a Marine, you went to war," she says, holding up a finger for each point. "You're a cop and well on your way to the SWAT team. You're willing to put yourself in harm's way to keep others safe. Sounds like the definition of a superhero to me."

Well on my way? Am I? Doubt gorges on my ambition like an algae-sucking catfish. Thoughts of Dad hit me hard. He might be gone, yet I can't stand the fact that each time I fail, I let him down, just like I always seem to do. I run my hand over my head, feeling the scar on my temple. "You know, when I chose the Marines over college, I thought my dad would blow a gasket. He was an academic; education was his life. Teaching psychology at the collegiate level, it kind of had to be." I laugh humorlessly. Ren squeezes our intertwined hands and sets them swinging again—something she does each time we hold hands, a pendulum keeping our own time. "But, he didn't get upset," I continue. "He clapped a hand on my back, drew me into a hug and said, 'Son, I feel safer already, knowing you'll be out there protecting your mother and me.'"

Stopping at the elevator, Ren hits the button, and turns to me. "See, even your dad knew. He sounds like a great man."

I nod. "The best. I miss the hell out of him."

Bing. The elevator announces it's arrival and the doors open. I put my hand on the small of Ren's back and usher her into the elevator.

As the doors close, Ren sidles up against me and my arms have nowhere to go but around her. I hold her close, drawing on her strength. Our bodies complement each other perfectly. Her round curves fit neatly into the contour of my frame, like we were made for one another—two parts of a whole.

"I think it's safe to say, Cayden, your dad would have been extremely proud of the man you are," Ren says, her arms tight around my middle. "A superhero."

"There's nothing super in wanting to keep the people you love safe. It's what a man does." What my dad did for Mom…what I want to do for Ren. "But I'll take the hero part, as long as I get to be yours." I crush her to my side.

The elevator stops and we wait for the doors to open. Ren looks up at me, smiling. "We have got to work on your lines, Sinclair. Cheese city." She scrunches her nose up and shakes her head.

"Nah, I think they're working for me just fine." I run my hand down her hip and kiss her just as the doors open. I may not have gotten the job I wanted, but things can't be too bad when I get to end my day in the arms of a beautiful woman.

CHAPTER ELEVEN

REN

Cayden unlocks his truck, opening the door for me. I climb inside and watch as he rounds the front of the car, unable to keep my eyes off him. In my excitement upstairs, I hadn't noticed how delicious he looks in a dress shirt and tie. His massive arms pull against the confines of his shirt and my mouth goes dry. I'm suddenly very jealous of that shirt. The urge to rip it from his body, free those gorgeous arms, and run my hands (and my tongue) over the contours of his biceps hits me low in the belly, a radiant heat spreading through my veins.

I'm pulled from my lustful daydream when I hear the door open. Cayden slides in, his right arm, so close to my face, taunting me. He flexes, leans forward, and slips the key into the ignition. *God, you're torturing me. Why?*

The truck rumbles to life. "I forgot to tell you," he says, pulling onto the street. "You look stunning. That dress is…" He pauses, sneaking a glance in my direction. "It should be illegal for anyone to look that hot."

Oh, let's not talk about criminal, mister. Have you seen your arms lately? "Really? You didn't get any dates in high school, did you?" I sneer with laughter.

"The ladies couldn't resist," he says full of pride, puffing out his chest.

No doubt. I reach over and run my hand over his shoulder and slowly down his biceps, feeling the hard, sinewy muscles flex beneath my touch. *Shameless, I know, but it had to be done!* "I bet."

Cayden turns his head. "Sure you want to go to dinner?" he asks, raising an eyebrow. "I can turn this truck right around."

The butterflies in my stomach wake up all at the same time and start in on a Zumba routine. It's gotten damn hard to put on the brakes these last couple weeks, but I know the second I sleep with him, things will change. I may not remember what happened on the night of my birthday, but the fear and anxiety that accompany intimacy are real and tangible, and as much as I want to forget, leave them behind, I can't. I ache for Cayden's touch like my lungs beg for air, but I'm so fucking scared to taint "us" with my past.

I touch the silver charm at my neck. The day I found it, on our first date, I strung it onto a chain and haven't taken it off since. With Cayden, I feel more alive and free than I've ever felt with anyone. Things have changed. I can see a future with him, and it terrifies me that he may not want one with me when he finds out what secrets I keep.

The phone rings through the speakers of Cayden's radio: *Call from Mom* flashes on the dash.

"Sorry, Ren"—he pats his hand against my thigh—"I've got

to take this." Cayden pushes a button on his steering wheel and the call is connected. "Mom? Everything all right?" he asks.

"Cayden, are you busy tonight?" Mrs. Sinclair's voice is scratchy and weak.

Cayden looks to me, conflicted. I know he wants to please us both. I shake my head and mouth, *Dinner can wait. See what she needs.*

All the fine lines of tension disappear from his face. "Uh, no, Mom. You need something?"

"It's not a good night and Lacey can't come over."

My heart breaks for her, she sounds so weak.

"I'll be right there, Mom. I'm on my way. I've got Ren with me." He looks at me, a warm smile at his lips.

"I'm afraid I won't be very good compan—" Mrs. Sinclair breathes heavily through the speakers and starts coughing.

"Mom, what's wrong?" Concern drips from his voice and his foot presses down on the accelerator.

Yep, just like a superhero, flying in to save the day. My heart smiles at this.

Mrs. Sinclair's coughs fill the cab, distorted through the radio speakers.

"Mom?" Cayden says, louder.

"Sorry"—she coughs again—"I won't be good company. But I very much want to meet Ren. I'm glad she's coming."

"We'll be there in a few."

"Thanks, hon," she says and disconnects the call.

Cayden puts his hand on my leg. "Sorry about dinner."

I wave away his apology. "This is important."

"Ren Daniels, you are a special, special lady," Cayden says, shaking his head. "Thank you."

"No thanks needed. I like this change of plans. I'm excited to meet the other woman in your life." *Excited to meet the woman who raised someone as special as you, Cayden Sinclair.*

* * *

"And then," Katy says, huffing out a breathy laugh, "he cuts the cord of my curling iron, while it's on and plugged in, just so he could see what the wires looked like on the inside."

I look at Cayden, my eyes wide with amazement. "It is a wonder you're still alive."

He shrugs. "I was an inquisitive child." Bringing his chopsticks to his mouth, he powers down a mouthful of chow mein.

"Jumping off of roofs, dismantling toasters, cutting live wires? That's more than an intellectual curiosity, that's reckless."

"Oh, and when you got that scar." Katy points to Cayden's head.

I look at Cayden. "I've always wondered about that."

His jaw is clamped shut, a small tic visible low in his cheek. "I'd rather not talk about it," he says through clenched teeth.

Whoa. Found a Cayden Sinclair hot button. My curiosity spikes through the roof, not to mention my anxiety. What is *he* hiding? My mind touches on a dozen worst-case scenarios.

Katy nods, backing off. "Well, at least having Blake around made you a little more levelheaded."

Cayden shakes his head, like he's flinging off the weight of a bad memory, and he rolls his eyes. All conversation about his scar, dropped. *Am I okay with this?* I want to know what happened, what his secret is.

He has secrets, you have secrets. Get over it, Ren, the voice in my head reminds me.

"Blake," he mumbles.

I glance at Cayden just in time to see him rolling his eyes. The note of derision in his voice throws me. "What? I thought you two were close."

"We are, he's practically my brother. But, Blake and I were so different growing up. I was the 'reckless' one"—he air-quotes, giving me the side-eye—"and Blake was the cautious one."

"Yes," his mother adds, pointing at him.

Having known Blake for several years, I can attest to his prudent nature. Dylen is the wild one in that relationship, for sure. They balance each other out.

"I was glad to have Blake around, but it still wasn't the same. Sometimes, being an only child got lonely, which in turn fostered my inquisitiveness."

Katy smiles, but it doesn't touch her eyes, sadness lurks in the shadow of happiness. I know this look. A lie to yourself, a way to trick your mind into believing everything's okay. "Cayden always wanted a sibling," she says. "But after two miscarriages, Frank and I couldn't risk losing another child. Each loss was so difficult. The Thompsons helped us through those dark times, and over the years, Blake became like another son."

I can't begin to imagine the suffering Katy and Frank endured, suffering the loss of two babies. Between my job—having witnessed heart-wrenching sorrow when a couple loses a little one—and my own story, where my ability to have kids is questionable, I fight back tears. I don't cry often, but when it's the loss of a baby, I can't keep them at bay.

"Oh, honey," Katy says soothingly. "I didn't mean to upset you." Her worried gaze shifts from Cayden to me.

Cayden stands, swipes a tissue from the box on his mother's dresser, and comes to kneel in front of my chair. Putting his hand on my leg, he hands me the Kleenex. "Sweetheart?"

I wipe my cheeks. "I'm fine," I say, my voice thick with the tears I manage to hold back. "I have a hard time when babies don't make it."

"Ren's a maternity nurse, Mom."

I nod, swallowing the lump in my throat. My heart thumps in my ears, memories resurfacing. *Now is not the time to have a breakdown, Ren, pull it together.* I slap the lock back on my heart, trying to forget the pain and sadness of that night.

"Ren, I'm so sorry. I didn't know. Cayden mentioned that you were a nurse, but I didn't know what kind. "

"You don't need to apologize." I laugh weakly and run the tissue under my eyes, fearing I resemble a raccoon. *The one night I decide to put on a little makeup. Geez, Ren.* "I'm a hot mess." I force a laugh to lighten the mood.

Cayden rubs his hand soothingly over my thigh, a gentle smile on his face. "A beautiful mess," he teases.

"Thanks," I say, with a playful glare.

"Hold it right there, you two," Katy directs. "I need to get a picture."

I wave my hands. "Oh, Mrs. Sinclair, that's not a good idea. I look terrible."

With shaky hands, she holds up her phone. "Nonsense." She focuses her attention on her screen, centering Cayden and I. "Say cheese," she instructs, not taking "no" for an answer.

Cayden rests his arm on my leg, leaning his head against the side of mine. "Cheese!" we say in unison.

Katy taps her screen and admires the photo. "What do you think, Cayd? Do I still got it?" Flipping her phone around, Cayden scrutinizes the snapshot.

"Cancer can't take away your mad photography skills. One day, Mom, you'll have a house full of grandchildren to take pictures of," he says proudly, patting my leg and handing Katy's phone back.

Uhh…what? Is this something he hopes will happen with me? I should tell him that's not going to happen…at least not the old-fashioned way. I mean, there's always adoption, but what if he doesn't want that? Dammit. Pull it together, Ren, now is so not the right time to freak out about that.

Turning his attention back to me, his grin morphs from tender to joyful.

I give him a halfhearted smile in return; it's all I can do. If he wants a big traditional family, I'm not the woman for him.

"Ren—" Katy says, dissolving into a fit of coughing.

"Mom?" Cayden stands and is across the room in a flash. "You okay?" he asks, smoothing back her hair.

Patting his arm, she says, "Will you get—" She coughs some more, unable to finish her sentence. "Water," she finally croaks out.

I jump from my chair, wrapping a tight fist around the tissue. "I'll get it." I need to be alone for a minute, clear my head.

"Thank you," Cayden says, lines of worry creasing his face.

I head out of the room, thankful for the silence. Making my way down the spiral staircase, I notice at least fifty pictures lining the right side wall—the Cayden Sinclair Photo Gallery. Some are large photographs, others are small, but each placed with care and deliberation. I hadn't noticed them when we arrived having helped Katy to bed, but now, the hall light from upstairs shines on them like a spotlight.

The picture at the top step is Cayden in his dress blues, his mother and father proudly at his side—Cayden looks just like his dad. They both have the same tall frame, square jaw, and broad shoulders.

Taking another step, I see Cayden and Blake at their high school graduation, and another with Cayden in his cap and gown, his arm around other friends.

Worrying the tissue in my hand, I scan the length of the staircase: the photographic history of Cayden Sinclair lays before me. I could learn his whole life story just by traveling up and down the stairs a handful of times.

High school…sports…junior high…elementary school… Little League…friends…vacations…baby days…family… with each step, the pictures hypnotize me. I can't leave until I know everything about him.

A muffled, weak cough travels down the hall, drawing my attention back upstairs.

Oh shit! The water! Not earning the Nurse of the Year award tonight.

I sneak one last glance at a sweaty shaggy-haired (*Ahh!! He had long hair! So friggin' cute!*) Cayden in a football uniform, and race down the remaining stairs.

Jogging through the hallway, I search the wall for a light switch in the kitchen and flip it on. The kitchen is plunged into brightness and I squint against the shock.

I pad over to the fridge and pull it open, grabbing a water bottle from the shelf. Shutting the door swiftly, I turn and see Cayden standing in the entryway. "Oh!" I shout, putting my hand over my racing heart. "You scared me." I let out a huge breath.

A devious smile on his lips, all the tension and anxiety from when his mom brought up his scar has disappeared. He walks our takeout containers to the waste can, steps on the lever, and drops the empty boxes inside. "Sorry, didn't mean to sneak up on you. But, I'm not going to lie, I was enjoying the view."

"What? My backside?" I throw a self-conscious glance over my shoulder.

Cayden takes two steps and we're nearly eye-to-eye. Moving his hands to my waist, he presses his fingers into my side and pulls me against him. "This"—his hands roam to the small of my back...and lower—"is fucking gorgeous."

I swallow a sigh and try not to melt into a puddle at his feet. Forcing out the only words that come to mind, I hold up the water bottle . "Got the water."

He sways his hips, and mine in turn, teasing (and doing a damn fine job, at that). "Good. I was wondering if you got lost."

Nope, just distracted by your life's history along the staircase...and the lengthening hardness pressing between my legs.

"Sorry about earlier. I didn't think Mom was going to go into the miscarriage stories." He works his hands up my back, holding me closer.

"It's fine, really. I can't believe I turned into a blubbering mess." I lay my head on his shoulder and shake my head.

"I think my mom fell in love with you tonight. When you left the room, she couldn't stop gushing over you." His voice is deep and thoughtful. *Just your mom?* I want to ask, but, given the fact that I can't give him what he wants—his big family, lots of grandchildren for Katy—it's safer that I don't.

For three years, I've pushed away every guy I've dated, scared to let anyone inside. But everything is different with Cayden. When he touches me, I don't feel lost; I know where I want to go, and whom I want by my side when I get there.

Yet, even knowing I've found someone who centers me, I know I'm not good for him, and before things get more serious between us, I need to tell him…warn him, but the words stop at the edge of my tongue with no intention of falling beyond my lips.

"Ren?" he says, brushing his hand down the back of my head. "You okay?" He kisses the top of my head.

I nod, mumbling against his shoulder, "I'm okay." Looking up, I flash him a reassuring smile. "Let's get this to your mom."

Cayden grabs my hand and we turn to leave, flipping off lights as we head back up the stairs. Snippets of Cayden's life flash along the wall, one catching my attention. Halfway up the staircase, I stop. Cayden, still holding my hand, pauses the second he realizes I'm a step behind.

"Ren?" He backtracks, coming to stand beside me.

I point to the photo. "Is that you?"

He takes a closer look and nods. "Yeah, why?"

Drenched in sunshine, a young Cayden—not more than ten or eleven—stands in the middle of a forest clearing bowing his head over his folded hands. "What's this a picture of? You look so peaceful." I shift my gaze from the picture to Cayden.

A wistful smile touches his lips as the memory carries him to the past. "Dad took that picture. My first time using a compass," he says longingly. "We were hiking, Dad made me navigate our way back to the campground."

"Did you make it?" I want to be where he is. *Take me with you, Cayden.*

His eyes still glued to the picture, he nods. For a few quiet seconds more, Cayden visits with his dad. I can imagine he's recalling the rustling noises of the forest, the summer sun on his skin, and his dad's patient voice guiding him as he navigated them back home.

CHAPTER TWELVE

CAYDEN

I pull into an empty space in front of Ren's apartment and kill the engine. Opening my door, I step out just as a patrol car whizzes past, sirens blaring. How does she stand to live down here? All the crime, the constant noise. Her building has good security features, but it still makes me nervous knowing she's down here, alone.

Jogging around the front of the truck, I pull open her door and offer my hand. "You know," she says, slipping her hand into mine, "you don't always have to open the door for me. I won't think you're some kind of insensitive bastard, or anything." One heeled foot at a time, she steps down.

"Noted." I tap my index finger against my temple. "But as long as you're my girl, be prepared for the chivalric code, sweetheart." If there's one thing I learned from my father, it's how to treat the woman who owns your heart. "Oh, and you should note that I will never stop opening the door for you," I whisper, my mouth at her ear. "When I'm a hundred years old and you're ninety-nine, you might have to wait a good long while, but I will make it around the car to open your door."

"Noted," she says, touching her temple, and biting the corner of a coy smile.

Sweetheart, I'd open the doors to the world for you, if you'd let me.

I kiss the top of her head and inhale deeply, getting lost in the tropical scent of her hair. Tonight was just what I needed. Even though they don't know it, Ren and Mom kicked my foul mood in the ass.

Hand in hand, we climb the stoop and enter through the double doors of her apartment. Ren rummages around in her purse and pulls out her keys. "Do you want to come up?" she asks, her eyes locking on mine for a brief second before she turns to unlock the entry door.

Oh, sweetheart, do I. I want to pick you up, carry you into your apartment, kiss you senseless, and not stop until we're satisfied and tangled in each other's arms. "I'd love to."

With the door unlocked, I pull it open, and let her lead the way. Walking to the elevator bay, she presses the button and we wait.

Electricity charges the air and the hairs on my arms and back of my neck stand on end. My muscles flex, needing to touch her.

The elevator opens and Ren steps inside, me at her back. Sliding to the left, she pushes three on the panel of floor numbers, and leans against the wall as the doors close.

I've got to get my hands on her. Bursting her personal bubble of space, I slip my hands around her waist, our eyes locked. I wait for her frightened bird response, the one that tells me I've pushed her as far as she's willing to go. But right now, it doesn't come. The usual fear I see in her eyes is replaced with dark pools of desire, and I'm ready to dive in. I don't go slowly, crushing my lips to hers. She heaves a rapturous sigh, arching her body in offering.

I work my mouth over her lips, moving down the side of her neck, across her chest, placing a kiss over the charm she found on our first date.

Ren moans, her chest heaving as she wraps her arms around my head, allowing me to worship at her altar.

"Cayden…"

She's killing me. My name comes out of her mouth dripping in sex and it takes all my restraint not to take her right here. "I fucking love it when you say my name like that," I say against her mouth. Cupping her glorious tits, I'm praising and cursing this red dress. "Ren, I want you."

The elevator lurches to a stop and the doors open with a high-pitched ping.

"Fuck," I growl, forced to cease my ministrations. "Why don't you live on the thirty-third floor?" I breathe a harried laugh.

"God, why don't I?" she sighs, straightening her back, a wanton smile tugging at her swollen lips.

Pushing my fingers through her luscious curls, I bring her head to mine and kiss her again, one last time before we need to leave the elevator for good. "We should—"

The elevator cuts me off with an unceremonious, *ding*, and the doors slide closed.

I rest my head against her forehead and laugh. "We could travel up to the thirty-third floor." I wag my eyebrows.

She presses the open button, saying, "I have a better idea."

The elevator opens again and she grabs my hand, hauling me toward her apartment.

Inside, Ren kicks off her heels and we're no longer the same height. I've got a good five inches on her now. Taking her by the elbow, I spin her around, and pull her close. Not wasting another minute, I kiss her, reclaiming the intensity of what we had in the elevator. Stalking forward, I pin her between my body and the door. "You're right," I breathe against her mouth, "this is a better idea." My hands roam over her waist and down her hips, as my fingers work her dress upward. It's an amazing dress, but is has to go.

"Uh-huh," she moans, nodding. Bending down, I drag my lips over her cheeks, her jaw, paying close attention to her neck, with a gentle bite. Pulling my hands upward, her dress sits at her waist, giving my hands enough access to what's underneath.

Trailing my hands along the seam of her closed legs, I climb higher and higher, increasing the pressure, wanting her to open for me. "It's okay, sweetheart. Relax." My index finger meets the silk of her panties and I rub against her.

Ren turns her head, cutting off access to her neck and pushes on my shoulders, hard. I step back.

"Can I get you anything?" she asks, shoving her dress back in place. "A drink?" She walks toward the kitchen, not meeting my eye. *What the hell just happened?*

Still breathless and damned confused, I reply, "Uh, no

thanks. I have to be at work in eight hours." I follow her into the kitchen, needing her to talk to me. If I'm doing something wrong, I want to know. "Ren," I say, touching her elbow. Gently, I pull her toward me, careful to keep my distance.

She turns around, looking up at me with her sad, dark eyes. "You can talk to me. You know that, right?"

She nods, biting her lower lip. "Just give me a minute, okay?" she whispers. "I'm okay, I promise. I just need to take things slow."

"I can do slow." I give her a reassuring smile. Whatever haunts her, I don't want to be the person that dredges up those memories.

"Coffee?" She holds up the two mugs, one in each of her hands.

I nod, letting her set the pace. "Sounds good."

I walk around the counter and slide onto one of the barstools. I cross my arms, watching her move about the kitchen. It's such a strange dichotomy: even though she put the brakes on, the pull to put my hands on her is overwhelming, and yet I'm content to sit here and watch her all night, if that's what she wants.

It's unreal how well Ren fits into my life. I was so worried that having a love life would interfere with my job and take time away from Mom, but tonight proved that I can have it all. As a matter of fact, having Ren with me tonight made the blow from Captain Fuller bearable. Until she showed up, I didn't know how empty my life was, which is what Mom had been telling me all along.

Ren picks up a small remote on the counter and points it into the living room. A slow ballad with a heavy bass fills the room. Definitely not country.

"Oh, no. We cannot listen to this." She cringes and mashes her thumb against the buttons. There's a lull in the music and a song I recognize comes on, the song to which she lead me around the dance floor at Blake's wedding.

"What was wrong with the other song?" I rest my elbows on the counter, memorizing every facial expression, every line and curve of her body. I can't get enough of the graceful sway of her hips as she pulls a box of coffee pods from a high shelf. What makes this whole scene perfect: she has no clue how fucking sexy she is.

"You really don't know who that was?" She looks over her shoulder.

"Not a clue, sweetheart. My name-that-tune knowledge is best if the performers hail below the Mason–Dixon line."

"Hmm…" Bemused, she pops a coffee pod into the Keurig and closes the lid. "And here I thought everyone in the bi-state area knew that group."

"Not everyone. Who is it?" I'm beginning to wonder if I should know.

"It's Mine Shaft. My brother's band. They're alt-rock." The Keurig sputters and Ren pulls the steaming mug from beneath the spout and passes me the first cup. I take it off her hands and she quickly starts the next.

"Guess that's why I've never heard of them." I shrug, pressing the rim of the coffee mug to my lips. Sipping carefully, I wince, the bitterness and the temperature assault my tongue, a double whammy. "That's a strong cup of joe, sweetheart." Coffee's not my caffeinated beverage of choice, but when there's paperwork to be filed, the clock's ticking slow on the late shift, and there's no Mountain Dew in sight, it fits the bill.

She smacks her palm against her head. "I'm such a dope. I drink mine black, so I didn't even think to offer you any cream or sugar." She bites her lip, suddenly shy. "I don't do a lot of entertaining, either, so I'm not the best hostess. I'm used to Dylen making herself at home."

I stand and make a slow jaunt around her counter, our gazes locked. "Shhh…" The granite countertop is cool under my fingers. One foot in front of the other, I stride closer to where I want to be, hoping she won't push me away this time.

Three…two…one…

Ren shuffles backward, leaning against the counter, staring up at me.

Calm yourself, Sinclair. Take it slow. Don't rush this. Don't scare her.

"Is this okay?" I ask, slipping a big, floppy curl behind her ear. All evening, I've watched that curl fight a losing battle, hanging over her left eye only to be shoved back in line with the others. It's determined though, refusing to give up the war. "I've wanted to do that all night."

Ren nods. There's still apprehension in her eyes, but she's not pushing me away.

I drag my thumb over the curve of her soft bottom lip. "We'll move at your pace, okay?" Her mouths parts and she exhales, her hot breath fanning out over my hand. A flame ignites inside me. Tracing the curve of her mouth, where skin meets lip, it takes all my strength not to throw her on the counter and bury myself deep inside her.

Eyes still locked on one another, I feel the tip of her tongue sweep over my thumb as she slowly licks her lips. My dick throbs, begging to be freed from the confines of my pants.

Setting my hands at her waist, I lift her onto the countertop, gently running my hands down the smooth fabric of the red dress that's teased me all night. Hell, who am I kidding, *she's* tortured me all night.

I brush my fingers along the tops of her thighs, like I did earlier. With unhurried, deliberate movement, I gauge her reaction. I've seen apprehension, disquiet, and unease reflected in her dark eyes, something plaguing her whenever sex is on the horizon. It breaks my heart to see uncertainty and doubt in her eyes when she looks at me. I don't know what happened in her past, but I know she lived through something frightening. I want her to know I'm not that guy; I would never hurt her. I want my touch to silence her fears.

Ren parts her legs and moves her hands up my arms, inviting me in. Her eyelids close as she tilts her head, and I meet her halfway, our mouths barely touching. "Are you sure?"

She nods. "It's okay...I'm okay."

Dragging my lips against hers, more blood rushes south. My body urges me to speed up the pace. I want to be inside her more than I want to breathe.

I slide my hands beneath her dress, working my way languidly up her thigh, every nerve ending in my fingertips firing at once. The roundness of her hips filling my palms, the curve of her ass...my fingers don't meet panties. *I know she had panties on when we walked through the door?* I slide her forward, desperate to flip her skirt up and get a better look.

Her fingers roam over my close-cropped military cut, the hair on my head prickling beneath her deft hands. I dip my tongue into her mouth, teasing. *In...out...in...out...* Each time a little farther. "Ren," I groan. "God, the things I want to do to you."

She pulls back, just a fraction of an inch. My mouth is cold without hers. *Fuck, I pushed her too far.* She searches my face, her eyes wide and dark. Licking her lips, she whispers, "I want you to."

"Ren?" I shake my head, unsure, remembering how scared she looked moments ago.

She nods with a sigh. "I'm okay. I want this...with you." Drawing my head back to hers, our foreheads pressed close. "Take me to bed, Cayden."

Ren, please be sure, because I fucking need you. My heart pounds in my chest, ready to burst through my rib cage, dying to get as close to her as humanly possible. "Like I said before, you're in control, sweetheart."

Gently, I slide my hands under her backside and beneath her legs, scooping her off the counter and into my arms. She nuzzles the crook of my neck, kissing her way to my ear. "My room is down the hall, second door on the left."

A growl rumbles in my chest and I turn my head, seizing her mouth, kissing her senseless as I stalk toward the bedroom.

The door's open and I walk in, oblivious to everything but her. I set her down on the bed, unwilling to give up her mouth. She lies back and I cover her with my body.

Wasting no time, Ren tugs at my shirt, pulling it from my pants, and slipping her hands beneath. Her hot fingers touch my skin and my abs flex in response, while other parts of my body ache for her attention.

This is a first, a side of Ren I've never seen, confident, demanding, and sexy as fucking hell. I'm tempted to sit up and rip my shirt off, Hulk-style—buttons popping and flying in all directions—to give her better access, but like I told her before, she's in control.

Sitting up, Ren beneath me, I work my way down, fitting each button through its hole, revealing myself to her. I shrug the shirt off and toss it to the ground, basking in the glow of Ren's lustful gaze.

"Cayden," she says, praying my name. Her fingers hover over my stomach, like she's afraid I'll disappear, or burst into flames, if she touches me.

I wrap my hands around hers and bend, kissing the inside of each of her wrists. "Sweetheart, I'm yours." *Let me be your superhero. Let me go to war with your unspoken nightmares.*

I place a kiss on her palms and guide them to my torso. "Touch me, Ren." Fanning her fingers against the planes of my chest, she inches her hands downward, her fingertips dipping into the cuts of my muscles.

"What's this?" she asks, fingering the tattoo inked at my side.

"A reminder of what I am. Always faithful. Always a Marine." I run my fingers over and between hers, the emblem of the United States Marine Corps beneath our hands.

She lifts off the bed, puts her hands on my chest and pushes me back. I fall onto the mess of pillows stacked against the headboard, thinking this is the end of our tryst, but as always, Ren surprises me, swinging her legs over my body, straddling me.

Leaning over, she kisses me quickly. "Cayden Sinclair"—she trails kisses down my jaw…my neck—"you are the sexiest man alive."

More kisses. Down my chest, her tongue slipping between her lips every so often, catching a taste of my skin…swirling around my nipple.

My breath comes rapid fire. "I have no idea what you just said, but keep doing what you're doing, sweetheart."

Her mouth moves southward, licking across my tattoo. My hands twitch at my sides, wanting to touch her and my dick throbs.

Trailing her tongue lower, she plants tiny kisses at my navel and her hands move to my belt buckle.

"Ren," I breathe. "Are you sure? I need you to be absolutely sure."

She straightens, locking her eyes on mine. "Abso-fucking-lutely," she affirms, popping the button of my fly open and lowering the zipper.

Holy. Fucking. Shit.

My hands are on her, under her skirt, working their way to her center. I'm shocked when I feel lace between her legs. "A thong. Nice." I palm her bare ass, giving it a playful smack.

She shimmies and flashes a sex-kitten smirk. "You like?"

"What do you think?" I raise my hips, pressing my raging hard-on between her legs. I'm twenty-five and I'm going to die of a fucking heart attack. This girl will be my end, my kryptonite. "This"—I trace a finger over the thin slip of fabric rounding her hip—"is sexy as hell." I drop my hand between her legs again, rubbing my finger over her panties. She's so wet.

She grinds against my hand. "Please, Cayden," she begs.

I pull her panties aside and run my finger along her slick folds. "Oh God!" she whimpers, throwing her head back. "Cayden!" Her body gyrates on my hand.

"That's it, sweetheart. Take what you want."

As she moves, her body picks up rhythm, and I press my thumb against her sweet spot and slip a finger inside her…two fingers.

"Cayden, I'm going to come," she breathes, bringing herself home on my fingers.

"Go ahead, sweetheart, then I'm going to make you come again."

Her face flushes and a gasp catches in her throat. Ren in the throes of ecstasy is the most gorgeous sight I've ever seen. "That's it, Ren."

Breathless, she collapses on top of me. Pulling my hand free, I roll us, putting her beneath me, and brush her sweaty hair off her face. I need to see her, drink in her glow.

My desire for this girl goes beyond physical. Her smile, her laugh, the healing touch of her fingers on my skin, the way she comes to life when our bodies unite, with no effort, she sets my world right again. In such a short time, she's taken my battle-torn soul and weaved it back together, stitching herself into the pattern.

I'm not me without her.

CHAPTER THIRTEEN

REN

That was fucking amazing! That was just his hand? He is a goddamn superhero. Captain America and Iron Man have got nothing on this guy! I stare up at him. "Make love to me, Cayden." I tug at the sides of his pants, eager to have him inside me.

I don't have to ask twice. Cayden stands, plucks his wallet from his back pocket and withdraws a foil packet. Oh, thank God, he's prepared. Even though there's no risk of getting pregnant, I still have issues with unprotected sex.

Dropping the wallet, pants, and boxers into a heap on the floor, he climbs back on top of me and runs his fingers through my hair. "Ren, I want this with you."

"I want this, too." My eyes travel south, over his massive erection. It's been a long time since I've wanted to see a penis, and good God, am I glad I waited. *Super-friggin-man!*

Planting my hands on his laddered abdomen, I smooth my fingertips over each delicious muscle. *Damn. He's a breathing piece of artwork.* His muscles quake, rippling beneath the dark hair that points the way to his dick. I trace that line.

He exhales, eyes rolling to the back of his head.

I continue my descent, lightly brushing my fingers over him. His hips jerk and his head snaps forward, locking his gaze on mine. "I fucking love this dress, but it has got to come off."

He lifts the sides up and I sit forward, allowing him to undress me. Running his hands over my breasts, he moves around back, flips the hooks on my bra and eases the straps down, freeing me.

Another article of clothing lands in the heap on the floor.

"God, you are beautiful." Reverently, he bows his head, kissing the valley between my breasts, paying attention to every inch of my skin.

Lightning strikes, it's a bolt crashing through my body, setting a fire ablaze between my legs.

His fingers, his tongue…is there any part of this man that isn't pure magic? Nah. I think not.

I arch my back, giving my body over to him. I want him to consume me, become part of me. He's already discovered parts of me I thought were lost forever, and now, he's writing his name on my soul like on a log from a geocache.

Cayden leans down, his body weight pressing me into the mattress. He captures my mouth with his, biting at my lower lip. "Ren…" I love when he grinds out my name, his voice thick with longing.

I'm ready. More than ready. I lift my ass off the bed, his dick pressing between my thighs.

"Fuck," he moans, pushing against me, harder.

I yank the sides of my black thong down. Cayden sits up,

rips open the condom, slides it on, and is back on top of me. His green eyes are stormy with concern and even in the darkness of the room, I can see the muscle in his jaw ticking, contemplating his next move.

It's time to calm his fears and put an end to mine. Reaching up, I place both my hands on each side of his face. "I want this, Cayden. I know you won't hurt me. I trust you."

In one glorious thrust, he's inside me.

For a beat, neither of us moves. Our eyes lock together in silent communication. Me, reclaiming what I thought I'd lost all those years ago—taking back my control. Cayden, he just watches me, searching for any sign that I'm going to push him away again.

I raise my hips, pushing him in farther. Testing my boundaries. *It's okay. I'm okay.* I exhale, breathing easy for once, getting comfortable with my body again. *I want this.*

I want my actions to speak for me. I want to show him that I'm with him, body and soul.

Relaxing my hips, I sink back down on the mattress, Cayden sliding out just a little.

He inhales sharply and bites his lower lip. The struggle not to move is visible, written in the taught lines on his face. He's holding back with every fiber of his being, giving me the control, just like he promised.

Placing my hands on the back of his head, his shorn hair tickling my palms, I bring his face to mine, and whisper in his ear, "Make love to me, Cayden."

Needing no more reassurance, with one large exhale, he sinks back into me, giving into his need for more friction.

Holding me close, he sets a slow, blissful pace, one that I can keep up with. Our bodies move in unison, mine remembering exactly what to do, and how damn amazing sex can be when it's consensual.

Running his fingers through my hair, Cayden kisses me, his tongue matching the rhythm of the rest of our bodies. I drink him in, tasting his mouth.

Trailing my hands down his spine, feeling the strain of his back muscles each time he pushes into me, I smooth my hands over his ass, pushing against him, forcing further inside. Wanting…needing…more. "Harder. Deeper, please," I beg, consumed by the growing pressure between my legs.

Cayden obeys, swiveling his hips, grinding into me as picks up the pace. "Ren, you're so tight…so wet," he moans against my mouth. "Fucking…God."

Overcome with desire, he lifts slightly and grabs my hands from behind him. Stretching them up and over my head, he clasps his hand on top both of mine, pinning them to the pillow.

I'm at his mercy, and that's just fine. I trust him implicitly. I want to give my body to him, watch him come apart because I got him there.

Spreading my legs wider with his, Cayden uses his leverage, pushing in and out of me. *In and out. In…out.*

In, out. Over and over. "I'm so fucking, close," he moans, biting my earlobe.

Not lessening his pace, he works his way down my neck and lower. Circling my nipple with his tongue, pinching it between his teeth, he relinquishes my hands, he grabs my breasts, sucking and kneading. "Goddamn, Ren, you are so fucking gorgeous."

So many emotions…sensations. *I'm so close.* The scratch of his five o'clock shadow against my chest, along with his hot wet mouth, sends desire pooling between my legs. My hips grind against him, faster. "Don't…stop," I breathe.

Oh my God!

"Come for me, baby."

Trading sides, he gives my left breast some much-needed attention. Hips pumping, he fills me so perfectly.

"Yes! Oh my God! YES!" I cry out. "Don't. Fucking. Stop." His dick hits a spot inside me and that's it, I'm gone. I'm free. A bird riding the air currents, high above the land. Only this time, I'm not alone.

Cayden thrusts harder. And harder. He gives me everything he has, following my order not to stop. "That's it, come for me." His mouth is back on mine, his breath becomes my breath. He rocks into me and the pleasure high I'm riding doesn't stop.

"I…can't hold—" Two more deep thrusts and Cayden drops his forehead to mine, and growls, "*Fuuuuuuck.*"

Shoulders heaving, he opens his eyes, staring into mine. "Sorry, baby. I couldn't hold on any longer," he sighs, shaking his head against mine. "Did I get you there?" Worry clouds his face. "Are you okay? Did I hurt you?"

My lips pull into a smile. I love that he hasn't pulled out of me, that we're still connected so intimately. I bring my hands to his face, smoothing over his sweat-slicked skin. "Oh my God did I come. I'm so far beyond okay, it's ridiculous." I giggle, bringing my mouth to his. I want to kiss away his anxiety. "You could never hurt me."

"Never," he says, kissing me, pressing his whole body into mine.

I want to stay like this forever, Cayden on top of me, but my lungs burn, begging for air. "Cayd—" I squirm beneath him, breaking my mouth away from his. Lifting his head, he looks down at me. "I. Can't. Breathe." I manage to get the words out.

"Oh, shit!" Pushing up, he slides out of me, and rolls onto his back. Throwing his arm over his eyes, I watch his chest rise and fall with each breath. "Trying to suffocate you right after I get finished telling you I'd never hurt you"—he turns his head my direction—"not a good move."

Boneless and satiated, I giggle again, and snuggle up next to him. "Trust me. I'm cursing the fact that I actually need oxygen, because I did *not* want you to move." I drape my arm over his chest and draw lazy circles through the thin dusting of dark hair with the pads of my fingers.

His heartbeat still hasn't calmed and taps a rhythmic pulse under my hand. Similarly, Cayden's languid touch on my back and shoulders keeps me being putty in his hands. It's like the fate of the world rests with us, all of humanity is safe as long as we keep touching one another.

I watch his chest rise and fall with each breath and try to sync mine with his, finding joy in our peaceful existence.

"This is exquisite." Cayden brushes my side, tracing my tattoo. "This wasn't some drunken college ink. What's the story here?"

No one, except for Dylen, has seen my tattoo…and now,

Cayden. "A reminder." I choose his words; the same ones he used to describe his ink.

There's no way around this conversation. I can't tell him the significance of my tattoo without letting him in on the darkest part of my history. I don't want to contaminate our placid corner of the universe by opening the door for pain and sadness, but Cayden needs to know. I want him to know.

He's quiet, patient, allowing me to gather my thoughts…anchor myself to him, so I don't get lost in the past. I hug him tightly and he responds in kind, squeezing me closer.

"On the night of my twenty-first birthday, Dylen and I went out to celebrate. We decided to hit up a frat party." With the one arm I have slung over Cayden's broad chest, I hold on to him with all I have.

Sensing my growing anxiety, Cayden shifts, sitting up so he can draw me closer. "I'm here, sweetheart," he whispers in my ear.

I look at him and gather strength from his vivid green eyes. His lips pull up in a gentle smile giving me courage to continue my story.

"Dylen and I were having a fabulous time, dancing, trying different kinds of drinks, it was a great birthday. Then, close to midnight, things changed. I remember sitting on an ugly purple couch, reading a text from Dylen. She'd met some guy and was headed back to his apartment. She didn't want to leave me, but I insisted, I told her to have fun, not to worry about me. I was going to call my brother to pick me up and take me home, all was good." I pause, catching my breath…and my courage. "That's the last thing I remember. The rest of the story is a still a painful mystery."

"You don't have to tell me, Ren. Not if you don't want to. Not if it hurts too much."

I shake my head, not giving the fucker in my story any power over me. "I do want to." *I need you to know, Cayden, why I've been so cautious.*

"It's hazy, but I think someone offered me another drink. In my head, he's a blurry figure with a voice that's low and distorted, like the sound in a slow-motion video. The next morning, a vise gripped my temples, trying to squeeze my brain through every orifice of my head. I was alone, in a strange room, on a futon, naked. Whomever that mystery guy was, he slipped something into my drink, I passed out. And he raped me." It's taken years of sessions with my therapist to get those words to come out of my mouth, but each time they do, I feel a little freer.

Cayden stills beside me for a beat before turning me toward him. Settling his hands on my face, his thumbs caressing my cheeks. "Ren." A mixture of emotions crosses his face…horror…sadness…anger…fear…devotion.

"I don't remember a thing from that night. Just waking up so scared and alone. It was a long time before I told anyone what happened that night." *Now's your chance, Ren, tell him the consequence of your silence, that you can't give him children.*

After what we just shared, knowing that we won't ever get to do that to make a baby together is the saddest, most painful part of my story. Tears puncture my well-composed façade.

Cayden bows his head, pressing our foreheads together. "Ren, sweetheart," he whispers, prayerfully. Kissing the tip of my nose, he drags his lips to my cheek, catching a falling tear. "Please tell me I didn't hurt you."

I pull back and stare at him. "Hurt me? Cayden, I haven't been with anyone since after that night. I haven't wanted to. But you"—I grab the sides of his face and force him to listen, to understand what he means to me—"you...with me...I'm not facing the big bad world alone for once. I know I'm safe right here."

He inhales, drawing my breath into his lungs. Four...five heartbeats pass before he exhales. "I've had buddies of mine say they're fine, then they hear a car door slam, or a clap of thunder, and bam, they're not fine. They're lost, thrown back into the war. The smallest trigger sets them off." He shakes his head. "I don't want to send you back to your nightmare."

"Cayden," I say with a little more force. "You can't. What we shared was amazing. Never once did I leave you. See this"—I point to my tattoo—"they're bluebirds of happiness. In ancient Chinese culture, the bluebird was said to be a fairy queen, a protector of women. The Navajo believe bluebirds represent the rising sun." I grab his hand, lifting his index finger to my skin, I guide his finger, making him trace the cursive script that leads to the branch the birds are perched on. *R-I-S-E*. "I got this tattoo as a reminder that I rise each day with a fresh slate. I rise each day, and like the sun, I get to bring light into this world. I'm a survivor, dammit." I smile, filled with so much joy right now. "To me, birds symbolize something brighter on the horizon. They would know, from their vantage point, they get to see what's coming before the rest of us."

Cayden puts his hand over my heart, on the charm lying against my bare chest. "Is that why you chose this from the cache?"

I climb onto his lap, straddling him. "You gave me wings on our first date, Cayden."

He sits up and brushes my hair behind my ears. "What do you see on the horizon?"

I wrap my legs around his waist, locking our bodies together. "Us."

* * *

Adulting sucks. It's been three days since I've gotten to see Cayden. Three days. THREE DAYS since he rocked my freaking world! I finally choose to end my sexual hiatus and our jobs and the universe conspire to keep us apart. *Ugh! What is this life?* Why can't our work schedules play nice?

Yawning, I tap on the door and push my way into my patient's room. "Knock, knock!" I put on my cheery nurse voice. "I've brought someone with me."

"Hi, Emily," Dr. Stevenson says. "Ren tells me your labor has slowed." Dr. S studies Emily's chart, then checks the readout from the fetal heart rate monitor.

Emily nods, tiredly. "Yeah."

"She's made very little progress since early this morning," I inform Dr. S.

"Mom and baby's vitals look good," she comments, eyes scanning the readout. "Yet, I would like to get things moving a little faster." Looking at Emily, Dr. Stevenson smiles and says,

"I'm going to break your water, that should speed things up."

I notice Emily's face darken with worry as she looks to her sister Justine. I've seen the same reaction from countless mothers. "Everything's fine, Emily. Nothing to worry about." I give her a reassuring smile and collect the amnio hook for Dr. Stevenson.

Justine brushes Emily's hair off her forehead and squeezes her hand. "It's okay, Em. You're in good hands." Emily nods, a halfhearted smile on her lips.

I can't imagine what Emily's going through, her husband on deployment. She's got to be worried sick about him. And now she's giving birth to their child while he's gone. Bittersweet set of circumstances. Justine tries to be a good stand-in, trying to ease Emily's anxiety. It's good that Emily has her sister, that Justine's touch is enough to alleviate a portion of her fear, it's better than any drug Dr. S could offer. Even though her husband isn't here, Emily knows she's safe…home…as longs as her sister is by her side.

Dr. S pulls a stool up to the end of the bed. "Emily, this procedure won't hurt you or the baby. At the onset, you'll feel a little pressure. When the sac ruptures, you'll feel a gush, and it will be over."

"Okay," Emily breathes.

I pass Dr. Stevenson the hook and help Emily get situated on the bed.

Carefully, Dr. Stevenson preforms the amniotomy and breaks Emily's water.

Dr. S turns to me, "Ren, I need an OR setup, stat. There's meconium in the fluid."

"What's wrong?" Emily's voice wavers; she's on the brink of tears. Justine moves closer to Emily, the crushing need to protect her sister, share her pain, her fear, and be her partner.

"Emily, the amniotic fluid wasn't clear, the way it should be. It's best for the baby, at this point, to be delivered by C-section. Nurse Daniels will get you prepped for surgery." Dr. Stevenson stands and pulls off her gloves. To me, she says, "I'll meet you in the OR in five minutes."

"Yes, Doctor."

Before Dr. Stevenson leaves the room, she looks at Emily. "Everything's going to be fine. It's time to have your baby!"

Once the doctor is gone, I hit the call button on Emily's remote. "Kenna, I need assistance in two forty-three, stat."

Through the intercom, Kenna's voice fills the room: "On my way."

The crackle of the pager goes quiet; we're in the eye of the storm. I have mere seconds to calm this terrified mother and aunt before fear of the unknown sends them both into a panic. Once Kenna arrives, there won't be time for explanations.

With a cautious smile, I look to Emily, then to Justine. I need my words to comfort them, transfer hope. "Like Dr. Stevenson said, everything's going to be fine."

Tears well up in Emily's eyes. "I don't want a C-section. I need Vince here." Her voice wobbles with fear. No new mother wants to hear that there is something wrong with her baby. The terror in her voice is palpable, a monster with its claws wrapped around her throat.

"Dr. S has delivered hundreds of babies this way. She knows what she's doing. Trust her." I squeeze Emily's hand.

"Do you know what you're having?" I need to put Emily's focus back on her child, make her remember that there is something good and perfect waiting at the end of this scary blip on the map.

Emily shakes her head, but Justine answers, "They want to be surprised."

Every couple that has passed through the hospital's doors, has left their mark on me, and Emily is no different. Even though her husband isn't here, I can see how much she loves him—the flash in her eyes when she said his name, the way she cradles her belly, holding her baby and in turn, a part of her husband. And then there's Justine. Vince isn't here, so it falls to Justine to be his intercessor. Justine has to be the one to drive away the darkness, the scary and unknown with her words and her touch.

"Hear that, sis," Justine says, wiping Emily's sweaty hair off her forehead. "You finally get to meet your little person." Emily smiles through her tears.

"Ready?" Kenna asks, standing at the door.

I nod. "Justine, you go with Kenna, she'll get you ready for the OR. I will stay with Emily and get her prepped. We'll see you in there in five."

Justine looks at Emily, sweeping a hand across her forehead. "This is it, baby." Her voice is thick with tears. "You're doing so great. I love you, Em."

My heart clenches. Coming in a close second to the little ones I get to see come into this world, I also get to witness awesome displays of raw emotion.

I wheel Emily's gurney into the OR. The operating room is

clinical, bright, and full of commotion, much different from the intimate ambiance of the birthing rooms. "You're going be fine," I say, reassuringly.

Once I have Emily's gurney locked into place, the surgical team preps the doctors' work area, hanging surgical drapes.

"I'll wait with you until Justine comes in."

"Thank you," she says, her voice low and scratchy. I know she's terrified. I wish there was something I could do to reassure her, but until she gets to hold her baby, nothing will make any of this okay.

Kenna ushers Justine to Emily's side. Immediately, she grabs Emily's hand, their fingers intertwine, and lock together: an offering from Justine. Just by her actions, I can hear Justine's unspoken words: *I've got you, sis. We do this together.*

"All right, Emily," Dr. S says, "I'm going to begin. Dr. Baird is going to assist in the deliver, too. All you're going to feel is lots of pressure and some pulling and tugging."

I watch Emily's head bob up and down as she listens to Dr. S describe the C-section process.

Dr. Stevenson bends her head and takes the scalpel to Emily's lower abdomen. "Here we go."

I hang back and let the surgical team do their thing. My fun starts once the baby's born.

I'm mesmerized by how in sync Dr. Stevenson and Dr. Baird are, the way they move around each other, it's like a choreographed dance. They've worked together so often, they know each other's movements almost by heart.

I watch the clock. Three minutes into the surgery and I already see the baby's head. With a quick suction of the baby's nose and mouth, Dr. Stevenson slides her hands around the slippery bundle and pulls the baby out. I note the time on the clock, calling out, "Time of birth, ten twelve p.m.," and scribble the time on the dry-erase board.

I step toward Dr. S as a high-pitched wail fills the room. "Happy birthday, baby girl Harris!" Dr. Stevenson shouts, passing the newborn to me. My heart swells. This part never gets old.

"A girl?" Justine cries. "I have a niece?"

"Nurse Daniels is going to weigh her and get her cleaned up, then she'll bring her over to you," Dr. Baird informs them.

Taking the pink wiggling little girl in my arms, I usher her to the radiant warmer, perform her Apgar test, put an ID bracelet on her tiny ankle, and clean her up for her mother and aunt.

The infant wriggles and cries as I sponge her off and swaddle her in a blanket. I've done this so many times, I make quick work of the task, knowing the new mom is beside herself to meet her baby.

While Emily is sewn back up, I present the seven-pound-four-ounce, twenty-one inch bundle of joy to them and place her in Aunt Justine's arms. "Here she is," I sing.

Justine cradles her niece's head as if she were made of glass.

"What's her name?" I ask, watching them cuddle and kiss the little girl.

A pang of sadness hits me in the gut. This happens to me every time. But since Cayden came into my life, it hurts even more. The blissful unease on Justine's face when she took the baby in her arms is the same expression I would love to see on Cayden's face one day. But that's all it will ever be, only a dream…that will never come true. Sometimes, I don't know why I stick with this profession. Being around newborns all day is like bathing in the ocean with no skin to cover my muscles and nerve endings.

"Gabriella." Emily's voice, full of pride and love, pulls me from my pity party. "After our mother"—she smiles at her sister—"and Rose," she adds, reverently. "After Vince's mom."

"Gabriella Rose, that's a beautiful name." I pat Justine on the back, happy to be a part of this family's special day, remembering again why I did choose this profession, despite the pain.

I may never have children of my own, but being a small part of all the families that come through the hospital doors helps temper the sting.

CHAPTER FOURTEEN

CAYDEN

"I'm here to see Emily Harris," I say to the security guard outside of the maternity wing. "My name's Cayden Sinclair."

"What is your relationship to the family?" the guard asks.

"Family friend."

On a sticker with yellow and red balloons, he writes the room number, along with my last name and passes it over the counter. "Wear this while you're on the floor, please."

I take the sticker and say, "Thank you," while he opens the security doors, granting me access to the maternity wing. It's comforting to know that Ren is working in such a secure environment. This place is locked down like Corps base, Camp Pendleton.

Slapping the sticker on my shirt, I glance at my watch. I have an hour and a half before I have to pick Mom up and take her to the oncologist. Nothing like spending the day inside of hospitals.

Pulling my phone out, I type out a quick text to Ren, hoping I will get to see her before I have to leave. *I'm at the hospital, visiting a buddy's wife. Hoping to say hi.*

I'm not sure if she carries her phone while she's working, but hopefully she'll get the message. Since the night we slept together, our schedules have done their level best to keep us apart.

Turning left down the main hallway, the walls are covered in hundreds of pink and blue footprints, with names written next to each. I wonder if Emily and Vin's little one has her footprint on the wall yet.

Halting at Emily's door, I knock. A few seconds later, a woman pulls the door open. She's older than Emily, but they share similar features. "Hi, I'm Cayden, a friend of Emily and Vin's?"

"Oh, hi. Come on in. I'm Em's sister, Justine." She pulls the door open wider, welcoming me inside. "The baby's in the nursery, getting a bath. They're supposed to bring her back as soon as she's cleaned up."

"Great." I walk into the room behind Justine, and see Emily propped up in bed. She looks tired, but happy. Among all my close friends, Emily and Vin are the first to have a kid. It's so surreal.

"Em, you have a visitor," Justine announces, like I'm towns-folk being presented to the queen. "I'm going to grab some lunch, give you guys time to visit." Justine picks up her purse. "Do you need anything while I'm out?" she asks her sister.

Emily shakes her head. "No, thank you, Just."

Justine waves. "Back in a few. Give my niece lots of kisses for me."

"Will do, sis. Love you," Emily calls down the hall.

Once their family business is taken care of, I step closer to the bed. "Hey, Em."

Her blue eyes light up. "Cayden! It's so nice to see you!" She holds her arms out wide and I sit on the corner of the bed, hugging her.

"Congratulations, beautiful." I squeeze extra hard, for Vin. "Here"—I pull back—"these are for you and the baby." I present the bouquet of pink and white carnations and roses.

"Oh, they're gorgeous." Pressing her nose to one of the carnations, she inhales deeply. "Thank you. I'll have Justine put them in some water when she gets back." Emily sets the bouquet on table beside the bed and frowns. "Gabriella isn't here, she's in the nursery getting a bath."

"Your sister said she should be back in a little bit. I'd love to wait, so I can meet her, if you don't mind."

"Not at all. Please stay." She smiles. Yet, it's met with somberness. The birth of her child mixed with the absence of her husband. "Having you here makes it feel like Vince is a little closer. You're part of his Marine family."

"Have you heard from him?"

"When Gabriella was born, two days ago, we were able to Skype for about ten minutes, when I got out of recovery. He got to see her." Emily's eyes fill with tears. "He was so proud. He got all choked up when he talked to her. It shredded my heart," she chokes out.

"He is proud. And I know it's killing him not to be here." I draw her back into my arms, giving her my shoulder to cry on.

"Knock, knock," a voice says at the door. A voice I recognize instantly. Ren. "Someone's here to see her mommy," she coos, coming around the corner.

Emily pats my back and I sit up. "Thanks, Cayden." She wipes her eyes with the back of her hand and sniffles, brightening, as Gabriella gets closer. "There's my sweet girl."

Wheeling in a little rolling crib, Ren's smiling face lands on Emily, then on me, sitting at the edge of Emily's bed.

Ren has her hair pulled into a short ponytail and her cheeks are flushed a bright pink, she is so damn beautiful. My whole body screams to touch her. It's been a damn long five days since she's been in my arms—five days too long. And, shit. Those Minnie Mouse scrubs she has on, cute as hell.

"Cayden?" Her eyebrows pull together in shock. I'm the last person she expected to see in one of her patient's rooms. It's her smile that speaks the loudest, though.

"Ren"—I stand, walking over to her—"this is a pleasant surprise." I wrap my arm around her waist and kiss the top of her head, breathing in coconuts.

"You two know each other?" Emily asks, pointing at us.

"Uh, yeah—"

"Yes." We answer together.

Ren stares at me, dumbfounded, but snaps out of it when the baby squeals. Her eyes flick to crib. "Oh, goodness! I'm sorry Miss Gabriella. I didn't mean to keep you from your mommy." Wheeling the cart to the other side of the bed, she scoops the baby into her arms, passing the tiny bundle to Emily. "I'm sorry," Ren says, "Here's your sweet girl."

Two seconds.

In the two seconds Ren had the baby in her arms, I'm hit by

how much I would love to have a family. How much I want to build that family with Ren. To see her holding our baby.

"So, how do you guys know each other?" Emily asks again, tucking Gabriella's blanket around her.

I open my mouth to answer, but Ren beats me to it. "Cayden is my boyfriend." She walks around the bed and comes to stand beside me, proudly putting her arm around my waist.

Emily looks up from Gabriella and smiles hugely. "Really? Small world, huh?"

"It really is," I mutter.

Ren looks up at me. "How do you and Emily know each other?"

"Emily is married to one of my Marine buddies, Staff Sargent Vincent Harris. Vin is on deployment right now, but I told him I'd check in on his girls."

"Wow, once again, the universe throwing us together. I guess we're meant to be, Cayden Sinclair." She winks.

You don't know how true I want that to be, Ren Daniels. "So it would seem. Did you get my text?"

Ren shakes her head. "I don't keep my phone on me. It's in my locker, I check it on breaks. Did you need something?"

"No, I just wanted to let you know I was at the hospital. I hoped I'd get to see you."

"Well, I guess we have little Gabriella to thank for this fortuitous turn of events."

I look at Emily who is grinning from ear to ear, beaming down at her newborn. "I haven't gotten to see her, yet. Mind if I hold her?" I ask Emily.

She glances up at me. "Not at all."

Leaving Ren's side, I skirt the bed, and Emily passes the football-size bundle over, gently placing the baby into my arms. Little Gabriella stares up at me, blinking. She smells like baby powder—the same delicate scent that clings to Ren. Gabriella's cheeks are rosy pink, she has a head full of jet-black hair like Vin's, and eyes just like her mommy's, a clear, ocean blue.

It's awe inspiring that this little lady is part Emily and part Vin. Makes what Vin is doing right now, all the more important—making the world better for his daughter.

Gabriella smacks her lips, a tiny pink tongue sticking out. "Hi there, Gabriella," I coo, trying not to sound like I'm talking to a puppy. "Such a pretty little girl."

As I talk to Vin's daughter, it smacks me in the gut that he hasn't gotten to hold her yet, to touch the soft skin on her face. Gabriella wiggles, stretching one of her arms out of the blanket. I look to Emily, concerned. "Is this okay? Does she need to be retucked?"

Emily laughs. "It's fine. She wiggles out of the blanket all the time."

Gabriella's fist comes to her mouth and she sucks on it, lips smacking loudly.

"She's hungry," Ren says, standing over my shoulder.

I look up to see Ren smiling down at Gabriella. Reaching over me, she puts her finger to the little notch in baby's chin. "Hungry, yes. I know."

Ren has got the baby talk down. Her voice is squeaky and high pitched and cute as hell. Gabriella's eyes zero in on Ren's like she cast a magic spell over her. Ren is a natural with babies.

It's her job, idiot. The voice in my head, so kindly reminds. Even still, she's going to make a hell of a mother someday.

"Well, I hate to leave this little party, but I am on the clock," Ren says, squeezing my shoulders. "I'll talk to you later, Cayden? I know you're taking your mom to her appointment later. Let me know how that goes."

I hand Gabriella back to her mother. "I should go, too."

"Cayden, it was so lovely to see you, please don't be a stranger. Come by the house whenever you like. I know it'd make Vince happy."

"I will." I lean down and kiss her cheek. "She's amazing, Emily." I touch Gabriella's cherubic face one more time.

"Emily," Ren says, "do you need any help feeding Gabriella? I can have the lactation consultant step in to assist you."

"I'll try it myself this time, since we don't have an audience. See how it goes. If I need help, I'll hit the call button."

"Perfect. Let me know if you two need anything."

"Will do, Ren. Thank you," Emily says.

Ren moves toward the door. I give Emily a wave and follow Ren out the door. In the hallway, she glances to the left, then to the right. "Let's go to the break room," she says, tipping her head toward the long corridor behind me.

Walking at her side, it's so hard not to grab her hand and hold it, but I know she's at work. I respect that professional line.

"What an awesome surprise, getting to see you." She glances up at me, beaming.

"I had hoped I'd get to see you."

We stop and she opens the door to a room that's practically

a closet, with a small sofa, refrigerator, and a microwave, nothing else. Ren closes the door behind us and turns, wrapping her arms around my neck. Her lips are on mine, slow and sweet. "God, I've missed you," she sighs, leaning into me.

My arms are around her in seconds, loving how all of her round soft curves mold to my hard edges. "Fuck, yes," I moan in agreement.

"I can't be gone long; I'm not on break, but I had to see you." Her tongue licks across my lips, hesitant…teasing.

"I will take every minute I get." Sucking her bottom lip into my mouth, I push the limits of how much I can take while she's at work, my tongue brushing against hers.

So many inappropriate thoughts crowd my head—locking the door, throwing her on that tiny sofa, stripping her naked, and having my way with her, just to list a few.

"You sure it's not break time?"

"I'm sure," she mumbles against my lips and pulls away.

Dammit!

Frowning, she shakes her head. "I really need to go. But damn am I glad you had a reason to be at the hospital. Got any more friends who are having babies? I could get used to seeing you around here, Officer." She runs a finger over my lips.

Fuck. I love when she calls me "officer." I grab her wrist, sucking her finger into my mouth and biting it between my teeth. "God, I want you right now," I growl.

She swallows, her eyes wide. "I want you, too." She pulls her finger from my mouth with a *pop*. "But, I have to go."

"*Fuck.*" I nod, brushing my knuckles over her soft cheeks, trying to ease the wanting, pained expression on her face.

"Let me know how your mom's appointment goes this afternoon," she says.

"I will."

"Don't forget, I told Lexie and Shae that I would go out with them tonight. Lexie was pretty adamant that I go."

"I remember. I don't know what Lacey is up to tonight, so I might have to stay with Mom."

"Keep me posted."

"Will do." Leaning in, I kiss her one more time, needing one more taste.

Before we get carried away again, Ren steps back and opens the break room door, and together we slip out undetected. No one the wiser to our impromptu make-out session.

On my way out of the hospital, I smile, brushing a finger over my lips. Ren, kissing, babies. So many thoughts swirl in my head, but my most favorite: family.

CHAPTER FIFTEEN

REN

Trading my Minnie Mouse scrubs for a short black cocktail dress, I head out the door to meet Lexie and Shae. Walking to my car, I shoot Lexie a text, *Be there in a few.*

Her response is immediate. *Can't party without you. Hurry up!*

I also text Cayden. *How is your mom? Please call me. I'm worried.* His mother's appointment was hours ago. Why hasn't he called?

Sighing, I toss my phone in my purse, and yank out my keys. Clicking the button on my keychain, my Miata flashes its lights in greeting.

The short drive to Belle's—the hole in the wall bar that was our hangout in college—is uneventful, as I keep my lead foot from leaning too far on the gas pedal. After paying that last ticket, I don't need to get busted again...unless it means Cayden would be the one doing the busting. The thought crosses my mind for a split second and then I remember I don't have a spare hundred dollars lying around.

There's always a chance he'll get you off with a warning. My conscience waggles her eyebrows seductively. I have sex with Cayden once, and it's all I can think about it. But, it is nice to enjoy sex again.

Pulling into the parking lot, I notice Shae's Acura parked in the front row. My late arrival means that I'll be parking in the back.

Finding a well-lit space, I lock my car and head inside.

Belle's is hopping tonight. Scanning the bar, I see Lexie near the back, waving her hands above her head. "Ren! Over here!" she shouts.

I weave through the high-top tables and sidle up to the one occupied by two of my best friends. These ladies have been with me through thick and thin.

Lexie's long blond hair sweeps over her shoulders and down her back in gorgeous messy beach curls. Standing up, she holds her arms out to me. "You made it!" she squeals, folding me into a hug.

"Ugh. I didn't think I was ever going to get out of work. I had an emergency C-section right at the end of my shift."

Shae screws her face up, wrinkling her nose. "I don't know how you stand to watch that." She pretends to shiver and takes a long pull on her beer.

"It's certainly not as glamorous as CPA life." I nudge her with my shoulder and plop onto the stool next to her.

"I never have to worry about my calculator peeing, pooping, bleeding, or vomiting all over me, thank you very much. How's the saying go … 'there is safety in numbers'? Yes, there is."

I shake my head. "Oh, Shae. You are too prissy for your own good." I laugh.

"What'll you have, sweetheart?"

At the sound of a low rumbling voice behind me, I turn around. Looming over me, the waiter stands ready to take my order. He's kind of cute, resembling Clark Kent with his black-framed glasses and neatly styled hair.

"I'll take a Coors Light. And my name's not 'sweetheart.'" There's only one man in this world that gets to call me that.

"Got it. One Silver Bullet coming up." He salutes and with a wink he heads to the bar.

"So, what's new, ladies?" I ask, folding my hands on the table.

Lexie bites an olive off the plastic sword garnishing her martini, smirking and holding her hand at a really awkward angle. Why the hell is she doing that?

"What is that look, Lex? You okay?"

"Go on, Lexie, tell her," Shae prods.

My gaze passes between the two of them. "Tell me what?" Then I see it, the massive sparkling rock on Lexi's left finger. That explains the awkward hand position, an attempt to get me to notice her bejeweled left hand.

"Holy shit. When did this happen?" I snatch her hand off the plastic sword and examine her new bling. "Lex!" I turn my attention back to her, eyes wide.

"Friday night."

"And I didn't get a single Snapchat?" I cock my head and stare at her.

Shae bumps Lexie with her shoulder. "She and Ollie have been locked in the bedroom for the last two days."

My cheeks warm at the thought of being locked in Cayden's room for two days.

Lexie shrugs with a smug grin, casting her baby blue eyes on each of us. "We had some celebrating to do."

The waiter returns, setting my beer in front of me. "One Coors Light."

"Thank you." I nod.

Putting the bottle to my lips, I take a long drink. "Ahhh, now that's good." I sigh, swallowing. "Lex, we need details," I demand, setting my bottle down with a *thud*.

"Um...I don't think we need *those* details, Ren. I do not want to know what kind of kinky, *Fifty Shades* shit Lex and Ollie are into."

I roll my eyes. Sometimes my friends are so dense. "Not that. How did he *propose*?"

Lexie chews on the end of the plastic sword, smiling. "We were at the baseball game. The jumbotron caught the whole thing during the seventh inning stretch."

"Oooh, look at Oliver busting out the moves," I croon. "Nice."

"Ahh! I still can't believe it!" Lexie shuffles her feet under the table. "It was so cool!"

Shae chimes in, "You know Ollie's a keeper when a Cubs fan, purposes to his diehard Cardinal-loving girlfriend, at a Cubs versus Cards game, at Busch Stadium."

"And the Cards won," Lexie adds. "Our union is blessed by the baseball gods."

"Not sure Oliver would agree with that," I say, taking a drink.

"Psssh"—Shae waves her hand—"Lexie has got that man so whipped."

I don't know if that's the right adjective; I wouldn't say

Oliver is whipped, but is he in love? Yes. I've seen the way he watches Lexie, like the stars rise and fall in her eyes.

Shae vacuums up the dregs of her fruity drink with her straw. "What about you, Ren, what have you been up to? I saw you getting cozy with fine piece of man at Dyl's wedding. The one that promised me a dance, but never came through. What's his name? Chris?"

I shake my head and swallow the last of my beer. "Cayden."

"Caaaayden," Shae drawls. "Sexy." Her shoulders dip suggestively. "And to think, I could have had him draped over me all night. So sad," she says, pouting.

Damn straight he's sexy! And I'm not sharing. My heart thumps out an extra beat.

"How are we doing, ladies?" the waiter asks, stepping up to the table. "Another round?"

We glance around the table, each of us giving a silent nod. God, I've missed my friends. "What the hell," I say, "let's do it."

"Awesome. I'll get those right out." He slaps the table with a stack of menus, flashes a smile, and turns to leave.

"Okay, spill it, Ren. What's up with you and Cayden?" Lexie asks.

What's up with Cayden? I know what's up! I laugh inwardly. I've never been one to kiss and tell; it's not my thing. But, I do want Lexie and Shae to know how happy I am. Only my family and Dylen know what happened three years ago, but Shae and Lexie are aware that I haven't dated or even hinted at wanting a relationship with the member of the opposite sex in years. So, the fact that I spent any time with Cayden at Dylen's wedding is enough to pique their interest.

I bite my tongue between my teeth, fighting an impish grin and schoolgirl giggles. I nod. "We've been seeing each other." *A lot of each other!*

"Oooooh!" they say in unison.

"How much of each other?" Shae's lilting voice teases.

"Enough." I'm not sharing any more beyond that. I don't want to jinx anything by speaking it out loud.

Aren't you jinxed anyway? Doomed? Once he finds out you're broken, he's going to dump your ass. Enjoy it while you can, sweetheart.

"Enough? What kind of freaking answer is that?" Lexie chides.

"Here we go, ladies," the waiter says, returning with a tray balanced at his side. "A Coors for you." He sets the bottle down in front of me.

"Thank you."

"No problem, love." He picks up the next drink, depositing it in front of Shae. "A strawberry daiquiri, aaaaanndd a dirty martini." He sets Lexie's drink on the table.

"Thank you," she says, picking up the black plastic sword.

"You bet. I'll check back in a bit." And he's off to the next table.

"Dude, he was totally flirting with you, Ren," Lexie says, smirking, popping an olive into her mouth.

I cock my head. "Yeah, right."

Shae kicks my chair, her eyebrow pulling up. "He didn't call the rest of us, '*love.*'"

"Whatever. You two are full of it." I reach for my beer, my cheeks burning. I press the mouth of the bottle to my lips and take a swallow, hearing my phone ring in my purse.

Setting my beer on the table, I unzip my purse, and pull my phone out: *Officer Sinclair* is lighting up the screen. Can a heart smile? Yes, yes it can, because mine just did. I accept the call and my heart flares, sending a warm glow cascading through my body. God, I miss him.

"Cayden?"

"Ren"—his voice is rough, gravelly—"can you come over?" he asks, a desperate heaviness strangling his words.

Worry bitch slaps the smile off my heart. "What's wrong?"

"I just need…" His voice trails off.

Lexie taps me on the arm. "Everything okay?"

I cup a hand over the receiver and pull it away from my mouth, whispering, "I don't think so. I'm going to take this outside."

Lexie and Shae give concerned looks and nod while I stand, headed for the exit. "What's wrong?"

Silence.

My pulse quickens. This is not like him.

"My mom's not well." Fear paints his voice black.

"I'm on my way." I pull the door to Belle's open and march back inside. "I'll be there in in a few."

The call ends. No "goodbye," no "see you soon," only silence. Not good. Sooo not good.

I fling the door open and run back to the table. Snatching my purse from my chair, I shove my phone inside. "I've got to go. Something's wrong."

Lexie and Shae look to one another, nodding in understanding. "No, go. We've got this," Shae says, waving me away.

My once smiling heart sags like an old lady's jowls. "Thanks, guys." I pull each of them into a quick hug. "Love you. I'll keep you posted." I toss a twenty on the table and call over my shoulder as I leave. "For my drinks. Thanks, loves."

Keys in hand, I race out of Belle's, my heart in my throat. I've never heard Cayden like this. *Sorry, Cayden, I'm going to speed.*

CHAPTER SIXTEEN

CAYDEN

I set the nearly empty bottle of bourbon on the table and peel my ass off the couch, stumbling toward the door. A jackhammer pulverizes my skull. Knowing Ren is on the other side is the only thing that keeps me upright.

Ren is on the other side…

Each step, I'm closer to her.

Ren is on the other side…

Ren is on the other side…

One more fucking step…

Ren is…

I yank the door open.

Here.

The jackhammer quiets.

"Jesus, Cayden. Are you all right?" she gasps, stepping over the threshold.

A shot goes off in my head. The first shot of a war. I war to hold her, make love to her, kiss her, cry on her shoulder, fuck her, and collapse in a heap of tears in her arms. My body sways, pelted with the shrapnel of Mom's cancer.

"Ren." Thank fucking God her name is one syllable, because that's all I can grind out.

She slips her hand on my shoulder and pushes past me with the gentleness of an angel. I know she's been sent here to save me. I'm not the superhero, she is. I watch her glide across the room in blurred slow motion and the jackhammer resumes it's excavation at the crown of my head. My skull is about open.

"Cayden"—she pats the cushion beside her—"come sit." Her voice is soft and sweet, like Mom's homemade cinnamon rolls, icing melting into the swirling crevices.

Mom.

I'm not drunk enough. The oncologist's voice…still a spike driving through my head, piercing my heart. *Terminal.*

Ren, like a tractor beam, pulls me toward her. I drag my heavy feet across the carpet, flopping onto the cushion. Draping her arm over my shoulder, I collapse against her, my head falling into her lap.

"Oh, Cayden"—her voice soft as a cloud—"what happened?" With the lightest touch, she brushes her hands gently over my close-cropped scalp.

My muscles yield to her touch, uncoiling like frayed yarn. The tension in my neck and back release, and I exhale for what seems like the first time since I dropped Mom off at home.

"Mom went to the doctor today," I mumble, focusing on her touch; the lazy path of her fingers traveling through my hair. *Forward and back. Forward and back….* "Not good."

Between Ren's fingers and the bourbon, I'm almost numb.

"I'm here. You can talk to me," she whispers.

My brain clicks over the words, forcing them into a coherent response. "Treatment's not working."

"Did the doctors suggest another treatment? There are so many experimental options available."

I shake my head. "Not for the type of cancer Mom has." Rolling onto my back, I look up at her. "She's terminal, Ren. They can't help her anymore."

Her face falls. "Cayden..."

I close my eyes. Her sadness, along with my own, is heavier than gravity at the moment, and it's crushing me. "I can't do it. I can't watch her die."

Ren puts her hand against my forehead, stroking back over my hair. "I am so sorry."

My body weighs a million tons. Sleep...I need sleep. "When she's gone. I won't have...anyone." When I wake up, will this nightmare be over? "You're lucky," I mutter, slipping beneath the weight of sorrow and bone-tiredness, "having a brother, a sibling. You're not alone. You have a family."

"You're not al—"

I think I hear Ren's voice, soft and angelic, floating somewhere above the amber sea I'm drowning in, but it can't be. I'm alone and lost in the dark.

* * *

A ray of light filters between the slats of the blinds and shoots me in the eye, sending a fireball of pain through my optical nerve and incinerating my brain. *Fuck.* I press my eyes closed against the burning light and stretch my legs out.

Umm…what the hell?

My feet push into legs. Warm, smooth, legs. Cracking open an eye, I wince and lift my head. *Ren? What is she doing here?*

Pushing up on the couch, I peel the other eye open and suck in a breath through closed teeth, my head ready to explode. I scoot my ass to the edge of the couch cushion and rest my elbows on my knees, cradling my head.

Breathe, Sinclair. In and out. Nice and slow. What the hell did I do last night?

My body is a live grenade, any sudden movements, and I will explode.

The blankets beside me stir and the cushion sinks as Ren sits up. "How you feeling?" she asks groggily. I appreciate her thoughtful whisper, but the state I'm in, she may as well have shouted into a bullhorn pressed right against my ear.

I give an almost nonexistent shake of my head and attempt to speak, "Not…good." My voice is gravel, wrapped in sandpaper, covered in Tabasco.

"What can I get you?"

Drunk off my ass last night. Massively hungover this morning, and she's still here. She didn't leave. I do not deserve this girl.

"Nothing, sweetheart. Just give me a minute." Massaging my temples, I try to piece together the events of last night. The empty bottle of bourbon explains why my head feels like the Super Bowl game ball. The last time I polished off a bottle of bourbon was when I found out my dad passed away. It wasn't one of my finer moments and sure as hell had been asshat stupid. Had my CO found out about my bender…dear God. At least this time, I wasn't on duty.

Ren stands and walks toward the kitchen, disappearing around the corner. She opens the freezer. Ice clatters into a glass, followed by rushing water. My stomach churns, anticipating the unwelcomed invasion of hydrogen and oxygen molecules. Although it would be good for me to down a glass of water—alcohol is coming out of my pores—I can't stomach it at the moment.

Ren comes back into the room with the offending glass. "You need to drink this." She holds the ice water out to me.

I lift my head, slowly, so I can look her in the eye. "Baby, thank you." *Please know I mean it.* "But I can't."

Gently, she sits beside me, careful not to rock the cushion. "I know you feel like jackal vomit right now, but you really need to drink something other than fermented corn. Nurse's orders."

I strain, turning my head to look at her. "Jackal vomit? That's a first."

"Jackal vomit is the worst. Trust me. I worked at the zoo in high school, jackals are disgusting creatures."

Even hungover, she manages to make me laugh. "Can you assure this water will make me feel less like jackal vomit?" I take the glass from her hand.

"Maybe an upgrade to a kitty fur ball. Only slightly better." She confirms with a nod.

"And that's a professional diagnosis?"

She pouts her lips and gives me the stink-eye. "Are you questioning my mad nursing skills, Officer?"

"Never, sweetheart. I've seen them in action." Putting my lips to the edge of the glass, I tip a swallow of water back. The cool liquid flows over my thick, dry tongue, washing down my irritated throat. *Fuck. Was that bourbon laced with fire?*

Setting the glass on the coffee table, I mumble out a choked, "Thank you," and fall back on the couch, closing my eyes as I wait for the room to stop impersonating the Disney World teacup ride. "Remind me to never consume bourbon again."

"I'll do my best," she says, patting my leg.

"By the way, you look stunning." That black dress hadn't escaped my attention. I make a mental note to lose myself in Ren from now on; the aftereffects are far more enjoyable, and she can make me forget better than any goddamn liquor. Ren is the perfect distraction to the bigger issue…Mom's dying and there's fuck all I can do about it.

Her wavy hair is pointing in a zillion directions; she tries to tame it, running her fingers through the snarls. I wish I'd put them there another way. God, sex with her is so fucking amazing, I can't stop thinking about it. She makes me horny all the time.

"What's the plan for today?" she asks, unaware of my current train of thought. "I took the day off, thinking you might need help with your mom."

Opening my eyes, I sit up, staring at her, drinking her in…my hangover cure. She is goddamn perfect.

"I don't think any newborns will mind me being Katy Sinclair's nurse today," she says, smiling faintly.

"I really want to kiss you right now, but in my current state, that's probably not the wisest course of action." I twist my body around. Despite the agony of my screaming head, I need to touch her. Resting my hand against her cheek. "Thank you."

"I'll take a rain check." She taps my nose with her finger. "Why don't you jump in the shower." She waves her hands around, referencing my horrid drunken mess. "I'll attempt breakfast—don't hold out for anything fancy, I usually burn water—and we'll spend the rest of the day with your mom."

Yep, she's an angel.

"What did I do to deserve you?" I say this out loud, but I'm really speaking to myself. Truly, how did such an amazing woman come into my life just when I needed her? And the best part is, I didn't *know* I needed her. Vin was right, the most important things always come into your life when it's least convenient.

I lost Dad…and now I'm going to lose Mom. It's nice to have someone on the path beside me now, to share the happy moments, and help carry the burden of the sad ones. My internal compass, my heart, points to Ren, the best treasure I've ever found.

"Can I show you something?" I hold out my hand to her, needing her strength to help me stand.

Laying her palm in mine, she moves, pulling me up gently. "Sure. Lead the way."

Down the hall of my little ranch, the second bedroom on the right is where I keep my collection of compasses. After getting lost in the woods when I was nine, Dad gave me my first one for my tenth birthday, not too long after the incident. Ever since then, my fascination with them hasn't wavered. In fifteen years, my collection has grown to over two hundred. Some large, some small, brass, wood, gold, liquid, marine, prismatic, I don't discriminate when it comes to a compass; they all hold a unique beauty—and safety. It's the same as having someone you care about at your side.

Our entwined hands swinging like a pendulum, we enter my compass room. I've never shown anyone this display. It's private, something I only shared with my dad. When I came home from Afghanistan, I couldn't bear for any of these to be buried in boxes…like Dad. I needed to bring them out, free them…set him free.

I flip the light switch and watch Ren's already large eyes widen even more. The floor-to-ceiling lighted display cases I built flicker to life, spotlights shining down on the navigation tools.

"Cayden," she says, exhaling. "This is breathtaking." Letting go of my hand, she tiptoes around the room, examining the contents of the cases.

"My dad and I put together most of the collection." I glance around. So many memories. "He always said, 'Cayden, with this tool, you'll always know your way home, where you belong.'"

Peering into a case, she glances over her shoulder. "They're gorgeous."

Stepping up behind her, I set my hands at her waist, my mouth at her ear. "Not as gorgeous as you."

Ren turns, our bodies press together. Her dark chocolate eyes capture me like magnetic north holds the needle of every one of the compasses in this room. "I have so many tools to help me find my way home," I say, brushing her bangs out of her eyes. "The funny thing is, I didn't know I was lost, until you found me."

For a second, I see a hint of her frightened bird response, then it flutters away. "Technically, you found me. Speeding down the road." She lifts her brow.

"My cheesy lines are rubbing off on you, sweetheart."

She cringes. "God help me." Running her finger down the scar at my temple, her eyes soften. "Why do I get the feeling your scar has something to do with why your dad gave you your first compass? I remember the picture on the wall of your mom's staircase. That night, you wouldn't let your mom talk about what happened."

I clench my teeth, hating the story and the scar that is a constant reminder of that night.

I nod. "I've always had this overwhelming desire to please my dad. Even now that he's gone, I still fear disappointing him." I keep a strong hold on Ren, drawing strength from her.

"When I was nine, Dad took me on an overnight camping trip. I was such a shit as a kid, always getting in trouble. You've heard the stories." She nods in affirmation.

"I looked up to my dad. He was a big guy, never afraid of anything. I wanted to be tough, just like him. To prove how manly a nine-year-old I was, I took off into the woods, determined to bring back dinner—a squirrel, rabbit, some fish, anything I could kill, and show my dad I was a big, strong outdoorsman, just like him.

"It got dark. I couldn't find my way back to our campsite. But I refused to give up—Dad wouldn't have given up. I kept moving. The terrain became treacherous and that's when I tripped and fell. My head met the side of a fallen tree, a branch slicing up the side of my temple."

Ren touches my scar with a tender finger.

"I can still feel the pain, white-hot and blinding. And the thing about head wounds? They bleed a lot. I crumbled in a bloody heap on the dirty ground. That's the last thing I remember, until I woke up in the hospital. The first person I saw was my dad. He had tears in his eyes that spilled over and ran down his cheeks. That was also the only time I ever saw him cry. My stupidity made the strongest man I know cry."

"Cayden," she consoles. "I'm sure those were tears of joy. That you were okay."

I shake my head. "Dad told me how scared he'd been. First, that it took him so long to find me, and then because I was injured and unconscious. He thought he was going to lose me."

"I'm sure he was scared to death. But, in my experience, fear is what keeps us going. So we don't give up. It's the way out of a nightmare, it sets us on the path toward home, safety. That fear of losing you is what kept him searching, kept him praying that you would be okay," she says.

"I hated being the cause of his pain. This scar is a reminder that I broke him that day." My throat constricts and tightens.

Nausea flares, the sour bourbon in my stomach rearing its ugly head.

Ren cradles my face in her hands, forcing me to look at her. "Cayden, I don't know your dad, but I'm certain you didn't break him." Her voice is soothing, like a warm summer breeze. I can almost believe her words.

"I made a promise to myself, and to Dad, that I would never let him down. Never be the cause of his tears and disappointment. Lately, it seems that's all I'm capable of…disappointment."

Ren caresses her thumb over the lines of tension at the corner of my eye. "Cayden Sinclair, what are you talking about?"

"I can't save Mom. I didn't get the SWAT position. Everything I came home for, everything I told my dad I would protect and work for, gone."

"Your mom is lucky to have such an amazing son. She knows that and so did your father. Sometimes saving someone is as simple as just holding them. Letting them know they're not alone. And what do you mean, you didn't get the SWAT position?"

Shaking my head, I run a hand over my thumping head. "Not enough time with the force to be eligible."

"Why didn't you say anything?"

"I didn't want to see your disappointment in me."

"In life, there are going to be disappointments. The world's an ugly place. I've lived in that ugly place. But, it's places like this"—she latches her hands behind my neck and puts our foreheads together—"safe in the arms of someone you care about that make the ugly places a little less scary.

There's no disappointment here. You are an incredible man, Cayden Sinclair." She puts her hand over my heart. "Go easy on yourself."

I breathe her words, absorb them into every cell of my body, and for the first in my life, I don't feel lost. The needle of my soul stops spinning and points a direct line to her.

CHAPTER SEVENTEEN

REN

Who knew "terminal" was synonymous with "fast"? Within a week of finding out she was terminal, today Cayden is moving his mom from her home of twenty-eight years into a hospice care facility.

Cayden texted right before my shift ended, asking me to swing by his mom's house and pick up her Bible. On my way to the house, silent tears work their way down my cheek. I haven't known Katy long, but I still feel the hurt, the consuming grief, and double-edged sadness like a scalpel slicing through my guts. One look at Cayden's face when I show up at the hospice facility is all it will take; I'll be carved, hallowed out. So, so empty.

The Sinclair family home is dark, already mourning Katy's absence. Cancer's shadow is wide and all consuming. Pulling into the driveway, gravel crunches beneath my tires, quieting as the car rolls to a stop. Getting out, I slam the door shut, the *clang* echoing into the night.

Cayden shared with me the location of the hide-a-key, safely stowed under an extra landscaping brick behind an overgrown bush in the front yard. Upending the brick, I pluck the key from the dirt and skirt around to the front door, letting myself inside.

Being here without Cayden is so strange. I switch on the foyer light as another tear slides down my cheek. The walls… the tables…happy family memories stacked up feet high. A tsunami ready to pummel anyone who opens the door.

I run up the stairs, eager to get Katy's Bible and be on my way. I know Cayden is putting up a strong front for his mom, giving her someone to lean on, someone to carry her through this ordeal. But right now, Cayden has no one. I need to be there for him. He's Superman to so many people, it's time for him to come down and let me carry him.

Mrs. Sinclair's room is just the way I remember it, tidy and carefully decorated with more family snapshots. It's interesting to see what people collect, what holds meaning and value in their lives. Me, I collect birds, my brother collects music. Mom loves her cookbooks, Dad, anything football related, and Cayden has his collection of compasses. Katy collects memories. She reminds me of old Rose in *Titanic*, unpacking all of her picture frames when she arrives on the deep-sea vessel. I smile at the thought. A lifetime of wonderful treasures.

Snap out of it, Ren, get the Bible and get to Cayden.

I shake my head and step over to the nightstand, where Cayden said his mother keeps her Bible. Sure enough, there it is, lying right on top. I pull it out and shut the drawer. It's old and falling apart, the pages stuffed with so many loose papers and pictures.

Standing, I open the flap to my purse, ready to drop the Bible inside, just as a photo and a piece of yellowed paper drift to the floor. Bending over, I retrieve the articles. The snapshot is of Cayden, his parents, Blake and his mom and dad, and two black labs. The boys don't look more than twelve or thirteen. Blake has Cayden in a headlock, giving him a noogie and the parents are suspended in eternal laughter.

A smile pulls at my lips. Pushing the photo back between the pages, I flip the folded yellowed paper around, an elegant cursive script on the front: *Baby Two and Baby Three.*

Mrs. Sinclair had suffered two miscarriages after having Cayden. Whatever this paper is, it's meant for those two babies.

A morbid curiosity to unfold the paper and read grabs hold of me, but I resist. The contents of this Bible are Mrs. Sinclair's deepest, most cherished thoughts and memories…her soul. I couldn't invade her privacy like that.

Another tear slips down my cheek and I press the paper back between the pages of the gospel.

I get it. On her deathbed, she wants *all* of her family.

* * *

"Cayden?" I push open the door to Mrs. Sinclair's room, keeping my voice hushed. "Cayden?"

Stepping inside, Cayden comes around the corner, greeting me at the door with a kiss. "I'm so glad you're here." Relief drips from his words.

"Sorry it took so long. I've got her Bible." I hold up the battered book.

He takes it from my hands. "Thanks."

"How is she?"

"Sleeping. She sleeps a lot."

In my profession, death comes with the territory, albeit, I see life more often, but I have seen death, too. When the body begins to slow, periods of inactivity and excessive sleep are normal. Metabolism begins to shut down, dehydration sets in, it's all part of the process of dying.

I take Cayden's hand, squeezing hard, letting him know he's not going through this alone. "Keep talking to her," I say, knowing that even those who are in comas or close to death, experts believe they can still hear. The familiar sound of a loved one is comforting. "She can hear you."

"I know," he mumbles, enveloping me in a tight embrace.

The last few nights have taken their toll on Cayden. He hasn't shaved, the beginnings of a scruffy beard darken his face, along with matching circles under his eyes. Katy is sleeping for the two of them.

"Sit with me?" he asks in a hoarse whisper.

"Always."

His fingers inch between mine, holding on for dear life. Silently, we push farther into Katy's room, the dim lights casting long shadows on the walls. Strange, the birthing rooms at the hospital and this room have the same ambiance, the low soft-white lighting, generic landscape paintings, and floral wallpaper, yet, the difference in atmosphere is striking—the buzz of electricity in a birthing room is palpable, a hospice room leaks breathable oxygen, death slowly suffocating everyone inside. How can nearly identical rooms be so different—one bursting at the seams with life, and the other shriveling like a rosebush past its season?

Cayden pulls another chair over for me, and we sit. He slips the Bible into her right hand, and holds on to her left—a lifeline. "What am I going to do without her, Ren?" he whispers, grabbing for my hand with his free one.

I squeeze. Can I transfer my energy, my life, to him...to Katy? If I could, I would freely offer it. Anything, everything, all that I have, it's theirs to take. But I have no superpowers. The best I can do is hold him and be his anchor when the hurricane comes.

We sit like this for almost an hour; not speaking, holding each other, and watching the rise and fall of Katy's chest.

Cayden pops up from his chair and brushes a hand over her head. "Mom? I'm here." His voice is like soothing warm tea on a scratchy throat—calm and inviting...a healing balm. "Mom?"

Behind the deep timbre of Cayden's voice lie the remnants of the boy he used to be. I can hear it when he says, "Mom." The sound of a child lost, searching for his mother, missing his safe harbor in the big scary world. The real meaning behind that one word...*Don't leave me.*

Katy stirs.

"Mom?"

"Frank?" she croaks, her eyes still closed.

Tears prick my eyes. Cayden flinches.

"No, Mom. It's me, Cayden. I'm right here." He sits on the edge of her bed, pressing both of his hands into hers.

Katy's eyes flutter open, heavy lidded. "Baby," she breathes.

Cayden's smile is brighter than the Milky Way on a clear night in the middle of the ocean. "It's okay, Mom. I'm here. I'm not going anywhere. Ren brought your Bible." He lifts it off the blanket, holding it up for her.

Katy turns her head. "Thank…you, Ren," she manages to say.

I stand, joining Cayden at her bedside. "You're welcome."

Katy smiles, her eyes shifting from Cayden to me. "This"—she lifts a bony finger, pointing at us—"makes me happy."

Cayden glances at me, draping his arm around my shoulder.

"My family…" Katy trails off, clutching the Bible close to her heart, drifting back to sleep.

I turn my eyes to Cayden; he has the most striking profile. A single tear slides down his bearded cheek, but it's the smile on his face that says everything I need to know. He is seeing our future—children, laughter, picnics, Little League, skinned knees, bikes with training wheels…a family.

It's time to grow a pair and tell him, Renata.

I see me, shattering his dreams.

CHAPTER EIGHTEEN

CAYDEN

"Let us know if she needs anything else, Mr. Sinclair." The nurse tucks Mom's blanket around her and moves toward the door.

"Yes. Thank you."

I slump into the chair next to Mom's bed. No one can give me a definitive answer as to when it will happen...when she'll draw her last breath. They say five minutes, or tomorrow, or seven days, or a month. It's cancer's call. And it's biding its time, lurking in the shadows with one more bullet.

Her chest rises...

I hold my breath, waiting for it to fall. Waiting. Is this the last one?

She exhales.

And so do I. Only to play the waiting game again.

As a Marine, battle tactics are ingrained in me: know your enemy, be one step ahead of your enemy, know when your enemy will strike. Eliminate the enemy.

I know Mom's enemy. But how am I supposed to stay ahead of a silent killer, know when it will fire the kill shot? None of my training, none of my talents, nothing I have in my arsenal will defeat this foe.

I am useless.

My phone vibrates, the noisy buzz filling Mom's quiet room. I dig it from my pocket and glance at the message. *How is she? How are you?* It's Ren.

Same. We're both the same. I hit send.

Her response is immediate. *I'll be there as soon as I get off.*

I slide my fingers over the screen, typing back.

"Cayden?" Mom croaks.

I'm on my feet, stuffing my phone into my pocket. "Mom." Scooping her hand into mine, I squeeze, but not too hard, she's so frail. "What can I do?"

Moms know everything, right? They always have the answers. Voices from the past fill the silence.

"Mom, where is my football uniform?"

"Middle drawer, left side, under your Hard Rock Café T-shirt."

"Mom, what's twelve times twelve?"

"One hundred forty-four."

"Mom, are we out of milk?"

"No, it's on the door, bottom shelf. Get a glass, don't drink from the carton!"

"Mom, how do I know if a girl likes me?"

"If, at school, you're the same kind, charming, helpful boy I see at home, then she likes you. And I'm a girl, and I like you."

"Mom, what can I do?" I'm twenty-five years old, and I need my mother's wisdom more than ever.

She smiles, giving my hand a weak pat. "Baby."

"It's good to see you smile."

"You have always been my smile."

I cough, swallowing the lump in my throat. I'm a grown man, a Marine, I don't cry.

Mom shifts, struggling to sit up. "Let me help you." I put my hands under her withered body and slide. She weighs nothing. I might as well have been moving air.

Wheezing, she's out of breath from trying to push herself up. The same Katy Sinclair who climbed Mount Kilimanjaro unassisted.

My eyes sting.

"I need…something," she says

"Anything. Tell me and it's yours."

Closing her eyes, she draws in a deep breath. Mustering the strength to speak.

Five…six…seven breaths.

I'll wait until she's taken a hundred breaths as long as she keeps breathing.

She opens her eyes again, and smiles. "I need a promise."

"A promise?"

She nods, wincing. Breathing. "Find peace in the simple things."

"Okay? What do you mean?" I hook my foot around the leg of the chair and drag it closer, not willing to give up her hand for a second. Sitting beside her, I wait for more.

She remains quiet. *Please, Mom, keep talking. Keep fighting.* "Take your time. It's okay." My thumb slides over her cold hand, over the hills and valleys of bones and tendons right below the skin.

Her eyes lock on mine, fierce and determined. A look I've seen many times before. Her "mom" look. The one that says, "You better listen, or I'll have your ass." Even as sickly as she is, she can still deliver that special, loving brand of "mom fear" in my grown man's heart.

"You've always been so ambitious, Cayden. Big dreams." She pauses for a breath. "There's nothing wrong with dreaming, it keeps you excited for the next turn of events. Spurs you on. But…sometimes those big dreams overpower our simple, most precious realities.

"Don't let your big dreams, your ambitions, blind you. Find peace in the simple. Grab on to it and don't let go."

I clutch her hand a little tighter. "I promise."

Her faded green eyes plead. "I had big dreams too, Cayden. When I was pregnant with my second child, I imagined all the things you and your little brother or sister would do. I fell in love with those dreams. I clung to them so tightly. And then I miscarried."

That memory still drives a nail into Mom's heart. I can see it on her face. "You don't have to do this. Save your energy."

"You need to know this. It's important. Let me finish."

I nod.

"You were only three, too little to remember, but when I lost that baby, I fell into a deep depression. Scared your father to death. He didn't know what to do, how to help me.

"One day, I was curled up in bed, it was a bright spring day. A robin had built its nest in the gutter, right outside my window. Those obnoxious birds chattered all day long." She smiles at the memory. "Anyway, your dad came in and announced that he was taking you fishing. I knew what he was doing, trying to get a rise out of me, playing on how much I loved to fish. I told him to have fun and I threw the blankets over my head and went back to sleep. Do you remember that fishing trip?" she asks.

I shake my head. "I don't. I wish I did. So many other fishing trips come to mind, but you were always there."

Mom coughs, bringing her hand to her mouth. "Sorry."

"Don't be sorry, it's okay. Can I get you something?"

She moves her bald head side to side. "No." Pulling in some more oxygen, she dives back into her story. "On that trip, my sandy-haired little boy"—she pats my hand—"caught his first fish. And I missed it. I was at home, pining for dreams that weren't going to come true. I was missing life, my simple realities.

"That's why I love my pictures so much. They remind me to find the peace and joy in the simple. I see so much of myself in you. I'm not going to tell you to stop dreaming, Cayden, but don't be like me and let those dreams become false realties. Hold tight to the treasures you have. Find peace in them, because *they* are your life."

"You have my word, Mom."

She sinks down into her blankets and closes her eyes. The fervor and intensity of her message left her drained. "I say this because I see the lofty dreams in your eyes. You're still clinging to the hope that I'm going to make a miraculous recovery and be fine." Mom shakes her head. "I'm not. I'm dying, Cayden."

"Mom—"

Lifting her hand, she says, "Stop."

I close my mouth and let her continue.

"You haven't gone home in days. You only eat when Ren brings you food." She points to the door. "You're life is out there, Cayden. I want you out there living it, enjoying all your treasures, not in here, clinging to a false reality. I will not let you hide in here and miss something amazing."

She's saying goodbye. I won't let her. Not yet. My vision blurs.

I want to tell her how strong she is, that she shouldn't give up yet, but the second I open my mouth, the words will pour from me along with the tears pooled in my eyes.

No tears, man.

"I hurt, baby. I'm ready." A tear rolls down her cheek. "I'm ready to see my Frank again," she says, a weak smile on her lips.

I press my thumb and index finger hard into my clenched eyes, holding my breath. *FUCK!*

"I love you, Cayden. You are the greatest treasure of my life."

Lacing my hands behind my head, I look up at the ceiling, pulling in a big lungful of oxygen through my nose. It takes a minute, but I manage to compose myself enough to look at her. "I love you too, Mom."

"Go, baby. Go home."

I suck my lips in and give my head a fervent shake.

"You promised, Cayden."

A single tear runs down my face. I don't break my promises.

CHAPTER NINETEEN

REN

"Ren..." Cayden chokes on my name.

Oh, God...

I hit the emergency stop button on the treadmill, wrap a towel around my neck, and hop off the machine. "What is it?" My chest heaves; I'm breathless from my workout and strangled by the word I fear is coming.

"She's gone."

"I'm on my way." I jog to my room, pulling open drawers and yanking out any clothes I can find.

"I'm already on my way to you. I'll be there in five." The line goes dead.

Dead. Katy's dead.

Three weeks in hospice and now she's gone.

Stripping out of my sweaty tank top and sports bra, I trade them for a clean bra and a Mine Shaft T-shirt. Five minutes. He'll be here in five minutes. And his mom is gone.

The waterworks are churning—inevitable, I know—but I

hold them at bay. *You have to be strong for him, Ren. He needs you right now.*

At my small kitchen table, I shove my current therapist-suggested art project—mosaic glass tiles and glue—into a box, tidying up a bit. Not that I think Cayden will care if my apartment is a mess—I know he won't—but I need something to keep myself busy or I'm going to break down in a heap of blubbering sadness, and that's the last thing Cayden needs from me right now.

I really loved Katy. I wish I had known her before she got sick. But most of all, my heart breaks for Cayden. The bond he had with his parents was unique and special. I think of my parents, how devastated I will be when they're gone—how broken I was when Griffin almost died. My family's still whole, intact. Cayden's isn't, he's all that's left. And as much as I want to lie to myself, say he has me, it's not the same. I'm not enough.

Distractions don't work, tears sting my eyes anyway.

Bzzzz… the door sounds.

I run to the speaker by my door and click the button to open the security entryway.

Stepping into the hallway, I watch the elevator bank.

Bing.

The doors clang open.

Cayden steps out, still in uniform, shoulders hunched, shuffling toward my apartment.

"Cayden." My strangled voice punctures the silence.

Don't cry, Ren. Don't cry. Be strong for him.

A tear rolls down my face, betraying me.

Cayden lifts his stormy green eyes, locking them on me. His steps quicken.

Another tear…

I run, crashing into him. He throws his arms around me, holding tighter than he ever has before.

Cayden folds me into his body, steel arms press behind my head, crushing me. Grief and anguish contort his body like a soda can in a vacuum.

He doesn't breathe. Doesn't move. Just holds me—a tether tying him to this world. If he lets go, he'll drift away into a dark oblivion.

I shift in his vise-like arms, circling an arm around his middle to support his weight. One foot in front of the other, I lead him the few steps to my apartment, and kick the door shut behind us.

Inside, I don't stop until we collapse, entwined together, onto the couch. Inertia or the burden of sadness, Cayden's head falls back, his eyes squeezed shut. He lets go of me to press the heels of his palms into his eyes. "I wasn't fucking there," he growls.

I can give him the whole "You were there in spirit" speech, but I know that sentiment won't be of any comfort. Nothing I say will make this better. But, if I can get him talking, he won't feel like a pressure cooker on the verge of exploding.

"When?" I keep my voice blanket soft.

"Hospice called the office just after noon. I was out on patrol." He drops his hands but keeps his head back, not making eye contact. "Riggs radioed, told me to come in." He pauses, his shoulders moving up and down with each breath. "Cap met me at the door, hauled me into his office and delivered the news. Told me to take some time off."

Cayden lifts his head. Storm clouds brew in his usually placid green eyes. "I came straight here. I know I should have gone to her...but I couldn't face her. Not after I left her alone...when she needed me."

There are no words. I place my hand on his clean-shaven cheek and stroke my thumb under his eye. Tilting his head, he leans into my touch, closing the distance between us. His lips seal around mine, a soft, gentle kiss, a summer breeze rustling the leaves of a tree. A kiss with a hint of pleading, whispering, *Find me.*

I scoot closer, my pulse kicking up a notch when his hands migrate to my cheeks, cradling my head. His tongue traces the seam of my mouth, more insistent, pushing my lips apart.

He takes, kissing harder, a desperate frenzy. Dropping his hands to my side, he tugs at the hem of my shirt, unrelenting and urgent. I can't keep up, he's moving too fast.

"Wait," I say, my hands on his chest, pushing back.

His shoulders heave and he continues his silent pleading.

I know what he wants. Hell, I know *why* he wants this. To lose himself, to forget his pain, a reminder that he's not alone. But, is this the right time? I don't want him to regret it later...to have me be a reminder of one of his most painful memories. I know what it's like to have sex linked with something awful, scary, and sad. I don't want that for him.

"Are you sure?"

Cayden brushes away some of the curls that escaped my ponytail, the storms in his eyes subsiding a bit. "I've never been more sure of anything in my life. I need you, Ren. I'm so fucking lost, but I know you can find me." He moves in again, pressing a single, heavy, demanding kiss on my mouth. "Please," he exhales.

I'm still not sure this is the best idea. But, the need to take his pain away, hold him, and show him how loved he is takes over.

"Okay." I breathe.

Locking our fingers together, I stand, bringing him with me. My toes sink in the plush carpet as I lead him toward my bedroom. With a quiet *snick*, the door seals us away from the ugly world. It's just the two of us. In here, we can right wrongs, share heartache, breathe life, heal wounds, and find the other half of our broken spirits.

Cayden lifts my shirt, crushing his lips to mine. He's not wasting any time. His fingers make quick work of the hooks of my bra, pulling it down my shoulders. His right hand gropes, palming my breast while his left grabs my ponytail, yanking my hair free of the elastic.

He's rough—sharing his pain. My nerves ratchet up, the idea of fast, hard sex scares me, but I trust Cayden; he'd never hurt me. His words from several weeks ago sound in my head: *I'm in control.*

If I tell him to stop, he will.

Matching his fever pitch, I stumble over the buttons of his shirt, unable to get them undone fast enough. He rips his mouth from mine. "Fuck, I forgot I still had this on." His fingers annihilate the last few buttons, shrugging his blue uniform to the ground as he moves to unbuckle his belt. He walks his gun to my dresser.

Cayden, half naked and armed, is seriously fucking hot. A shiver runs down my spine watching his lats shift and flex as he moves. Pressure builds between my legs, throbbing.

Turning around, Cayden smiles devilishly. "God, you're gorgeous." It's the first time he's smiled since he arrived.

A thrill runs through me...I put that smile there.

"Not bad yourself, Officer," I tease, finding my inner sex goddess.

He stalks toward me, hunger on his face. "Have I ever told you that I love the way you say 'Officer'?"

I shake my head.

Snaking his arms around my back, the hard ridges of his chest press firmly against the swell of my breasts. "I fucking love the way you say, 'Officer.'"

Dipping his head, he drags the tip of his tongue from the sensitive skin below my ear to the pulse point in my neck. It ticks against his mouth, and he lingers there before moving lower, exploring every inch of my breasts.

"Cayden," I rasp, inching us backward. My legs bump the mattress and I fall back, breaking free of his grasp. He looms above me, breathing hard. *What other parts of you are hard, Officer?*

I don't break his gaze, but move to unbutton his pants. I lower the zipper, slipping my hands into his boxers...pushing everything down...freeing him.

At his navel, I trace the path of dark hair that leads to his dick, first with my finger, then with my tongue.

Cayden pulls in a sharp breath. "Ren," he says, thrusting his hips toward the warmth of my mouth. "You don't have to do this." His words are strangled; a war between wanting me to swallow him whole and being a gentleman.

"Relax, baby. Let me take care of you." I don't know where this confidence is coming from, but with Cayden, I know I'm safe. He'll protect me. With him, I can be free.

I run a finger over the length of his shaft, hilt to head, aware of his every response, each quiver of muscle. His legs quake. I grip him with my hand and wrap my mouth around him, loving how I make him come undone with just my touch.

"*Fuuuuuck,*" he drawls, his knees bending in pleasure.

Sliding my hands up his ass, I push farther, taking all of him. Slow and steady…in…out…in…. I swirl my tongue over his dick at the same time.

He thrusts to match my rhythm. I'm not sure if I'm giving or he's taking, but my head spins out of control with lust.

"Ren…" he chokes, his hands on my head, guiding me. "You've got to stop, baby. I want to be inside you when I come."

I suck him in a few more times before Cayden steps away, breaking our connection. "Jesus, Ren, you are damn good at that." Crouching, he lifts his wallet from a pants pocket, taking out a condom.

He stands, chest heaving, staring down at me. "Sorry, babe, I've got to be in you." Giving my shoulders a gentle shove, I fall back on the bed. His fingers press into my hips and he yanks my shorts and panties down together, collapsing on top of me.

Pulling up to rest on my elbows, lust consumes me, I skip past the chaste kisses and plunge my tongue in his mouth, devouring him. Cayden bites my lower lip, sucking it hard, pressing his body weight into me. We're not gentle with each other.

I want him…I need him…

Bring me home, Cayden.

I drag my short nails over his back, arching mine, I spread my legs, welcoming him. This gorgeous, hot man is all mine. Shivers tingle down my spine and out to the rest of my body as I watch him rip open the condom wrapper with his teeth, and slide it over his length. At my opening, he nudges.

White-hot heat pulses between my legs.

"*Ren…*" My name falls from his lips like a prayer and he pushes inside. Sliding…sliding…filling and stretching me. A second ago, we nearly tore each other apart, now, the connection complete, our bodies revel in the oneness. Neither of us moves, luxuriating in the possession of each other's souls.

He shifts his head to the side, blowing across my ear. "So. Perfect."

I feel him move inside me, a twitch, then a slight thrust, pushing deeper.

My eyes flutter closed and I bite my lip. *Fuck me.* My hips move of their own accord, begging for more.

Slowly, our rhythm builds. Our lips find each other again and our tongues join in on the action.

I wrap my legs around him, burying him deeper inside me. Cayden touches a place in me, no one ever has, or ever will.

"*Oh,*" I whimper, my body clenching around him. "Ohmygod!" My words run together.

Harder. Faster.

I…Need…More…

Our bodies move, frantic, wild, and sweaty.

My release is on the horizon.

"Ren, I'm going to come," Cayden groans against my mouth.

From darkness to light, the sun breaks through, and I scream his name, "CAYDEN!"

Convulsions wrack my body, keeping me in the stratosphere. Cayden pumps faster, until he's joining me. "Ren. Fuck. Me."

Two more thrusts and Cayden's spent, collapsing in a heap of satiated male.

He's crushing me, but I don't care. I trace lazy circles on his sweaty back. I'd give up breathing if it meant that I could lay like this forever.

"Ren?" he mumbles, his chest vibrating against mine.

Eyes closed, I'm still basking in the sunshine of best orgasm I've ever had. "Yeah?"

Cayden lifts onto his elbow and props his head. My body's cold without his and I open my eyes, pouting. "Lay back down. You're ruining my afterglow."

"That was fucking great." He traces a finger from my collarbone to the valley between my breasts. "You're going to think I'm crazy when I say this, but I can't wait until we get to do that to start a family." His finger moves lower, until his palm is resting on my stomach. "That's something I've always wanted. And I want a family with you."

Oh, God…

Is it possible for words to slice your heart clean from your chest? Because mine is gone. It's on the floor, trampled, and lifeless.

Now's your chance, Ren, fucking tell him. That's a pipe dream. There won't ever be a little one…a family.

But I keep quiet. Hold on to my lie for another day.

And the lie that he'll still want me to be his family when he knows the truth.

CHAPTER TWENTY

CAYDEN

The lid is closed. The end of Katy Sinclair's story. No matter how many flowers the florist drapes over her casket, it's not enough. Mom deserves more…better. Life.

"I admire Katy's passion for life. She lived big," Lacey says, standing at the front of the church. "From her marathons to the mountains she's climbed, Katy never slacked, never took the easy way out."

I close my eyes and squeeze Ren's hand, hard. She squeezes back. My anchor.

"It was the same with her battle with cancer," Lacey continues. "Katy stared cancer down with the same ferocious tenacity that she did every obstacle in her path. She was ready to go to battle, to show cancer that she was the boss. I watched her fight with dignity and grace every day.

"On my last vis—" Lacey sniffles, blotting her eyes with a tissue. "Sorry. I hoped…I'd get through this," she cries.

My own tears are lodged in my throat, and the more of

Lacey's eulogy I listen to, the more they beg to be freed. As long as I hold on to Ren, I'm fine.

Composed, Lacey continues, "On my last visit with Katy, she told me she got so much more out of life than she ever dreamed, she accomplished so much more than she ever thought possible. And her greatest accomplishment was her family. All of you, sitting here. Katy's not gone. Cancer didn't win. It didn't take her away. She lives in each of our hearts. Forever."

Lacey steps down from the podium and walks back to her seat. Mom would have liked her parting words. A little piece of Mom does exist in every person in this room. Not enough to bring her back, though. No one can replicate her victory arm raise at the finish line, her one of kind whoop of excitement when she caught a fish, her infectious laugh when I told a joke, the way she taught me to be the change in the world.

The reverend gestures to me and the other pallbearers, it's time to take our place at Mom's side. I stand, letting go of Ren's hand, already feeling lost. Alone.

I stand beside her. Mom carried me for so many years; my shield from the cruelties of life. Bending my knees, I lift; it's my turn to carry her. It sickens me, though, knowing I couldn't shield her from the illness that put her in this box. Along with Mom, I carry my failure.

Walking to the back of the church, I keep my eyes focused, my jaw set, yet nothing helps, one tear breaks free, making its way down my cheek.

* * *

"Aunt Sunny, thank you for coming." I bend down, placing a kiss on my great-aunt's wrinkled cheek.

"Bless you, dear." Aunt Sunny pats my arm. "It was a lovely service. Your mama was a great lady."

More than great. Perfect. How does Aunty Sunny live well into her eighties, but Katy Sinclair's body revolts, putting her into the grave at fifty. How is that fair?

"Take care of yourself, Cayden." Aunt Sunny hobbles past me, on her way to sit down.

"I will."

I glance around the room, at all of my mother's friends and family. The funeral this morning had been nice, so many people. And it was great of Mom's church to provide lunch for everyone after, but I'm ready to call it a day. Putting Mom in the ground with Dad was the hardest thing I've ever had to do. I need a stiff drink. Sticking a finger in my collar, I pull, trying to loosen it. The damn thing has gotten tighter all day.

Across the room, my eyes fall on Ren. My own Persephone—a breath of fresh air in hell.

I've always done well in high-stress situations—it's what makes me a top-grade Marine and police officer—but, it's the quiet after the storm I can't handle. Mom's passing, organizing the funeral; I'm good at getting shit done. Tonight, with the war over, returning to the deafening silence of civilian life, I'm glad I have Ren waiting for me, or I'd be a drunken train wreck.

Ren tosses her head back, laughing at something Blake said. I could use a dose of her laughter.

Leaving my post at the head mourner's table (I don't know if that's what it's called, but I'm going with it), I stroll over to Ren, circling my arms around her waist as I come up behind her. I'm hit with the flowers and coconut scent of her shampoo and my mood lifts out of the underworld.

"Hi, babe," she says, craning her neck over her shoulder and clasping our hands together over her belly. "Blake was just telling Dylen and me about the time his family and your family went on vacation to the Grand Canyon."

"Ah, the 'Legendary Grand Canyon Calamity' as Mom called it." I smile at the memory.

"That's the one," Blake says. "I'd never seen your mom so angry."

"Well, when her son unfastens the latches of the backseats in the minivan, and her best friend's son goes sailing backward into the cargo area when Dad brakes at a red light, it's certain to grab her attention."

Ren shakes her head and looks over her shoulder. "You were such a shit."

"You don't even know the half of it," Blake groans. "I can still feel my head hitting the back of the van." He pouts, rubbing a hand over the back of his head.

I wrangle my hand from Ren's grip and slap a hand on Blake's shoulder "Glad there was no permanent damage, man. Thanks for being here."

Blake pulls me into a brotherly hug. "I loved Katy like a second mom, I wouldn't have missed it."

Ren taps the arm I still have pressed around her. "My brother and his girlfriend just walked in, I should go say hi."

"I'll go with you. I haven't seen Griffin in forever," Dylen chimes in.

I step back, letting Ren pass as she and Dylen take off toward the door.

"I can't compete with the rock star," Blake commiserates. "But hey, looks like you and Ren are hitting it off. I leave for my honeymoon and you're a proud bachelor, I come back, and your Facebook relationship status is changed."

"Six weeks, man." *She sped into my life and right to my heart.* "It's soon, but damn, I want that woman in my life forever, Blake."

"When you know, you know. I'm happy for you, bro." Blake claps a hand on my back. "Look at them." He raises his chin in their direction. Ren is cuddled up next to her brother, along with Dylen on the other side. "We're damn lucky."

I nod in agreement. "Truth."

"We should probably join them. You don't have to worry about Ren, but Dylen might decide to replace me with him." Blake points in Griffin's direction, a worried expression on his face.

Griffin Daniels, Ren's little brother and rising star of the rock world. I can see why Blake's nervous, having his woman hanging all over Ren's brother—the Daniels family is passing along some seriously killer genes.

"Nah, from what Ren says, Griffin only has eyes for one woman, the little blonde standing on Ren's left."

"So be it, but I'm not taking any chances." Blake slaps my arm and moves in on his bride, and I follow behind.

Ren's face lights up when I join her little family circle.

"Cayden, this is my brother, Griffin. Griffin, my boyfriend, Cayden."

Boyfriend. *God, if you only knew how much I want that title to be something else.*

I extend my hand in greeting. "Nice to finally meet you. I've heard a lot about you." Griffin gives his sister a sidelong glance, and wow, do they look alike. Ren has given me that same glance at least a hundred times since we met. Makes me wonder if my siblings and I would have looked alike, shared the same mannerisms. I envy their relationship. It sure as hell would have been nice to have a brother or sister at my side, to get each other through Mom's death. Carrying this weight alone is damn tiring and fucking lonely.

"Likewise. Hope my sister didn't give you too bad an impression of me." He shakes my hand in return. "And I'm sorry for your loss, man. Wish we could have met under better circumstances."

"Ren speaks very highly of you. Thanks, for being here. I'm glad you could make it."

"And this is Jillian. We grew up together," Ren says, stepping out of Griffin's embrace and throwing her arm over the shy blonde's shoulder. "She's like the sister I never had."

"Nice to meet you, Jillian. Thanks for coming." I shake her hand, too.

"I'm so sorry to hear about your mom." Her face turns somber, genuine sorrow reflected in her dark eyes.

"Thanks."

Griffin steps behind Jillian, his arm going around her waist, as Ren comes to stand beside me, and Dylen joins Blake.

I glance around our small circle. A combination of Ren's family and friends, and mine, blended perfectly. It amazes me how our paths never crossed before the day I pulled her over, and then again at Blake and Dylen's wedding, but I'm glad fate decided to throw us together twice that weekend. I can't imagine my life without her.

CHAPTER TWENTY-ONE

REN

I'm worried. I've never seen Cayden so…lifeless. Cayden is always so calm, levelheaded, able to handle any problem that comes his way. I knew Katy's death would gut him, but he's just not coping. He's not doing anything. I've never seen him this way.

I wish the police station hadn't given him two weeks bereavement leave; work would do him good, give him something else to focus on.

Two days after Katy's funeral, after a twelve-hour shift at the hospital, I went right over to his place. I wasn't surprised to find him on the couch, wearing the same basketball shorts and Nike T-shirt he'd put on the night we came home from the church.

Day three, and he's still in the same clothes; the only difference is they're a day smellier. Cayden needs a distraction. And a shower. I've got to get him out of the house.

Fiddling around in his kitchen, attempting to make him

something edible, I roll ideas around in my head. I have two days off, that's enough time for a short getaway; give him time to mourn Katy's loss outside of these four walls.

I take the lid off the pot of boiling water, giving myself a steam facial. The water is rolling. I guess it's ready for the noodles. Why didn't I just stick to microwavable food? The stove and I are not friends. My mother, I am not.

Taking the box of macaroni, I track the words with my finger, reading very carefully. For the average person, macaroni and cheese isn't a difficult meal to prepare. For me, it may as well be salt-crusted fish.

When water comes to a boil, add noodles. Stir frequently.

I dump the noodles into the water and stir. Circling the spoon in a clockwise pattern, I zone out, mesmerized by the swirling motion of the noodles riding on superheated bubbles.

Where can Cayden and I escape for two days? Someplace quiet...out of the way...something he loves to do...

A fly buzzes by my ear and I swat it away. "Stupid fly!" I friggin' hate bugs.

An idea boils to the surface of my mind. *I hate bugs...*

Of course! I'm going to take Cayden camping. We'll roast hotdogs on a stick, make s'mores, pitch a tent, enjoy the close quarters of a sleeping bag. Images of what we can do in that sleeping bag roll through my head and my cheeks flush.

It'll be perfect. Cayden can free his mind and enjoy doing something he and his parents loved. It's the perfect way to honor Katy's life. God knows she wouldn't want him moping around like he is.

The hiss of water hitting a hot burner pulls me back to reality. Bubbles and noodles topple over the brim of the pot. Steam and the acrid scent of burning starch fills the kitchen. "God. Damn. Shit." I drop the spoon on the counter and scramble to turn off the burner. I grab the handle of the pot and scream, "FUCKME!" yanking my hand away.

I grab my wrist, holding my burned claw, and dance around the kitchen whimpering. "That's it. I quit. I'm never cooking again." My hand throbs, heat radiating off my palm.

Hopping over to the sink, I twist the cold water on, and run my hand under the stream. "Ahhhh," I sigh, my clenched muscles relaxing.

"Ren?" Cayden says in the doorway. "What's wrong?" He's at my side in a matter of seconds. "I heard you scream."

"I burned my hand."

Cayden puts his hand in the water and pulls my curled fingers away from my palm. "Just a little pink." His fingers examine my injury with the care of a seasoned nurse. "I think you'll be all right, Gordon Ramsay."

"Thanks." Disappointment colors my voice. I wanted so badly to make him dinner. Albeit, macaroni and cheese from a box isn't gourmet or anything, but it still pisses me off that I couldn't accomplish this one menial task for him.

Cayden turns the water off and wraps a cool damp paper towel around my hand. "I have a first-aid kit in the bathroom." He tugs on my elbow, leading me in that direction.

Shaking my head, I stop. "It's fine, Cayden. Minor burns don't require a dressing. It'll heal better on its own."

"You sure?"

"I am a nurse, remember."

He sighs, struggling against his protective, got-to-fix-every-thing mind-set. And I do a little happy dance inside—my injury got him off the couch!

"Well, I screwed up lunch. And managed to destroy your kitchen in the process." The stove is a mess. Thin wisps of smoke rise from blackened noodles still lying on the hot burner. I move toward the sink, thinking he might keep some cleaner underneath, but he grabs my waist and pulls me back.

Turning around, I look up into his sad eyes, the dull green of a plant that hasn't been watered in days. I wish there was something I could do to help him through this, but unlike a plant, it's not as easy to water a broken heart.

"Don't worry about the mess," he says softly. He folds his arms around me in a protective, tight embrace. Resting his head on top of mine, he holds me. "Thank you."

I pull back, not enough to break our connection, but enough to see his face. "For what?"

"For being you."

"It's the only thing I'm good at." I wink.

"Sweetheart, you're good at a hell of a lot." He smiles. It radiates from his lips, through the light blush of his scruffy cheeks, and touches his eyes. No longer droopy and sad, but a life-filled, vibrant green.

Huh. Maybe a soul can be watered.

"You know, I was thinking. I have the next two days off, and you"—I tap my index finger against his chest—"have a lot of time on your hands."

"God, don't remind me," he moans.

I shake my head. "No, we should get out of town. Go somewhere, just the two of us. I was thinking, camping." I bite my lip, hoping he doesn't think my idea is stupid.

His eyebrow quirks up. "Camping? No offense, sweetheart, but you find one cache and you're ready to pack it up and call nature a day."

"I know. But this is something I really want to do…with you." I tighten my grip on his waist.

"There will be bugs," he warns.

"I'll bring thirty cans of bug spray."

His arms flex and a groan rumbles in his chest. "*Hmm*. You drive a hard bargain. I can't resist you covered in the smell of DEET. It's quite the turn-on."

I wrinkle my nose. He's so weird. "So, is that a yes?" My pulse accelerates with anticipation.

"Get your sleeping bag, sweetheart, looks like we're going camping."

"*Ahh!* Thank you, Cayden!" I jump, breaking the steel-cable hold he has around me. This will be so good for him. "Let's leave today. Right now."

He nods. "Okay. I've got a tent in the garage. But, don't you need to get some things from your apartment? As cute as your heart-speckled scrubs are, they really aren't meant for camping."

I glance down at my pink scrubs covered in tiny red hearts. "You're right." Dammit. I want to leave now, before he has time to reconsider and plop back onto his couch. "We can stop by my place on our way to the campground."

Cayden hugs me again, belly to belly. "I know you're doing this for me. And I thank you."

Smiling, I press up on my tiptoes and kiss him lightly. "You've been so sad, lonely. I'd do anything to make you happy, Cayden." I kiss him again. "Make you dinner." *Kiss.* "Burn down your kitchen." *Kiss.* "Sleep with spiders." I move in for another kiss, but his finger blocks my intended target.

"Hold it right there. I better be the only one sharing your sleeping bag."

A shiver runs down my spine. "God, I hope so."

* * *

Cayden punches in the code on the keypad of the garage and the motors kick in, raising the door. "Whose house is this again?" I ask, hoping we're not adding breaking and entering to our camping must-do list.

"My Marine buddy Taz lives here. Before he deployed, he gave me his key and entry code. I've been looking after his house while he's away. He's got a lot of land, it's secluded, and he won't mind if we set up our little campsite out back." With the tent, my bag, and his own slung on his back, and two chairs in his arms, he walks into the garage and motions for me to follow.

Dropping the chairs next to the door that leads to the house, Cayden opens it, and ushers me inside. "After you, sweetheart."

The fading daylight isn't able to penetrate the drawn shades, plunging the house into darkness until Cayden flips a switch and the kitchen brightens.

Taz's house is more hunting lodge than contemporary

home. The open floor plan leads from the kitchen right into the living room where five deer heads are mounted on the wall. The ceiling features the rustic exposed beams of a log cabin, and huge stone fireplace takes up one entire wall. It's a beautiful home and I can see that Taz takes a lot of pride in maintaining it.

"Too bad we can't just rough it in here," I say longingly, strolling through the kitchen.

"You're taking me camping, remember. I'm not going to let you beg out of it now. You've filled my head with too many pleasant images that I am planning on bringing to life."

"Taz has no neighbors?"

"Not for a couple miles in each direction. He's pretty secluded out here."

"Okay," I sigh, looking out the window. The wooded grounds, in all its bug-infested glory, stretches for miles. *Put on your big-girl panties, Ren. You're doing this for Cayden.*

"Which way to Camp Sinclair?"

CHAPTER TWENTY-TWO

CAYDEN

I lay the tinder in the fire pit and stack the kindling teepee-style before adding the firewood.

"You're really good at that," Ren says behind me.

I glance at her over my shoulder. "I've done it one or two times before." She crouches next to me. "Want to do the honors?" I offer the matchbook.

"I don't know," she says hesitantly, biting her lip.

I nudge the matches into her hand. "Go on. Give it a try. I'll walk you through it."

Flipping open the matches she tears one from the book and closes the flap. Setting the match head on the striker, she cringes. "This is so not a good idea. You saw what I did to your kitchen with water and a box of macaroni. Now you're giving me fire? I'm going to burn down Taz's whole setup here."

"Strike the match, Ren." *Doesn't she know that I wouldn't let anything bad happen to her? She's all I have left.*

In one fluid motion, she drags the match across the striker and the flame bursts to life.

"Here's the tinder." I point, indicating the dried leaves, dryer lint, and small twigs. "That's what you want to light."

She feeds the match through the small opening I left in the teepee, working the small flame over the leaves.

"Good," I coach. "You're going to need to work quickly and light the tinder in different places. We want the fire to rise up and catch the kindling."

The match burns down and Ren drops it into the tinder, hurrying to light another. "Now you've got the hang of it." I bump her shoulder with mine. "We make a good team."

She smiles at me. "Yeah, we do."

"Step back a second." With a long stick, I stoke the fire until it rises up in a crackling hiss, kindling sizzling. "Look at that." The firewood on top starts to burn and our campfire is blazing. Hypnotic flames lick and dance across the sycamore logs, giving off an earthy, sweet scent—the traditional campfire smell infused with vanilla and tea.

She rubs her hands together, then places her palms outward, testing the heat. "It's nice."

Giving the stick in my hand a little toss, I catch it near the top. "How about some dinner? I make a mean campfire hotdog."

When Ren turns her head, the flames reflect in her eyes, and I'm struck by how amazing she is. Just by being here, spending the night in the woods at the back of Taz's property, bugs and all, she's shouldering her fear to help pull me through mine.

"School me in the ways of roasted weenies, Campfire Chef. Stick me." She holds out her hand.

Wagging my eyebrows, I pass her a stick and a cold dog. "With pleasure."

She smirks, and takes the stick from my hand. "Always with your mind in the gutter."

With a low growl, I grab her, hauling her close. "Not the gutter, sweetheart. But you and me in that sleeping bag…I haven't been able to get my mind out of that yet." I kiss her hard.

Breathless, she asks, "Is that a promise?"

"I always keep my promises."

"Good. Because I'm going to hold you to that one." She winks. "But first, I'm starving. The terrible cook we had earlier, the one who tried to make mac 'n' cheese, she really fucked up lunch."

"Don't be too hard on her, she's a superhero in disguise."

Stepping out of my arms, she walks to her chair and snatches her faded red hoodie off the back. "Yeah, right." She rolls her eyes.

She pulls on the sweatshirt, her curls bouncing as her head pops through the neck. On the front is the Superman insignia and the word "nurse" printed inside the "S." She has no idea how super she truly is. She plops down in her camping chair and puts her hotdog on the end of her stick.

I point to her shirt. "I rest my case."

Glancing down at her chest, she gives a lopsided smile and shakes her head. I can't believe how fast I've fallen for this girl. Without her, I wouldn't have gotten through Mom being sick, and I sure as hell wouldn't have made it these last three days.

"O Campfire Chef," she sings, pointing her stick at me. "How do I cook this thing?"

Dragging my chair next to hers, I ready my stick. I love sharing with her all the things my family enjoyed. It softens the blow that they're gone and I'm the only one left.

"Like this." I put my hotdog into the fire. "You want to put it near the base of the campfire, where the flames are blue. That's the hottest part, your food will cook fastest there."

Ren pushes her stick into the flames, right next to mine. Together, we roast our hotdogs, side by side, just like I used to do with Mom and Dad. In a way, this is like a passing of the torch from one family to the next.

After only a minute, Ren takes her stick from the fire and holds it close to her face, examining the hotdog. "Is it done?" She gives it a tentative poke. "Whoa, that sucker's hot!" She pops her finger into her mouth.

I lean over and give it a once over. "It could go a little longer. It's probably still cold on the inside."

Wrinkling her nose up, Ren shoves the stick back into the fire. Two seconds later, she crosses her legs. Then her foot starts bobbing. I don't know why I never realized it before, but Ren can't sit still. Come to think of it, she's always in motion. When we hold hands, she always sets them swinging between us. After we make love, she traces circles on my chest or back. Even when she's asleep, she tosses and turns and her eyes flutter.

God, she makes me so happy. I love every single thing that

makes her Ren. I know what Mom meant when she said to find peace in the simple things. My fidgety Ren brings peace to my war-weary soul.

The warmth of contentment spreads through my gut, pushing out in all directions like a compass rose, eating up all the pain I've felt the last few days…months…years.

I put a hand on her knee and she stops moving. Twisting her head in my direction, she asks, "What's wrong?"

"Nothing, sweetheart. For once, there is nothing wrong."

She smiles, all white teeth and kissable lips. "We should play a game," she says. "When I was in college, my friends and I loved playing a game called Two Facts and a Fib. Ever played?"

"Nope."

She gasps, appalled. "You are lucky to have me around, Cayden Sinclair. Your fun-o-meter is embarrassingly low."

"You are so right about that." Laughing, I pull my stick from the fire. The meat sizzles, sufficiently blackened and ready for some ketchup, mustard, and a bun.

"Oooh, is mine ready, too?" She draws it out again giving it another close examination.

I have to laugh; she is such a nurse. "Should be."

"Great. Will you pass me a bun and the grape jelly?"

"Uhh, what did you just say?" My ears have failed me. *Grape jelly?*

She gives me a puzzled look. "Pass me a bun and the grape jelly, please?"

My face scrunches up in horror. "I did not pack any jelly, sweetheart."

Leaning over me, Ren latches on to our large picnic basket

and pulls it in front of her. Flipping it open, she rummages around and brings out a bottle of jelly and a bag of hotdog buns.

"You didn't"—she sneers—"but I did." Fitting her hotdog into the center of the bun, she turns her attention back to me. With the bun right in my face, she draws two generous lines of sticky, purple jelly over the hotdog, and takes a giant bite. "*Ahhh*…now this is a good dog," she mumbles through a mouthful of jelly-covered hotdog.

My stomach churns, disgusted. "I cannot believe you just did that."

"Mmm-mmm."

"What did that dog ever do to you?"

Swallowing, she fishes a napkin from the basket and wipes her mouth. "When I was little, my grandpa used to put jelly on hotdogs. I picked it up from him."

I run a line of mustard down one side of my dog, and a swipe of ketchup down the other side—because they can't touch. "Well, I can't fault you for keeping a family tradition alive. But later, we're going to have to keep a Sinclair family tradition alive."

"What's that?" she asks, taking another bite of her hotdog.

"We're going for a midnight swim."

Mid-bite, her eyes go wide, and she lowers the hotdog from her mouth. "Where?"

Fear and anxiety sweep over her face. I want to wrap her up in my arms and prove to her in every way I can, that I will always keep her safe.

"The river."

"Uh-uh. No way. I am not swimming in any river. Do you know how many *things* live in there?"

"The river that runs along Taz's property is completely safe. I've been swimming there before."

"No way. It's not happening."

Standing up, I step in front of her and squat down. I push her knees apart and lean in, our faces inches apart. "Do you trust me?"

Her eyes search mine, and she bobs her head reluctantly. "It's really a Sinclair family tradition?"

I nod. "Mom, Dad, and I would swim every night, after hot-dogs and s'mores."

Cringing, she rolls her head from side to side, warring with the idea of pleasing and refusing me. "Ooh, I really don't like you right now, Sinclair," she grumbles. "But I'll do it on one condition."

"What's that?" I smirk.

"You have to take a bite of the Daniels family hotdog."

"Lay it on me." I open my mouth, showing no fear.

Ren brings her half-eaten hotdog to my mouth. I take a hesitant bite. The sweetness of the jelly and the savory hotdog isn't the nauseating combination I expected. I chew more enthusiastically, mumbling around the food, "This isn't bad."

Ren's face lights up and it takes my breath away. Leaning in, I kiss her, tasting jelly on her sweet lips. "Look at us, blending family traditions."

"And making some new ones in the processes." Her lips part against mine, in a ravishing grin.

CHAPTER TWENTY-THREE

REN

W e power down a package of hotdogs—after one bite of my jelly concoction, Cayden chooses to stay with his traditional ketchup and mustard—and now we're onto s'mores, inching ever closer to my date with the river. Why did he have to eat my stupid hotdog? I've tried to change his mind: batting the eyelashes, pouting the lips, whispering all the things I'm going to do to him in the sleeping bag, nothing works. None of my ammunition is bring Cayden down. He's adamant about sticking to the Sinclair Family's Rules of Camping.

Well, I'm going to make this the longest lasting s'more on the face of the earth. I glance over my shoulder, toward the woods, knowing the river lies just beyond. Why on earth did I suggest *camping*? My stomach churns, nervousness twisting my guts into a pretzel.

Snuggling into Cayden's lap, I shove a marshmallow on the end of my stick, and put it into the hottest part of the fire, the blue flame at the base, just like he told me earlier. With his head resting on my shoulder and his arms in a protective circle around me, I watch as the marshmallow shrivels and bubbles, transforming from white, to light brown, before igniting into a yellow flame. I love that part, watching it combust, when the marshmallow can't take any more heat and it bursts into a glowing ball of fire. When Cayden makes love to me, that's how I feel, like I'll burn up in all of his desire. There's no better feeling in the world then to be consumed so wholly, inside and out, and every place in between.

Pulling the stick from the fire, I bring it close to my face, watching the flames transform the gooey sugar into a black, sooty char. When it's sufficiently blackened, just the way I like it, I purse my lips and blow, extinguishing the blaze.

"If I had known you like to eat charcoal, I would have packed a few briquettes for you," Cayden teases, his breath in my ear sending shivers down my back.

"Ha. Ha. Very funny. I like my marshmallows toasty."

"That is more than toasty, Ren, it's dead."

Suddenly, his arms cinch around me and he pulls in a deep breath. I'm sure his mind has settled back on the loss of his mom. "It's okay to think about her." I rub his arms, trying to ward off his sorrow.

He remains quiet.

"When I was a little girl, in the summer, my parents sent me to Girl Scout camp. At dusk, right before we'd go home, all the Daisy Scouts would gather around the campfire, roast marshmallows, and sing songs." My hope is that one of my childhood stories might help him feel better. "The first time I toasted a marshmallow, I stuck it in the fire, near the top, turning it a golden, toasty brown. When I ate it, I thought it was the most disgusting thing I'd ever tasted. I didn't understand what all the hype was about."

Cayden readjusts, shifting me on his lap, holding me tighter, but keeps quiet, listening. "I saw one of my friends turn hers into a torch. If marshmallows weren't good to eat, they sure looked like a lot of fun to burn. I stuck a second one in the fire, until it went up in flames. One of the other girls dared me to eat it. I slapped that sucker between a piece of chocolate and a graham cracker so fast, and popped it into my mouth. I've burned my marshmallows ever since. There's something delicious about the bitter tang of the charred marshmallow and how it masks the sweetness of the melted chocolate. Such a wonderful dichotomy."

"It's a lot like life and death," Cayden mumbles. "The sting of death, masking the sweetness of life."

"Or maybe their relationship is more complementary," I challenge. "You have to savor them together. By itself, the burned marshmallow is bitter and hard to stomach, but with the chocolate, it's easier to digest. The bitterness of death will always bring out the sweetness of life."

A sharp, cool wind blows through our little campsite, exciting the fire. It crackles, the flames licking higher in the sky.

"I don't know, but I'll take your word for it," Cayden says, his thoughts far away.

We sit quietly for a long time, staring into the yellow blaze, embracing the sweetness of each other's arms in the wake of so much bitter loss.

* * *

Cayden pulled his truck into Taz's backyard, near our camp-site, so we could store our food and belongings out of the reach of the local wildlife. Tossing the picnic basket into the back of the truck, I shut the door and turn around, a scowl on my face. "Why are you making me do this?"

"Because we're sharing our family traditions, remember. A midnight swim always comes after s'mores. And we had a deal." He kisses my nose and then bends down, pulling his swim trunks out of his bag.

Silently cursing him and his family traditions, I unzip my bag and rifle through, looking for my bikini top and bottom. It's bright pink, it should be easy to spot, even in the low light of the campfire. I pull out underwear, T-shirts, a bra, a box of condoms (never leave home without them!), shorts, bug spray, deodorant, my toothbrush, toothpaste, and a hairbrush. Everything I need for a camping trip…everything except a damn swimsuit.

My bag empty, the contents in a heap on my lap, I look up at Cayden who's already changed. My mouth goes dry…but not my other parts. Cayden is bare chested, sporting a pair of low-slung navy-blue board shorts. The V-shaped muscles on his sides, taper to a point just below the drawstring of his trunks, along with the dark line of hair that travels from his navel and lower.

"Ren? What's wrong?"

I snap my mouth closed, realizing it's a wide-open flytrap. "Umm…" *Words, Ren. Speak words.* Words are a lot easier to come by when all of Cayden's muscles aren't illuminated in the glow of firelight. *Holy hell, is he hot!* "I don't…" I avert my gaze from Super-friggin'-man, to the pile on my lap. It's safer. "I forgot my suit," I mumble.

I see his face in my peripheral vision. "Well, this midnight swim just got a hell of a lot more interesting," he snickers.

Turning my head, I nail him with a death glare. "What do you mean?"

"Looks like we're going skinny-dipping, sweetheart," he says, waggling his eyebrows.

Taking handfuls of my clothes, he starts stuffing them back into my bag. "This is gonna be fun."

"Says who?" I growl through clenched teeth. "I swear to God, Cayden Sinclair, if anything touches me in that water, I will scream bloody murder."

Cupping my cheeks, he kisses me, despite the savage grimace on my face. "Nothing will touch you, Ren. I promise." My lips soften. "But, I can't promise, *I* won't touch you."

His tongue pushes beyond the seam of my lips, pressing against mine. "Trust me," he breathes into my mouth. My eyes close and I relax into him, opening to kiss him back.

"Ready?" he whispers.

"No," I murmur.

"Yes, you are!" Cayden takes my hand and yanks me up, all the stuff on my lap, falling to the ground. Glancing at the mess, he notices the box of condoms, and picks it up, raising an eyebrow. "Didn't plan on sleeping tonight?"

I shrug. "Depends on what your definition of 'sleeping' is."

"Ren Daniels, you are too much."

Together, we pick up the rest of my belongings and hand in hand, we make our way to the river. Cayden shines the flashlight ahead of us and helps me down the hill.

The sound of trickling water becomes more noticeable the farther we get away from the safety of Taz's backyard. "Cayden, will you be able to find the way back? Because I'm lost." The forest around us is pitch black, dense, and looks exactly the same in all directions.

Shifting his gaze upward, he says, "See that bright star right there? The brightest one in the sky?" He points.

I follow his eyes toward the break in the canopy of trees. There is a bright, twinkling star. "Yeah."

"That's Polaris, the North Star. At Taz's, that star was to our backs. On our way back, we need to travel a southern route."

The woods are noisy, screeches, hoots, buzzes, whines, rustling leaves. I have no desire to come across a single creature that makes any of those noises and Cayden's confidence in star navigation doesn't bolster my confidence. "Not to call into question your celestial navigation prowess, but I was hoping for a more precise means of locating the house. You wouldn't have a GPS with you, or anything, huh?"

He holds up his phone. "You're safe, Ren. I won't let anything happen to you. Please trust me."

I do trust you, Cayden. I trust you so much, that I gave you my body, my soul, and my heart.

CHAPTER TWENTY-FOUR

CAYDEN

"This is it." The slow-moving river runs a couple feet in front of us, down a shallow embankment. Darkness swallows everything. I'll have to keep Ren close.

Apprehension rolls off her in waves. I know she'll love swimming at night, in the dark, once she gives it a try. I wouldn't push her if there were any danger. This part of the river is so tame. "When I was a boy, this was my favorite part of camping. There's nothing like getting in the water when you're surrounded by darkness. Your senses are heightened, adrenaline is pumping—such a rush." I grab the hood at the back of her sweatshirt, pulling her closer. "I've never been skinny-dipping," I whisper into her ear.

Her breath hitches.

I drop my shorts and walk bare assed toward the river, hoping none of Taz's neighbors have a midnight swim on their agenda. If I get busted for skinny-dipping, I can kiss SWAT goodbye for real this time. But damn if the idea of Ren's wet, naked body doesn't have me pushing the limits of the laws I'm meant to uphold.

My feet sink in the mud at the bank as I step into the cool water. "This would be a lot more fun with you, Ren," I call over my shoulder, knee deep in dark water.

"Is it cold?" she asks.

Pushing off the river bottom, I propel my entire body into the water. Holding my breath, I dive under, swimming against the light current. The water's glorious, cool, and refreshing. The only thing that would make this better is Ren at my side.

I break the surface of the water and whirl around, spotting Ren on the bank, a little closer to the water. "Babe, the water's great! Get your ass in here!"

"Are there critters?"

I swim in her direction. She's going to need a little help. Walking out of the water, I notice Ren's eyes roaming over every inch of my body. And I love every fucking second of it.

Stomping through the reeds and tall grasses, I stop in front of her. "It's not Loch Ness, Ren. Nothing is going to hurt you. Do you trust me?" I ask.

She nods, dread and panic in her eyes.

"I need to hear it. Do you trust me?"

Clearing her throat, she mumbles a weak, "Yes."

"Good. Remember, you're in control. Always." I grab the bottom of her sweatshirt and pull it over her head in one motion, tossing it by my shorts. "Still trust me?"

"Yes," she says a little more confidently.

"Nothing is going to hurt you. I'm here." Unhooking her

bra, I drag the straps over her shoulders, my fingers skimming over the sides of her gorgeous breasts.

Ren sucks in a breath.

"Swim with me, baby." Desire strangles my words. My dick throbs, aching for her touch.

Lowering her shorts and panties, she steps out of them. She is naked and so fucking gorgeous. It takes all my strength not to lower her to the grass and bury myself inside her.

I extend my hand toward her and she slips her palm against mine. "Okay"—she sucks in a huge gulp of air—"let's do this."

Leading her toward the water, she hesitates where the water laps the bank. "It's okay, Ren. I promise." With the next step, mud squishes between her toes and she cringes. "You're in control," I remind her.

Another step, and she's in the water, ankle deep. "Oh!" she gasps, smiling. "It's cold."

"Keep going, it'll warm up."

Pressing farther, we're both up to our knees. Ren lets go of my hand and sinks into the water, going under. My lips curl into a wide grin, so proud of her, overcoming her fear.

I lower myself, letting the water lap at my ears, waiting for her to resurface.

She pops up with a gasp. "Oh, whoa! This is awesome!"

"See, I told you. And I have to say; being naked makes it even better. Thanks for leaving your suit at home." I wink.

"You bet."

The river flows past us, taking with it all the shit of the last two months: denied promotions, cancer, nightmares of the past, death. In here, the world is forgotten; it's the water, Ren, and me…us—what matters the fucking most.

Ren swirls around about a foot away, her head bobbing on the surface.

"So, this isn't your first time camping, huh? You said earlier you went to Girl Scout camp?"

"Yeah, but it was hardly camping. We didn't spend the night, or go midnight swimming. Crafts, s'mores, sang songs, went home. That's it." She raises her arms out of the water and circles around. "This is the real deal." Overhead, an owl hoots, right on cue. "See." She raises an eyebrow, pointing upward.

"No owls at Girl Scout camp?"

"Probably not even bunnies. Daisy Scouts was my mother's attempt at to 'harness' my energy. I gave my parents, and countless teachers, a run for their money. You were a reckless kid, I was Dash from *The Incredibles*."

I swim toward her, hating that I'm not touching her. Looping my arms around her middle, Ren brings her hands down, splashing as she grabs hold of mine. "Dash?"

"I was unstoppable," she says, giggling. "I moved so fast, all my childhood pictures are blurry."

Roaring with laughter, I nuzzle her neck, kissing right below her ear. "And a Daisy Scout? That is the damn cutest thing I've ever heard of."

She leans her head back against my shoulder, staring up at me. "I was a Brownie, too."

"With all your scouting experience, I'm surprised you haven't made your peace with the outdoors."

Rolling her eyes, she scoffs. "I may have been a scout for

many years, but I will never get over my hatred of creepy crawling things."

God, I love her body pressed against mine, smooth and wet. "Well, you may not be a scout anymore, but I know what you are now."

"What?"

"Mine." The curve of her ass melds perfectly to me, my cock pressing right between her legs. I grab a handful of her ass. "And fucking gorgeous."

Ren spins around, her eyes are wide and dark, and my heart stutters, twisting and reshaping itself to enclose her inside.

"Cayden," she says.

My name hangs between us, an unfinished sentence. She stares. I know how she feels, wanting to say so much, but not having enough words to articulate the exact emotion.

Want consumes me, and I crush my mouth to hers. Ren opens to me immediately, pushing her tongue against mine, snaking her hands around my shoulders and up my neck, latching them behind my head.

I keep my feet rooted on the riverbed as Ren anchors her body to mine, wrapping her legs around my backside. She moans against my mouth when my dick slides between her legs and she bucks her hips, repeating the motion, taking her pleasure.

The water laps around us as Ren rocks her body against me. Fuck. *Fuck.* "God, Ren, I want you so bad," I moan. "Let me inside you," I beg, ready to lose my shit.

She continues grinding and my head spins. "Baby." Putting my hands under her ass, I pull her higher on my body. My cock is right at her opening. I could so easily slip inside. I thrust, nudging against her. "Please…"

"Cayden," she groans, "we don't have anything." Open-mouthed, our tongues tease. I lick mine over hers and suck her bottom lip into my mouth.

"I'm clean, baby. I was tested when I got back from overseas."

Ren stills in my arms, her heavy-lidded eyes focusing on mine. There's a pleading in her eyes I've never seen before…and fear. "I want you inside me, Cayden, but I need you to wear a condom. I just…I can't without."

I brush my hand over her head, loathing the fear that clouds her face. I don't want there to be any fear, not between us. "It's okay. I can wait."

"Thank you."

I know this fear stems from her nightmare three years ago, and it slays me that I wasn't there to protect her from that monster. "You're in control, Ren. Always."

She unlatches her legs from my waist, setting her toes into the mud. "Why don't we head back to camp, rip open that box of condoms, and finish what we started?"

"Yes, fucking, please." I give her a quick, hard kiss, grab her hand, and together, we run for dry ground.

CHAPTER TWENTY-FIVE

Ren

Mmmm... Cayden's body is so warm. I wiggle my butt against him and snuggle closer, not wanting to give up our splendid little existence. God bless the person who invented the king-size sleeping bag. Flexing and pointing my toes, I rub them against Cayden's, loving how splendidly sore my body is. He flexes, tightening his grip on me, and between my legs, he rises, again.

"Cayden?" I whisper. "Are you awake?"

"Mmm..." he grumbles, giving his hips a little thrust.

What kind of answer is that? In the confined space of our tandem sleeping bag—which was not designed for a man Cayden's size—I manage to twist my body around, so I can see his face.

All that glorious scruff darkening his jawline...perfection. I lay my hand on his cheek, feeling the scratch of his whiskers on my palm. Heat blooms between my legs. The corner of Cayden's lips pull up, but he keeps his eyes closed.

"Somebody's warm"—he rasps, sliding me closer—"and wet."

I squirm against him. "And look who's hard."

Cayden's dick twitches between my legs and his eyes pop open. "Morning wood, baby. He's just not used to you being this close to someone who can to take care of it, and he's *loving* it."

"Is that right?" Propping myself up on my elbow, I lean over his shoulder, and reach for one of the foil wrappers littering the bottom of the tent. Last night, when I said we should rip into the box, that's exactly what Cayden had done.

Snatching the wrapper between my index finger and middle finger I lift it up and see something move out of the corner of my eye.

My heart kicks up a notch, and it's not because Cayden is teasing me with his hard-on. I glance down toward the bottom of the tent and see it, a giant, hairy spider... *the size of my fucking hand!*

Paralyzed with fear, I can't move. I saw that horror movie, *Arachnophobia*, if I don't do something quick, that damn thing will end up killing us both.

"Umm... Cayden?" I say, as calmly as possible, knowing that if I scream, Cayden will be up faster than a cardiac patient receiving nitroglycerine, and that thing will attack. "Don't move."

He stops rubbing his dick between my legs. "Why? Am I not hitting the right spot?" Getting a firm hand on my hip, he readjusts and resumes his gyrations.

"No, stop," I say, through gritted teeth. "There is a ginormous spider in the corner of the tent, right by your feet.

Cayden freezes. His hand clamps down on my waist. "Okay," he says, exhaling. "Is it moving?"

I shake my head. "No."

"Good. This is what I need you to do. Turn around as slowly as you can. Unzip the sleeping bag, then unzip the tent door. You're going to slip out as calmly and slowly as possible. Got it?"

Ohmygodohmygodohmygod. No! I can't do this! I nod my response because my heart is lodged in my throat. I don't know if I want to cry or vomit, maybe both. As slowly as I can, I twist my body around, so that my back is pressed to Cayden's chest again. Grasping the zipper's pull tab, I lower it methodically, one tooth at a time.

"You're doing great, baby," Cayden reassures me. "Now slowly unzip the door."

Reaching for the door, I feel Cayden shift beside me. "What are you doing?"

"Trying to get a better look, to see if I can identify it, and make sure we're not pissing it off. Keep working on the door."

I close my eyes and take a deep breath. *Hold it together, Ren.* This nightmare will be over in a few more minutes...and then I'm never going camping again!

Two more inches...

The tent door flutters in the morning breeze, free, no longer zipped tight.

"It hasn't moved, Ren. You're doing great. Now, pull your feet out of the sleeping bag and climb through the door, real slow."

I bite down on my lip, hold my breath, and pull my knees

to my chest, rotating my body out of the sleeping bag. In one fluid motion, I roll through the door and two seconds later, Cayden's outside with me.

"Ohhh! Jesus H. Fu—" I bite off my swear, throwing my arms around Cayden. "Was that thing in the tent with us all night?" My voice squeaks. My whole body itches, like a million things are crawling on it.

Cayden rubs his hands up and down my back. "Shhhh, it's okay. Shhhh…"

I glare at him. "Okay? That thing could have eaten us for breakfast! Did you see the size of it?" I break free of Cayden's arms. "I need my clothes." Scanning the campsite for my bag, I remember that I stored it in Cayden's truck so nothing would crawl inside.

Smart thinking, Ren.

Stalking toward the truck, I climb inside, and slam the door, thankful to be out of nature. From now on, it is five-star hotels for this city girl.

Cayden climbs in the driver side. "Well, isn't that a hell of a good morning. Thank God Taz has no neighbors," he laughs. "They'd wonder what kind of kinky shit he's got going on over here, two naked people dancing in his backyard."

I glare at him, not finding the humor in any of this. At all.

"Oh, come on"—he nudges my shoulder with his—"that was funny!"

"No. Not funny." I yank a shirt over my head.

"There aren't going to be any more camping trips, are there?" He stares at me, trying to dissect my thoughts, knowing full well what my answer will be.

"The only tent sex you'll be getting is if we pitch one in the living room."

He nods, considering the idea. "That can be arranged."

Reaching over the back of my seat, he pulls his clothes out of his bag. Working around the steering wheel, he slips his feet into his shorts and tugs them up. In all my pouting and huffing and puffing, I hadn't noticed the gorgeously naked man sitting next to me. I could have climbed onto his lap and turned our failed attempt at morning tent sex, into morning truck sex. *Dammit, Ren!*

Shrugging a T-shirt over his chiseled abs, he leans across and kisses me. "Wish me luck, sweetheart. I'm going to wrestle with Shelob." With a twist, he's out the truck and jogging back toward Cirith Ungol.

While Cayden dismantles the tent and gives it a thorough shaking, setting our eight-legged tent-mate free, I pack up the camping chairs and carry them to the truck bed.

"I found it, Ren," Cayden calls across the yard. "Want to see?"

"I think I'll pass, thanks," I shout back.

Crouching in the grass, Cayden examines the vile creature. "It's completely harmless. It's just a nursery web spider."

"I don't care if it's a spider made of solid gold. Just get the condoms so we can get out of here."

He looks up from his spider-study and laughs. "Always with your mind in the gutter, Daniels."

"Hey, we could have had some epic truck sex this morning, had that thing not held our condoms hostage."

After picking up the foil packets from the grass, Cayden

stands, tent and condoms in hand, walking back to the truck, a huge smirk on his face. "Did someone say epic truck sex? You've got my attention, Daniels," he says, pointing to the noticeable bulge in his shorts.

I bite my lip. "Rain check? I really just want a shower right now, Cayden. Me and nature, we're on the outs."

"I am going to hold you to that, sweetheart." Cayden kisses me hard and pulls my door open. "Your chariot, my lady."

Climbing in, Cayden shuts my door and comes around to his side. "Thank you, sweetheart."

"For what?" I've never seen him so cheerful, upbeat. Camping puts him in a seriously good mood. A flare of excitement lights inside me, proud that I knew what would lift his weary spirit.

"For this. The last twenty-four hours…the last two months…for you." He puts his hands on my cheeks and pulls my face toward his, planting his lips on mine. This kiss is like the front seat of a roller coaster, a stomach dropping rush, wind in the face, three-sixty loop of pure joy.

When we pull apart I'm wide eyed and gape mouthed. "Wow. What was that for again?"

"Because you're perfect. So, so perfect."

And then the ride comes to an end and you know you're going to be sick. "I'm not perfect, Cayden. Not even close." *When I can't give you the family you want, you're going to find out how not perfect I really am.*

His eyes scan my face. I can almost feel the places they linger. "You have the most expressive eyes, Ren Daniels. When you're happy, they're bright, despite being the darkest brown.

It's exquisite. A lighthouse in the dark." Very gently, he touches my eyelid. "And then sometimes, that light is extinguished, doused by rolling storms. I know there are storms from your past. And it kills me. I want so much to break through them, to bring that gorgeous light back. To hold your hand and chase those clouds away. Whatever it is, Ren, you can tell me."

My body deflates. How can he read me so well? Now's my chance, tell him and get it over with. This camping trip could be our last hurrah, end on a high note. Except…I don't want us to end. Selfishly, I want more time, even though it's going to hurt a million times more, the longer I draw this out.

"I'm just not perfect. That's all." I bite my tongue. *Coward. Heartless. Liar.* So many adjectives to describe me. "Perfect" is the antonym.

CHAPTER TWENTY-SIX

CAYDEN

"Mr. Sinclair, this is Attorney William Golden, Mrs. Sinclair's estate lawyer, please call me at your earliest convenience. Thank you. Have a nice day."

Beep.

"Mr. Sinclair, so sorry for your loss. This is Angela McBride with McBride Realty, if you are in need of a Realtor, please call our office, we'd be happy to get Mrs. Sinclair's home on the market."

Beep.

"Cayden, it's Lacey, I hate to bother you, but I have a box of your mother's things. Give me a call when you're at your mom's house, I'll bring it over. Thanks, dear. If you need anything, don't hesitate to ask, we're thinking about you."

Beep.

"Cayden, it's Emily. I know it's a bad time, I'm sorry. But, I wanted to let you know that I'm having Gabby's christening on the fourth. Vince and I would really love it if you'd be Gabby's godfather. Hope you can make it. Bring Ren, too. I'd love to see her. Thanks. Thinking about you. Bye."

"End of messages."

Reality fucking sucks. Why do I have a landline? I rip the cord from the wall. Why can't I just take Ren and run away again?

You're a Marine, Sinclair. You don't run the fuck away.

Plopping down on the coach, I rest my hands on my knees, burying my face in my hands. From down the hall, I can hear the sound of Ren's melodic voice mingled with rushing water.

The anger in my blood subsides with each note she sings. She isn't bad, actually. Musical talent must run in her family, too. I'd love to join her, but I'm content to sit here and listen at the moment. Finding peace in the small things.

Thanks, Mom.

By the time Ren is finishes her ten-song shower concert, I've got the truck unpacked, and no hot water left. But, I'm good. Better than good. The camping trip did exactly what it was supposed to. I miss Mom. I miss Dad. I miss them like hell. But, it's time for this Marine to get shit done, and my first order of business is calling Emily back.

I dial the number and wait for her to answer.

"Hello?" Emily says.

"Hey, Em. It's Cayden. How are you?"

"Cayden, hi! I'm good. How are you doing? I'm so sorry about your mom."

Ren walks out of the bathroom with a towel wrapped around her and I can't pull my eyes away. "Oh, um…" I stumble over my words, distracted. "I'm hanging in there, thank you."

Ren looks at me, puzzled, gesturing to the phone. I mouth, *It's Emily.*

Ren's face lights up. It's got to be hard for her. I'm sure she gets attached to all the babies she helps deliver. When they leave the hospital, that's the last she sees of them. Seeing Gabriella again will be a rare treat.

"Cayden, Vince and I would love it if you'd be Gabby's godfather. It would mean a lot to us."

"Emily, I'd be honored," I say.

"Oh, thank you! The christening will be at Saint Paul's Catholic Church on the fourth, six o'clock."

"Ren and I will be there. We'll see you soon. 'Bye, Em."

"Bye, Cayden."

Disconnecting the call, Ren sits down beside me. "What was that all about?"

"Emily and Vin want me to be Gabriella's godfather."

"Oh, Cayden," Ren says with a smile. "That's wonderful."

"Yeah, it is." I grab Ren's hand, lacing my fingers between hers. "I think you were onto something with your s'mores metaphor. I'm beginning to understand. The bitterness makes the joy that much sweeter."

Leaning in, I touch my lips to hers. They're soft and warm from the shower, a stark contrast to the mint on her breath. I love kissing her. Being near her, breathing in the coconut scent of her shampoo, and the faint smell of baby powder that always clings to her. And how her heart races when we're close. I can't slow her down and I never want to.

* * *

After a busy weekend of meetings with lawyers, baby Gabby's christening, and a secret trip to the tattoo shop, I'm in serious need of a quiet night, just Ren and me. I can't wait to show her my new ink. Her shift ended an hour ago and she should be here any minute.

Opening the oven door, I pull out the pan of dark chocolate brownies, underbaked by just a few minutes so they're still gooey on the inside—Mom's secret brownie-baking trick.

As I sprinkle powdered sugar on top, the doorbell rings. I set down the shaker and wipe my hands on a paper towel walking to the door. Seeing her on the other side, my heart picks up an extra beat. "It's about time," I tease. Then my eyes land on her tank top and the way her breasts peek out the top.

She comes inside, flashing me an annoyed grin. "I can't very well speed. Bad things happen when I speed."

"Bad, huh?" I raise my eyebrow, unapologetically running a finger over her cleavage.

She glances down just as I stick my finger in the dip between her peaks, pulling the front of her shirt, hoping to get a better view. Giving me a little shimmy, she tosses the last Harry Potter DVD on the end table, and grins up at me. "Like what you see, Officer?"

I lean in, kissing her, running my hands down her back and over the curves of her ass. "Abso-fucking-lutely."

"What is that divine smell?" She breaks out of my hold and beats a hasty path to the kitchen. "Brownies?" Her eyes light up like a kid's on Christmas morning. "You're spoiling me."

"I may be hopeless on the dance floor, but at least I've got game in the kitchen."

Tearing off a small corner of brownie, she pops it into her mouth and twists around, her eyes wide. "Don't sell yourself short, Sinclair. You've got some serious game in the bedroom, too."

God, I love her. I do. I love every goddamn cell of her.

Joining her at the stove, I pick up the small knife lying on the counter and cut a square. Prying it from the pan with my fingers, I bring it to her lips. "Keep talking like that and we're not going to be watching any movie."

She opens her mouth, taking a bite of the sticky brownie. My fingers are covered in chocolate. I reach for the paper towels, but Ren grabs my wrist. Wrapping her lips around my index finger, she starts to suck. Her tongue swirls around and around.

My whole body shudders. *Dear fucking Christ.*

Other parts of my body beg for the same attention.

When my index finger is clean, she licks at my thumb, guiding to her mouth, too.

"What movie?" she says, smiling coyly.

Grabbing her hand, I lead her back into the living room, down the hall, and into my bedroom, kicking the door shut behind us. I pull her arm with a little force, and our bodies come together with a thud.

"Oh," she breathes.

I can't take it anymore; I'm dizzy with want. Spinning us around, I shove her against the door and claim her mouth. She tastes like chocolate and Ren and I want to get lost in every part of her. Driving my tongue deeper, my body presses against hers, my arms caging her in.

Caught up, she bites my lower lip, and the metallic hint of blood lingers in my mouth. I want her so fucking bad. "Ren," I moan, bringing my hand down, filling it with her breast. She leans her head against the door, panting, giving me access to her neck.

I lick the space just below her ear, loving the way her body rubs against mine with each heavy breath she takes. Working my way down her neck, I bite where her pulse beats out of control, feeling its rhythmic thump against my tongue.

Is it possible to crave another person? Need them like water, to sustain life? Ren is my life. And I will never stop needing…wanting…craving.

Ren trails her fingers across the back of my neck, her forearms pressing my head lower, guiding me to where she wants me. I drag my mouth over the tops of her breasts, kissing the charm that lies just above her valley. The faint scent of baby powder lingers on her skin, making my head spin.

Arching her back, her chest rises even more. "Cayden, touch me," she whispers.

I grab her chin between my thumb and forefinger, forcing her eyes on me. "Where? Tell me what you want."

Gripping her waist, I guide us to the bed and give her a gentle toss.

She bounces onto the mattress, her wavy hair landing in a mess against her face. Giggling, she sweeps her fingers through it, watching with wide eyes anticipating I'm going to do next.

"Tell me what you want, Ren," I demand, again. "I know

what I want…to please you. To touch every place that makes you quiver"—slowly, I stalk toward her—"to kiss every place that makes you cry out"—I crawl onto the bed, hovering—"to fill you and make you scream my name."

My dick throbs against the zipper of my jeans, pained in its confined quarters.

Ren reaches up, her fingers digging into my shoulders. She pushes me back and I fall against the pillows at the headboard. Watching her, she climbs to her knees and starts working the button of my fly open. Her movements at my crotch brush against my hard-on, sending shivers down my spine. Slowly, she lowers the zipper, licking her lips.

"Cayden," she says, tugging at the sides of my jeans. "First, I want to put you in my mouth. It's a fucking turn-on watching you come undone."

Fuck. Me.

I lift my ass off the bed giving her the leverage she needs to pull my pants off, my dick springing free.

She grabs hold and my hips move of their own accord, thrusting fully into her palm. I suck in a breath, "*Fuck, yes,*" I moan, through clenched teeth, my eyes rolling into the back of my head.

Slowly, she lowers her head, her mouth so hot and so close. She swirls her tongue around the tip, and my dick gets harder. Spasms of pleasure run through me. At this rate, I won't last very long. She's too much.

Licking the along my length, she hums. The vibration of her mouth sends heat pulsing at my core. Then like a lightning strike, she takes all of me, sucking my dick into her hot mouth.

Her lips tighten around me, and using her hand and mouth, she works me over, hard and fast.

My hips give in to the rhythm and I fuck her mouth, taking more and more until my vision blurs and my balls ache, needing release. I'm on the brink of losing myself.

"Ren," I growl. Digging my fingers into her shoulders, I push her off, and roll us so she's under me. Ren grins, pleased with herself. "Uh-uh." I shake my head. "I'm not coming that way."

"One of these days, I'll get you off," she teases.

"Don't doubt your mad skills, sweetheart. It's not that you can't." I lean down to whisper the last part in her ear, "It's that I like to be here"—I rub my fingers between her legs—"when I come."

She sighs, grinding against my fingers.

Gently, I tug her shorts down, my fingers brushing along the smooth skin of her round hips, down her outer thighs, knees, calves, and slipping them over her ankles.

I run my finger over her panties, they're slick between her legs. "Do I do this to you, sweetheart?" I say in her ear, touching her again.

She squirms and offers a raspy, "Yes."

I touch her harder, my thumb pressing on the bundle of nerves at her core. She grinds against my hand, begging. "Cayden…"

With the same unhurried motion I used to take off her shorts, I slip her panties off, giving me access to all her glorious wet folds. Skimming my finger over her, I glory in watching her shudder at my touch.

Her legs quiver. I slide my finger inside her. "Cayd—

uhhh…" My name, giftwrapped in her groans, is the sexiest fucking thing I've ever heard.

"What, baby?" I circle my thumb over her clit and slide another finger deep inside. Working her, watching the way her eyes flutter. I love the way she presses her head into the pillows as she writhes on my hand, taking everything I'm giving her. Her hands grope the bedsheets, kneading. Open. Closed. Open. Closed. "Tell me what you want, Ren," I breath, gliding my fingers in and out.

"I want…" she pants. "*Ohmygod!*" Her hips buck against my hand. "Cayden! Yes! Harder!" She moves faster. I move faster, harder, giving her exactly what she wants.

She is so goddamn beautiful. More than beautiful.

"Come for me, baby." Her muscles clench around my fingers. "That's it."

"*Cayden!*" she screams. I fucking love when she screams my name!

Her body slows, coming down off the high. Opening her eyes, she looks at me, a giddy, satiated grin on her face. "Damn, you've got some magic fingers," she breathes. "But, I'm greedy tonight, I want more."

"Ren Daniels, you are some kind of perfect."

She pulls her body up and kicks her leg over my chest, straddling me. "You're in control, sweetheart. Always," I remind her, never want her to forget. My body is hers.

Leaning down, she kisses me, insistent, taking what she wants.

Her ass fills my palms, and I work them upward, breaking us apart as I peel her tank top off. She sits up and I follow her, tearing off my shirt in the process. The gentle, steady rocking of her hips quiets as she notices the plastic wrap and tape on my chest, covering my new tattoo.

"What's this?" She runs her fingers over the series of numbers inked right over my heart.

I glance down. I've wanted to show her all night. I've been waiting for this moment, for her to unwrap it like a gift. "It's for you," I say, looking up at her.

"For me?" Confusion pulls her eyebrows close. "I don't understand?"

Running a hand over the plastic, I stretch it out. "It's coordinates. The coordinates of the place we first kissed. When I knew you would be the last woman I ever kissed."

Her eyes search mine. "Cayden," she mutters. Slowly, she leans in and puts a gentle kiss just above the tape, then sweetly, she closes her lips over mine.

Soft and languid, she fills my mouth, our tongues stroking, caressing. Ren moves her hand between us and lifts slightly, placing me at her opening.

I tear my mouth from hers. "Ren, what are you doing?"

Her eyes locked on me, she lowers her body at a slow, excruciatingly blissful pace, until I fill her completely.

Nothing between us.

Enclosing her in my strong arms, I stare, transfixed. "Ren?" I need to know what's going on inside her pretty little head. I don't want to hurt her, or scare her.

She places her palms on my cheeks, holding my face in her hands. "I love you, Cayden," she says quietly. "I love you so much." Circling her arms around my neck, she kisses me, pulling us closer and closer, like she wants nothing more in the world than to fuse our bodies together.

I'm drunk on her, needing to pour my body and soul into every part of her. My heart screams in my ears. At this angle, I'm at her mercy, and I wouldn't have it any other way.

Slowly, her hips begin to move and our mouths duplicating the rhythm. My fingers at her back, and I flip the hooks of her bra, sliding it down her arms. Pulling it out from between us, I toss it to the floor.

Now we're one. One body. One flesh. The same. Connected. Anchored. Found.

Ren wraps her legs around my waist, locking her ankles, and we move in concert. Where she crashes down, I meet her coming up. But, the urge to thrust builds each time we come together; I need her to have all of me.

Leaning back, I brace my hand behind me, changing the leverage just enough that I'm able to raise my hips, and push deeper inside.

"Oh, Cayden," she moans, her tongue caressing the tip of mine.

Dear. Fucking. God. My head drops to her shoulder. This should not feel this amazing.

I thrust again.

She's so…so…perfect.

Again. Again. I rock into her, hard.

"Cayden," she whispers.

"What, baby?"

Giving her all of me, I push again as she clenches around my dick. "*Ahh!*" she stifles a cry, biting down on my shoulder.

"Come. For. Me. Ren." Holding her with one hand and

bouncing us with my other, my words match our rhythm as I pound into her.

"*Ohhh…uhhh! Cayden!*" Smothering her words into the crook of my neck, she rides out her pleasure on me, and I follow right behind, spilling into her.

"*Rennnnnn….*" I drag her name out, my hips still pumping into her, my release, long and hard, the best fucking orgasm of my life.

Neither of us moves. Our bodies refusing to give the other up.

Panting, our shoulders rise and fall in sync. Ren looks up at me and I lean my forehead against hers, spent and so goddamn happy. "Baby, why'd you do it? Why didn't you wait for me to put a condom on?" I have to know.

Slipping off my lap, she collapses beside me. I yank the blanket from underneath us and pull it up, sealing our sweaty bodies underneath. Ren curls up at my side, resting her head on my chest. Like she always does, her finger traces lazy paths over the ridges of my abdomen, but this time, she traces around the bandage on my chest.

"I trust you with my life, Cayden. My body, my soul, every part of me. I wanted to feel us. Just us."

Just us. As I absorb her words, the reality of what we just did hits me hard. We had unprotected sex. That was probably a stupid thing to do, but the thought of getting her pregnant doesn't scare me. To see my child swelling her belly, a baby that I put there, a little human that's half her and half me…that would be so fucking amazing. I want what Emily and Vin have. My own little family.

"Are you tired?" I ask, feeling a second wind coming on.

"A little," she says, yawning. "Why?"

"Want to take a drive? I want to get out of here. Take you somewhere."

"Where do you want to go? It's so late."

I turn onto my side and catch her eye. "Someplace special."

CHAPTER TWENTY-SEVEN

Ren

Staring out the passenger window, the landscape blurs to a deep midnight blue. It's a clear, quiet night. So, so late. Sleep hovers over me. "Where are we going again?" I ask, looking at him. Waves of enthusiasm roll off Cayden and pummel me.

"You'll see." That's all he'll tell me; that's been his answer for the last twenty minutes. He's like a little kid with a new toy. I watch him drive, eyes on the road, a permanent smile on his face (that I put there, by the way), and singular focus to get us to our mystery destination.

Knowing I'm not going to get any more information from him, I shift my gaze back to the darkness outside. Entranced by the soft twang from the radio, Cayden's steady breaths, and the thrum of tires, my eyes flutter closed. I rest my head on the window. The heat left over from the late summer day, still warms the night. It seeps through the glass, warming my cheek.

Sleep covers me like a blanket, but not all the way.

In my half lucid state, I'm aware of the truck's movement… Cayden at my side.

But soon, the darkness from outside encroaches upon my peaceful nap. My heart races. I can't see anything; it's too dark.

I'm lost.

I feel something cold. Resentment. Cayden's.

I've waited too long.

The truck stops, and I jerk, sitting up straight. "I'm sorr—" I shout, the words dying on my lips.

Cayden kills the engine. "Ren? You okay?" His hand touches my leg, ending the nightmare and bringing me back to real life.

I rub my tired eyes. "Sorry, I must have fallen asleep." Glancing around, I don't recognize my surroundings. "Where are we?"

"You'll see."

I yawn and stretch my hands above my head, trying to rid myself of the remnants of that dream, and to get my blood flowing so I can wake up. "Okay."

"God, Ren," Cayden says, clapping his hand down on my leg. "I'm sorry. You sure you don't want me to take you home?"

I shake my head. "No, I'm good." *I want to be where you are, Cayden.*

"Good." He smiles, climbing out. Like always, he jogs around the front, coming to my door, and pulling it open for me.

Proffering his hand, he helps me down. "The place I want to show you isn't too far." Pushing his fingers between mine, he leads me toward a copse of trees.

I stop. More nature? After the run in with our eight-legged friend, I have no desire to do anything outside. "Are we caching?"

Cayden shakes his head. "No. It's not even that far a walk. What I want to show you is just beyond that row of trees."

"Okay," I draw out skeptically.

With a tight clasp on my hand, Cayden and I step into the stand of trees. It's so dark. I lose all sense of direction. I'm thankful for the flat terrain, though; it's a lot easier to navigate than when we'd gone caching. And no sooner had we stepped into the trees, we're out, standing in a large open field.

Trees circle the field on all sides, like tall sentries guarding the secrets this place holds.

Cayden leads me to the center of the field and plops down on the dewy grass, spreading his arms wide, and stares up at the sky.

Hesitantly, I do the same, hoping no critters decide to use me as their personal jungle gym. But, once my eyes travel upward, all thoughts of insects disappear. With no light pollution, the Milky Way is on full display. Stardust is splattered across the sky like a painter slashed a dripping brush across a black canvas, over and over again. This sky is a million times brighter than when we'd gone camping; there, the trees had obscured most of it. The magnificence steals my words, and all I can do is marvel. So much beautifully organized chaos.

Okay, I can appreciate that this is nature's way of making up with me after the spider incident.

Crickets chirp and frogs croak in the distance. A symphony for the stars.

Cayden is quiet. I'm dying to know where we are, why he was so adamant to come tonight, but I don't want to sully this place with my voice.

For a long time, I keep my eyes on to the heavens. Beside me, Cayden is so still I wonder if he's fallen asleep. Inching my hand to his, I connect us. I love the feel of his long fingers, stretching mine wide. If we were standing, I'd swing them. That simple motion makes me feel like we're moving forward, together.

It's stillness that scares me. If I keep moving, the past…my past won't catch up to us.

I drop my cheek to the grass, staring at his profile—the sharp line of his nose and how it softly gives way to his lips, the square set of his jaw, the scar he hates so much—he's so beautiful. He blinks. Eyes plastered on the heavenly show above. He's been through so much the last couple months. I'd give anything to repair the holes left in the wake of his parents' deaths, take away his hurting and sadness, but I don't have any magic or superpowers. The camping trip and Gabby's christening, those were good starts to patching his heart. But I know that my secret is just one more piece of shrapnel to puncture him. Another hole to add.

I keep telling myself it's not the right time to tell him, that the family he sees with me is just a rose-colored dream. And now that I've stupidly thrown out the "L" word, everything is so much more complicated. Reality sucks.

"Sorry." His voice resembles distant thunder, a low rumble carried on the wind. "I've wanted to bring you here for ages. Tonight seemed perfect."

"What is this place?"

Cayden lifts our hands, kissing the back of mine, before holding them to his chest. "It's the clearing where my dad brought me after I'd gotten lost in the woods. This is where he showed me how to use a compass, where he snapped the picture you saw on Mom's wall."

That night, I silently asked Cayden to take me with him as he recalled the memory, and not even knowing, he *knew* I wanted to share this place with him.

My hand over his heart, its rhythmic thump travels through my skin and into my body…

Bum bum.

Bum bum.

Bum bum.

Sometimes, if I think about how much Cayden has permeated my existence, I'm scared and excited at the same time. He consumes me so thoroughly. His heart beats in my body, he fills me, he's in my every thought. I'm not just Ren Daniels anymore, but one half of a greater whole.

That's all you'll ever be, the voice in my head reminds.

"With Mom and Dad gone, I've been thinking a lot about life," he says, breaking into my reflections…drowning the terrible voice in my head. "Did they get everything they wanted before their time was up? Mom was *fifty*. That's twice my life. Have I gotten everything I want? Hell no. What do you want out of life, Ren?" he asks, still gazing up at the sky like it will provide the answers he's looking for.

You. Me. Us. Forever. "I've got the career I want. I love nursing. And one day, I'd like to get married."

Cayden turns his head in my direction, quirking an eyebrow up. "Married, huh?"

I shrug. "You asked."

"I want that, too." He winks. "And kids. A big family," he says excitedly. "If there's one thing I've learned from my parents' deaths, it's the importance of family. I'm it. When I die, that's the end of Frank and Katy Sinclair. But, with a big family, their legacy lives on. It's not the end, it's a beginning."

A lump rises in my throat. I taste bile. I am so not the girl for him. What kind of cruel joke is this? I love him. I do. I *love* him. How can I not be his? Isn't love supposed to be the answer that rights every wrong?

If you love him, set him free. Give him the chance to have the life he wants.

The night has turned from dreamy to a nightmarish reality. Dew soaks through my dress, mosquitoes bite at my legs and arms, and the once soft blades of grass stab at my exposed skin.

It's time, Ren.

I pull my hand from his and sit up, hugging my legs to my chest.

Cayden follows me, wrapping his arm around my shoulder. "Baby, what's wrong?" he whispers in my ear.

How do I murder his dreams after he's been through so much? I shake my head, desperate to find the words that will deliver the blow in the least painful way. But I already know there aren't any.

"Do you remember when I told you about the night of my twenty-first birthday?"

He rubs my arm, drawing me in a tight embrace. "Of course

I do. It kills me that you had to go through that. I wish I had been there to keep you safe."

I smile, but it dies on my lips. "When I woke up in that room, I was so scared, Cayden. So upset. I got dressed and left without anyone ever knowing I had been there. I didn't tell anyone what happened, for a very long time. It ate away at me every day. I struggled to get out of bed. I lost an unhealthy amount of weight. My grades plummeted. And I pushed away everyone who loved me." Tears roll down my face, reliving the aftermath of that night. "Yes, what happened to me wasn't my fault. It's taken years of counseling for me to be able to say that and believe it. But my silence was my fault. I should have never given my attacker that kind of power, the power to shut me up. And by doing so, I lost something far more precious."

A sob catches in my throat. The very words I've been dreading to say to him.

"Ren…" My name, kissed by his mouth, probably for the last time.

"My attacker didn't wear a condom that night." I look at him. "That's why I always makes sure I have some around.

"For a few weeks, I worried that I might be pregnant. When my period came, I'd never been happier. I could shove the nightmare into the recesses of my mind and move on. Yeah, right," I scoff, wiping away my tears.

"Ren, you don't have to do this," Cayden says, hugging me with both arms, shielding me from the faceless monster in my past.

"I do, Cayden." I look at him. "There are things you need to know before this…us…we go any farther."

The lively chirps of the crickets has died away. The frogs no longer croak. Fall lurks on the breeze, chilling the summer night. Goose bumps prickle my arms, making me shiver.

"I didn't get pregnant but I did get chlamydia. Don't worry," I say, hoping he doesn't think I gave him an STI. "I've been treated and tested. I'm clean now. I haven't been with anyone for three years, and I see my doctor regularly. But, in not telling anyone for several weeks after it happened, that gave the bacteria enough time to wreak havoc on my reproductive system. I ended up with PID, pelvic inflammatory disease. My uterus and fallopian tubes are filled with scar tissue. I may never have children.

"If you want your big family, Cayden, I'm not the woman you should be with." I lick my lips, tasting hot, salty tears. The bitter taste of shattered dreams.

CHAPTER TWENTY-EIGHT

CAYDEN

It's probably a good thing that Ren doesn't know her attacker, because I would get in my truck, drive over to his house, and shoot the motherfucker right between the eyes. I don't condone murder, but in this case, I'd be doing the world a favor.

Rage and sadness, boil in my veins, but she wouldn't know. I'm an expert at keeping my emotions locked down. I embrace her, protective mode fully engaged.

I am so angry that she had to endure all of that by herself. So gutted by the fact that I can't fix this for her.

Broken. Disappointed.

Earlier, when we made love...I'll never see Ren's belly grow with my baby inside her.

Fear seals my lips shut. I don't want disappointment to bleed into my words. None of this is her fault. I don't want her to think I blame her.

She rests her head on her chest, quietly sobbing, murmuring,

"I'm sorry, Cayden. I should have told you sooner. I'm so, so sorry."

In Afghanistan, the guys called me Big Daddy. I earned the nickname because I was always taking care of people. I always put others before myself—like my father. But I don't know how much more I can take. I'm wearing down. Dad, SWAT, Mom, Ren...our future? I don't know how much longer I can be the strong one and hold everything together.

"Sweetheart..." I muster two syllables. "Come on, let me take you home." I set my hands under her arms, lifting her as I stand. She sways, unsteady on her feet, empty, and spent—and not in a good way. "Lean on me, baby."

Giving me her weary body, I guide her back to the truck. Our moods drastically changed from just an hour ago.

The ride home is quiet. I steer the truck back to Ren's apartment, throwing a glance in her direction every now and then. My fingers itch to touch her, seal the chasm that's opened between us, but I'm afraid.

How can a five foot nine, 138-pound woman scare me? I've seen men blown apart on the battlefield, yet, having Ren shy away from me, curled in on herself, shoulders rising with each muffled sob, it's the most terrifying thing I've ever witnessed. She's pulling away from me, and I don't have any strength left to grab her back.

For weeks I've been saying how much I want to have a big family. My flippant thoughts and big dreams were a rifle zeroed right on her.

"Ren..." Her name pierces the night like a sniper's shot. I reach across the canyon that is my truck's cab, my fingertips hovering just over her arm. She's a magnet, pulling…guiding me in.

Anchored. The thousands of nerve endings in my fingertips register our contact, firing at will, sending a barrage of impulses to my brain. *This is the girl you love. She is your future. Your family.*

You're home.

When I'm not touching her, I'm Odysseus, lost at sea, fighting to get back to his fair Penelope.

Ren glances at my hand, my stroking fingers gliding up and down her arm. Like a blooming flower opening to the sunlight, she unfurls at my touch, turning her body toward me.

"I'm so sorry, Cayden. I could never find the right time or the right words to tell you."

"Shh"—I lay my palm against her arm, more nerve endings fire—"you don't have to apologize." *I'm sorry, Ren. Sorry I wasn't there for you.*

Just after one in the morning, the parking spaces outside Ren's apartment are empty. I swing the truck to the curb, roll to a stop, and kill the ignition. Without a word, I hop down and come over to her side, but she's already out, shutting the door and walking up the sidewalk to her building.

She didn't wait. Is she telling me goodbye?

I follow in her wake, joining her at the security doors. Dark leaden eyes stare up at me. "Come inside?" There's pleading in her brittle voice.

Yes is on the tip of my tongue, but I'm confused and so fucking tired. She is the moon to my ocean, pushing me away and pulling me back in. And the loss of my family is a rip current, pulling me under.

I need to be alone for a while, to kick to the surface, get my head above water. When I'm with her, she consumes me—she's all I see, all I hear. I'm drowning.

With an infinitesimal shake of my head, I fire another shot. "It's been a long day, Ren. I just need some time."

"I understand." The wind blows a curl over her eye. She doesn't bother to brush it away.

A knot forms in my gut, a knee to solar plexus. I'm breaking this girl's heart, watching it crack under the weight of my refusal.

What about my heart? It's peppered full of holes. "Give you a call later?"

She nods. The shadows of the streetlamps dance over her features, running the gamut: despair, to confusion, settling on disappointment. She turns away, opening the door.

You love this girl. Don't let her walk away, Sinclair.

Stepping off the landing, I walk back to my truck, and watch her retreating figure on the other side of the glass door.

Go after her, you idiot.

I start the truck and guide it onto the street, pointing it toward home.

I can't stop the damn buzzing in my ears. Radio static.

Communication lost.

Alone.

MIA.

* * *

Bzzzttt…bzzzttt…bzzzttt.

Lifting my phone off the nightstand, I crack open one eye,

scanning the incoming message from Speed Racer. *Talk to me, Cayden.*

Beside the four messages from Ren, Blake has texted twice, I'm sure, on Ren's behalf.

Peeling my sorry ass out of bed, I stretch, arching my back. Tendons snap and pop as I lengthen my spine. I haven't worked out in a week, not that it matters, I pissed SWAT away weeks ago.

Listen to yourself, Sinclair. Pull your fucking shit together.

It's amazing how much my conscience sounds like a combination of my dad and my USMC drill instructor. They'd both pound my ass if they were here.

I need to get out of this house. The walls are closing in. I'd give anything to go back to work, but Cap was generous in giving me two weeks bereavement leave. Turns out, I have a lot more to bereave than just Mom.

Ren's voice sticks in my head. *I'm not the woman you should be with.*

Does she really believe that? Do I believe that?

For three days, I've searched my soul, only to come up with the same answer: Ren is perfect. I miss her enthusiasm for life—the littlest thing sends her skipping and dancing around, and I fucking love it.

Walking in the bathroom, I flip on the light, smiling at the memory of our camping trip. Seeing Ren so excited and happy when she finally overcame her fear and swam in the river. The sound of her laughter filling the night is something I'll never forget. And there's her devotion to all things Harry Potter and superheroes.

I flush the toilet and drop the lid; Ren hates it when I leave the seat up. She says all the stuff inside gets aerosolized when it's flushed, and she'd rather not breathe pee.

Huh. I can't even take a piss and not think about her.

Turning the taps to the shower, I adjust the temperature and hop in. I need to get over to Mom's place and start boxing things up. The Realtor wants to get the house on the market as soon as possible. Maybe a change of scenery will help me figure shit out with Ren.

I love her. But is that enough? I never thought the issue of children would be a deal breaker. I'd meet the right woman and a big family wouldn't be too far behind. And now I'm certain I've found the right woman, and she tells me a family may not be possible.

I don't want us to resent each other in five, ten years. Is it better to sever our connection now, while there's still love to get us through the pain of the breakup, or it is better to ride it out and call it quits when that love turns to hatred?

The thought of hating her sends bile rising in my throat.

I switch the water off and grab a towel. My forehead thumps with a migraine, the weight of so many giant life decisions looming on the horizon.

* * *

Twisting the key in the lock, I shove Mom's door open. A musty scent permeates the air, having been vacant a little over a month. The house's way of mourning Mom, I guess.

I glance around, Mom's pictures on full display, Dad's ships in bottles visible on a shelf in the next room. Twenty-eight years of memories built this home. Now it's my sole responsibility to dismantle it.

Maybe it's best to start upstairs, in my old room. The memories promise to be less painful there.

I sigh and climb the first step, paying attention to the pictures on the wall. My baby picture from the day I came home from the hospital. Faded from years of sunlight shining through the windows. I always hated that picture being front and center, but Mom refused to take it down.

Second step, Cayden Sinclair's toddler years. Third step, elementary school. Fourth, Little League, summer camps, peewee football. Fifth, junior high. Each step, my life history plays out in front of me. Braces, friends, tuxedos, graduations, awful haircuts; Mom didn't miss a beat of my life.

And then there are the photos I'm not in. Many of them, actually. She and Dad traveled the world before I was born and after I moved out—before Dad got sick. Rome. Paris. Mexico. They're so content…happy.

How did Mom choose which ones went up on her wall instead of being thrown into a drawer and forgotten? Why did she want to relive *these* memories each time she traveled up and down the stairway? "Why, Mom?"

Running a finger over the glass containing the photo of Mom crossing the finish line of her first marathon, I wait for an answer that I know won't come. Why didn't I ask her before she died?

"Doesn't really matter now, huh? They're all going in a box." I trudge up the stairs, ignoring the rest of the memories.

I reach the top, determined not to look at one more of Mom's pictures, but it's like I don't have control of my own neck. My head turns and there it is, the newest photo in Mom's collection. Ren and Me.

The night Ren and I spent with Mom when Lacey couldn't. Ren isn't the first girlfriend I've brought home to meet Mom, but she is the first to make it on Mom's wall.

Staring down the steps, it hits me. I get why Mom chose these pictures. Why she wanted to remember. This was her life…her family: me, Dad, the Thompsons, Lacey, my school buddies, aunts, uncles, cousins, friends.

Ren.

To Mom, family wasn't just a biological relation, but the people she loved unconditionally. These photographs are reminders of the people she needed in her life every day. Her home…her north. When she put away laundry, vacuumed the steps, dusted frames—every menial household task, Mom needed these people at her side.

And she needed Ren. As sick as she was, Mom still took the time to fit Ren into her family…because she knew.

Taz, Vin, Bull—my Marine brothers—Riggs. I've fought in battle alongside these men. I may not share blood with them, but together we've shed blood, and I would gladly give up my life for any one of them.

What defines family? Someone you would die for… someone you can't live without. Your reality.

Ren.

I'm a fucking idiot.

Racing down the stairs, I fly out of the door, locking up behind me. I've got to find Ren. Beg her forgiveness. That's the thing about the future; I won't have one if Ren isn't a part of it. Screw the what-ifs, the big dreams. So what if we can't have kids—doesn't mean we can't try, and have a damn good time while we're at it. Hell, there are other ways we can make a family—adoption, a surrogate. But right now, I need to make things right with her. Life will be all right, as long as I get to come home to Ren each night.

I text Ren, *I found north.*

CHAPTER TWENTY-NINE

REN

Three days. How long does he need to *think*? Either he can accept the fact that I can't have kids, and love me anyway, or he needs to get the hell out of my life. And my head. And my heart.

One last text, that's it. After this, I'm done.

Yeah, right.

I tell the stupid voice in my head to shut up. I can quit Cayden Sinclair. I can. I've given plenty of men their walking papers. If I don't hear from him after today, I will rip this piece of junk necklace off, delete him from my contacts, and deactivate my Facebook account. Go off the grid.

But you can't delete him from your heart, my conscience sings. Why is she such a coldhearted bitch? Isn't she supposed to be on my side?

Phone in hand, I type four words, *Talk to me, Cayden.* I press send and pray this is the one that will capture his attention. Direct. To the point. No beating around the bush. He needs to talk to me. He owes me that. Over my dead body will

I let him take the coward's way out. After I let him in, poured my soul out, and fell in love with his ass, he can at least aim his pistol at my heart and pull the trigger in person.

I wrench my hair into a ponytail, twist the elastic around, and give it a final tug. It's so tight, the hairs at my temples scream and I've got an instant facelift. If I inflict pain in other ways, I can forget about the knife currently lodged in my heart. A constant reminder of why I gave up dating in the first place…too, too painful.

I fluff my bangs and slather on some lip balm, out the door in record time. If I waste one more minute staring at my face in the mirror, thinking about Cayden Sinclair, I will lose my shit.

Well, what did you expect to happen? You let things go too far. You waited too long.

STAHP! Where is the angel on my shoulder? I want her back. At least she's nice.

I need Dylen. She'll know what I should do.

Slamming the door to my apartment, I throw my keys and phone into my purse and head to the elevator.

The drive to Shameless Grounds wasn't terrible, traffic was light for a Saturday morning. I walk in and notice Dylen isn't here yet. That girl will be late for her own funeral.

I place my order, a double espresso con panna (extra panna!). A generous serving of whipped cream can't heal a broken heart, but it can sure give it a nice fluffy place to recoup after it's been trampled on. I snuggle into my favorite spot—the window seat in the corner—and stuff a throw pillow behind my back, closing my eyes with a sigh. Glad some things never change.

In our early college days, Dylen and I would meet here to study. Nestled in a quiet neighborhood, we could get away from the constant noise of the city, which I think was piped into our dorm and amplified to keep us out of our room as much as possible. Plus, Dylen, having spent most of her summers with her father in France, said Shameless Grounds was the only place she could get a decent café au lait.

Waiting for the server to bring my espresso and whipped cream mountain, I pull my phone out of my purse and scan Facebook. Against my better judgment, I go to Cayden's page. His posts are vague most of the time, not wanting to share too much personal information, should a criminal come across his page. His last update was a little over a week ago, "Thanks to all who came out to celebrate Mom's life."

I resist temptation and don't click the like button. I don't want him to know I was Facebook stalking him.

Flipping back to my profile, I check in and update my post, "Reunited and it feels so good!" I tag Dylen.

"*Sœur!*" Dylen sings, stepping up to the table.

I look up and see my friend…my sister. "Dylen!" Standing, I throw my arms around her. She tightens her grip, and I can't breathe. "God, I miss you."

Her strong embrace makes my eyes water. At least that's the story I'm sticking to, even though I knew I'd crumble the second I saw her.

Holding my breath, drawing on her strength, I close my eyes and relax. I'm fine. I will be okay. I will rise another day.

When I've composed myself, I pull back, and look into her ocean-blue eyes. "I am so glad you're home."

"I just saw you a week ago, *chouchou*."

"I know. But, I had to share you at Katy's funeral. Now you're all mine."

"Let me order, then I'm all yours." With one last squeeze, she dashes toward the counter.

I sit down and stare out the window, unable to keep from wondering what Cayden's up to. I know he has the day off; the department gave him two weeks.

"Café au lait, acquired. Achievement unlocked!" Dylen announces, stuffing her wallet into her purse as she sits. "Pictures. I have pictures!" She whips her phone around.

When I told Dylen I was kidnapping her from Blake today, I failed to mention my apparent breakup. Had I told Dylen beforehand, she wouldn't be bombarding me with her sappy, love-drippy honeymoon pictures.

I've really got to work on rebuilding that protective wall around my heart. Happy couples and all their touchy-feely shit was so much more tolerable when access was denied. Now, romance of any kind feels like my flayed heart is submerged in a chlorine bleach–rubbing alcohol solution. Cayden didn't pay attention during our *Harry Potter* movie date nights—the Crucio curse is unforgiveable.

You'd forgive him.

Inwardly, I scowl at that insufferable voice. Dammit. I totally would. But not before some serious groveling.

"And here we are outside our beachfront condo. This cute old couple took the picture for us. They were there celebrating their fifty-ninth anniversary. So adorbs."

And before I can comment, she's onto the next picture.

"Coffee, girls," the server says, setting our drinks down.

Mine is heaped with whipped cream, making Dylen's simple drink look boring.

"Thanks," I say before pressing my lips to the edge of the cup. I don't care if I have a whipped cream mustache; it tastes divine, and sweetens my attitude so I can endure the rest of my ride on the newlywed carousel.

I set my cup down and wipe cream from my upper lip and the tip of my nose. "Dyl, these pictures are great. You look so happy."

Swallowing, Dylen cocks her head to the side. "What is this broody, sullen demeanor I'm noticing?" I can't put anything past my best friend. "Spill it."

"I told Cayden." I don't have to give Dylen any more details. She knows what I'm referring to and how big a deal this admission is. Outside of her and my immediate family, no one knows about my ordeal three years ago.

"Oh, *chouchou*," she whispers. "What happened?"

I suck my lower lip into my mouth and bite down hard. *I will not cry. I will not cry.* The silent chanting helps. *Just keep chanting, just keep chanting…*

"I really thought he was the one, Dyl," I finally get out. "I told him that I love him."

Dylen's cornflower eyes are petal soft. "A week ago you were inseparable."

"Yeah, until Cayden laid the whole 'I want a big family' spiel on me." Tears sting my eyes. I started the battle strong, but I fear I may lose the war. "I haven't heard from him in three days. I'm pretty sure it's over."

Dylen stands and comes around the table, sliding into the window seat next to me, arms wide open. "Ren," she says soothingly. "I can't imagine him saying your situation is a deal breaker. He seemed like a great guy, genuine and caring. Blake speaks so highly of him."

"He is all of those things. He didn't say things were over, but he's ignored my calls since Monday. He refuses to talk to me. He's wised up and dumped my broken ass."

"Knock it off, Ren." Dylen's gentleness gives way to the stern motherly voice. She never let's me go down pity lane. "You are not broken. There are other ways to have a family. What did he say the last time you talked?"

"I know that. But what if that's not what he wants. He said he needed time to think."

"Well, there you go. Give the man some time"—her gaze shifts to the door—"Don't be so quick to jump to the worst-case scenario." Giving me a sidelong glance, her eyes go wide, and she shakes her head toward the entrance.

What is she looking at?

Craning my head, I look over my shoulder. The door closes behind Cayden.

What is he doing here and how the hell did he find me?

"Umm, I just remembered I promised Blake I'd help wash the siding on the house. I should go." She grabs my shoulders and kisses my cheek. "*Salut!*" Standing, she picks up her coffee, chugs it, grabs her purse, pivots on her heel, and gives Cayden a congenial nod.

"Nice to see you again, Dylen," Cayden says, as she breezes by.

"Cayden."

Dylen slips through the door, and it's just him and me. Even six feet apart his jade eyes send an arrow straight through my raw heart. In three steps, he looms over me.

"May I join you?" he asks, gesturing to Dylen's vacant seat.

That voice…ahhh… I sigh, bathing in its rich deepness, so bold and commanding. My bones turn to jelly.

Lock it up, Ren. Don't let him in.

Now my conscience decides to bat for Team Ren. 'Bout frigging time.

I nod to Dylen's seat, keeping my demeanor calm and cool.

Cayden pulls out the chair and sits, folding his hands on the table. His eyes roam over my face and I stare back. This could not be more awkward. *Say something, dammit.*

My heart thumps. I inhale, and the faint scent of his woodsy cologne whisks me back to the night of Dylen's wedding, his strong arms holding me as we danced.

Muffled voices from the kitchen in the back make their way to the front of the coffee shop. Cayden shifts, sliding his right hand across the table until his fingers touch mine.

Ever have one of those dreams where you're falling and falling and can't stop? Your stomach is in your throat and your lungs can't contract to draw in oxygen? The ground rushes up as fast as you career downward, out of control? If you hit, you're dead.

The second Cayden's fingertips touch mine, I hit the ground. But it's not the deathly collision I expect. I land feet-first, in control, safe and sound. Anchored to my place on earth. Him.

The pads of his fingers glide over my knuckles and onto the back of my hand, where he grips hard, holding on.

Air catches in my throat and my thoughts spew out in a rush. "I thought we were over."

There's a brief flash in his eyes before his expression turn somber...contrite? "Ren"—he chokes—"please know how sorry I am."

I need to stop this whole "let me down easy" speech. There's nothing easy about the love of my life prepping to rip out my heart. "Cayden, please—"

"No, Ren, let me finish," he interrupts. "I need you to hear this."

Under the table, I ball my hand into a fist, my short fingernails biting into the heel of my palm.

"I hurt you," he says, green eyes searching, trying to get a read on me.

Lock. It. Down.

"And it kills me, Ren. I'm an idiot."

Oh?

My willpower is slipping, caving under his penitential gaze. "Cayden, it kills me that I can't give you what you want...that there's a woman out there that can."

His eyebrows draw together and three vertical lines crease the space between them. "That's what I'm trying to tell you. You've already given me what I want...*you*. No other woman is you." His hand clamps down harder. So hard, my bones grind together. "At least I hope I still have you."

Doubt feasts on hope. "I don't know. What happens years down the road, when you resent me? When you're tired of our quiet, lonely house. I can't handle the thought of you glaring at me over the dinner table each night."

The lines on his forehead smooth, softening his features. "I have thought about nothing but you for the last three days." Yanking on my hand, pulling my arm across the table, he says, "Come here, will you? You're too far away."

Obliging, I stand and come around the table, as he guides me to his lap. "That's better," he sighs. "Let me tell you what I know: family molds and shapes you, family has your back, family shares joy and eases sorrow, family is putting those you love ahead of yourself. Ren, I've lived the last three days of my life without you and I hated every fucking minute of it. I'm not me without you. I've found my family in you." Putting a hand at the back of my head, he presses our foreheads together. "I've found my way home. I love you, Ren. I love you and I want all the simple pleasures life has to offer, with you."

My head spins out of control with his words. I want to trust him. "I love you, too. So much Cayden." I test the waters, lightly touching my lips to his, cautious.

He returns my shy kiss and holds me tighter than ever before.

I measure time in heartbeats. *Nine. Ten. Eleven.* His. Mine. *Fifteen. Sixteen.* Pretty soon I lose count, unable to distinguish my pulse from his. It doesn't matter though, I gave my heart to him a long time ago, so the beats I'm counting are all his.

Pulling back, I ask, "How did you find me?"

He reaches a hand into his pocket and takes out his cell

phone. "You checked in here, on Facebook. You're my compass, Ren."

I can't help the huge grin that pulls at the corners of my mouth. Rising to my feet, I pull him up, too, and slip my fingers between his, swinging our hands together. "Let's go home."

EPILOGUE

CAYDEN

One year later....

Walking out of Cap's office, I pull my phone out of the holder, eager to text Ren the good news. My fingers fly over the screen: *Reporting for SWAT training Monday morning. Picking you up in ten, we're celebrating!*

Heading out the door, I make my way to my truck, unlocking it as I get a response from Ren, *OMG!!!! Cayden, congrats! Got my caching gear on, ready to celebrate on the trails!*

Smiling, I climb inside the truck and start it up. I'm ready to hit the trails, too. The last year has been one fucking thing after another—Mom dying, getting passed over for SWAT the first time, almost losing Ren—I'm ready to put it behind me and start the next adventure, with Ren as my wife. I dial Blake's number and wait for him to answer.

"Hey, bro, what's up?" he says, his voice pouring through my radio speakers.

Tapping the steering wheel, I pull out of the parking lot, on my way to Ren's place. "We still on for this afternoon?"

"Just waiting for the signal. Is it go time?"

"I'm picking Ren up in ten. It takes about forty-five minutes to get to the park. You should leave now, it'll give you some extra time to hide the ring before we get there. Do you have the coordinates? The ring?"

"I've got 'em, man."

"Hey, Cayden"—a female voice cuts in—"Ren is going to flip!"

"Thanks, Dylen. If I have the best friend's seal of approval, I must be doing something right."

"Blake and I leaving now. This is going to be epic!"

"Great. I'll text Blake when we're close and you guys can set it up."

"We'll be waiting for the signal," Blake says, coming back onto the phone.

As I weave through downtown traffic, listening to Dylen and Blake's excitement, I'm blown away at how amazing my family is. I wish I could come home today and show Mom and Dad Ren's left hand (assuming she says yes), but knowing that I get to share this day with Blake and Dylen it's all right that I can't.

"Thanks you guys," I say, humbled…proud to call them family.

"You bet, man."

"We wouldn't miss this for the world!" Dylen screeches.

I find a parking space just down the street from Ren's. "I'm pulling up to Ren's apartment, I'll see you soon."

"'Bye, Cayd, see you," Blake says, and a song from the radio comes back on, the call ended.

Stepping out of the truck, I walk down the street toward Ren's apartment building. As always, the street is noisy and busy, offering lungfuls of car exhaust in place of fresh air. Over the course of our year together, Ren has often commented on how much she loves her downtown loft—and it really is a great apartment—but, I would love to take her to the country, find a big piece of land, and build Ren the house of her dreams. One day, our home will be filled with the sounds of our kids slamming the screen door, hollering in the yard, dogs barking, and birds singing.

If Ren and I can't have a baby, there's always adoption. Plenty of kids need a loving home to call their own, and they need Ren as a mom.

God, I love that woman. Beyond everything else in this life, Ren is my family. If it remains the two of us forever, I will die a blessed and happy man.

Pulling open the door to her building, I find her name, *Daniels*, next to the buzzer and push it. I can't wait for her last name to be *Sinclair*; that is, if she wants to change her name. I hope she does, but as long as she wears my ring and I get to come home to her every day, it won't matter what last name she chooses. I'll be ecstatic that I get to begin and end each day with her.

"Cayden?" Her voice crackles, full of static.

I push the button and speak, "It's me, babe. You ready?"

"Sure am. On my way down."

My heart sinks just a little. I always love going to the door to get her, but I know she's flying down the hall right now. All her energy and excitement cannot be contained.

Three minutes later, Ren is bursting out the doors of her building and sailing into my arms. "CAYDEN!" she screams, arms wide, crashing into me. My arms are around her before my name is out of her mouth.

I breathe her in…coconuts and fruity tropical winds with a hint of baby powder.

"I am so happy for you!" Planting her lips on mine, she full on kisses me.

I return her enthusiasm, our tongues dancing together. I lose track of time, but it doesn't matter, we're together.

After a moment, she pulls back, kiss-drunk and blissed out. "I know how much that job means to you," she says with a smile. "I knew you'd get it."

"I wasn't so sure."

"Are you kidding? You've worked your ass off this year. You deserve it."

She's right. I did work hard, but not as hard as I did to win her back. "None of this would be worth anything if I didn't have you to share it with."

She doesn't say anything, but leans in and kisses me again. Actions speak louder than words. Now for my next act: to make her mine forever.

"You ready?" I ask against her mouth. "We have some treasures to find."

One final peck and she leans back, looking into my eyes. "Let's do it."

I grab her hand and twirl her out of my arms, leading her to my truck, my heart kicking into high gear. I hope she has a similar answer to the question I'm going to ask her later.

* * *

The ride through the Missouri countryside was peaceful, but now, the fun starts. I hop out of the truck, and like always, I jog my way around to Ren's door, opening it for her.

Extending my hand, I help her down. "Ready?"

Bouncing on the balls of her feet, she rubs her hands together. "Oh yeah. Pass me a GPS, baby. I'm feeling lucky today."

Shit. Panic settles in my gut. Does she know what I have planned? Did she find out? She can't know. Dylen better not have said anything. Today has to be perfect. "Hoping to find something in particular?" I ask, fishing for clues to see if she knows.

"In the last year, I've found some really cool things. My bird charm"—her hand goes to her chest, touching the charm she's worn for over a year—"the Luna Lovegood Lego, even that ridiculous bug thingy you insisted I take."

And your luck is about to get even better! I bite my tongue, trying to keep any and all signs of my plan buried inside. "Hey"—I point at her—"that bug thingy was a trackable. Those things are rare."

Rummaging through my backpack, I dig out the nav device, and hand it over. "Lead the way, sweetheart."

Taking it from my hand, she expertly plugs in the way-point's coordinates.

"Where are we going?"

She steps close, putting her hand on my chest, right over the coordinates tattooed on the skin covering my heart. "Let's visit our first cache."

The place where she found my heart.

As much as I would love to go back to that spot, I grab her shoulders and turn her forty-five degrees, due north. "Mind if we try to find a new one?"

Glancing over her shoulder, she lowers her brows and squints. "There's a lot of brush that way."

"Not up for the challenge, Daniels?" I play to Ren's competitive side, knowing it will not deter her from proving me wrong.

When I registered the cache, I listed the terrain with high difficulty to discourage novice cachers from trying to locate it. I know Ren goes for the caches that aren't buried deep in the woods, but I didn't have a choice with this one. I've got some junk trinkets hidden inside, just in case someone does decide to locate *She Said Yes*. (Okay, I'm being presumptuous, but I needed to name the cache when I registered it. It fits, hopefully). Blake and Dylen are going to deposit the real treasure as soon as they get the text from me.

"A challenge, huh? You get a fancy promotion at work and now you're going *American Ninja Warrior* on me?" she teases, turning around. "Bring it, Sinclair. But if we come across Aragog in there, you're carrying me out."

"I assure you, there are no giant spiders. But, I will carry you whenever you need me to." I bend down, kiss her quickly, and grab her hand. "Come on, let's go."

We start off on the trail, the coordinates for Ren's cache plugged in. As she navigates, I hang back and pull my phone out of the pack. Typing a fast message to Blake, I hit send.

"Cayden, where are you?" Ren shouts from up ahead.

Stuffing the phone back inside my backpack, I sling it over

my shoulder and jog to catch up. "Right behind you, babe."
Sneaking up, I throw my arms around her waist and nuzzle her
neck, nipping at her earlobe, knowing it drives her crazy.

"Cayden!" she squeals.

"I'm done. I've found my treasure." I blow across her ear.

Ren wiggles her backside against my crotch and my dick
points the direction it wants to go.

"But we haven't found the cache yet," Ren mutters.

"There's no one around. Care to take a break? A quickie
in the woods? I can press you up against that tree right over
there." I lay the seductive, bedroom voice on thick, working
my hands down her hips...toward the front.

She lets out of heavy sigh and glances around, uncertain. "We
shouldn't. I still have nightmares about Shelob in our tent."

If Ren's ring weren't hidden away in some cache for anyone
to find at the moment, I'd convince her otherwise. The
thought of taking Ren here in the forest is intriguing. "You're
right. Now's probably not the right time, but next time," I say,
waggling my eyebrows. "I'd like to cross 'Make love to Ren in
the woods' off my bucket list."

"That isn't on your bucket list." She slaps my arm lightly.

"Oh, it is now, sweetheart." I thrust my hips, pressing my
hard-on between her legs.

She sucks in a breath. "I guess it is."

I put my lips to hers and speak truth into her mouth. "I
want you everywhere, Ren."

My phone beeps loudly at my back.

Shit. That's got to be Blake. My heart drops into my stomach. I hope no one stumbled upon the cache.

I step backward and pull my backpack off my shoulders. "Sorry, babe. I've got to check this."

"Is everything okay?"

As long as that ring is still there and you say yes, everything is perfect. Crouching low, I pull my phone out, hovering over the screen so Ren can't see. *Where are you? Hurry up.* Blake's text illuminates the screen.

Ren and I have to pick up the pace. No more getting sidetracked. I will lose my shit if someone finds that diamond.

"Who was it?" she asks as I delete the message and stuff the phone back inside my bag.

I look up at her and smile. "Just someone from work congratulating me." Standing, I grab her hand and tilt my head toward the trail. "Let's keep going."

The sun shines down in beams through the boughs of the trees, striking Ren as she scales the rocky hill. "Remind me again why we didn't just go back to the treasure we found on our first date?" Swiping a hand across her sweaty forehead, she plants her right foot at the top of the rock as I give her backside a push.

"Any excuse to put my hands on your ass is good enough reason for me." I squeeze her cheeks and she hauls herself up.

Hands on her waist, she juts her hip out. "Always with your mind in the gutter, Sinclair."

"My mind is not in the gutter," I grunt, pulling myself up the steeply graded hill. My arm muscles burn against the strain, and with a final roar, I push myself upward as Ren puts her hands on my triceps, giving me some added help.

Sweat rolls down the side of my face, dripping onto the

ground. "My mind is always on you, and you are most certainly not a gutter." I kiss her nose. "Check the nav. Which way from here?"

Ren studies the screen, circles a few times, and points northwest. "We're almost there, ten feet or so, that way."

We start trekking in the direction she indicated. "Look at you, you're a seasoned pro."

"I'm not a muggle anymore," she says proudly. "Who would have thought my letter to Hogwarts would arrive in the form of a speeding ticket."

"I guess that's true. The magic in your life didn't begin until I showed up."

Ren punches my shoulder. "Ugh! You are so cocky. And your pickup lines still reek."

"Are they really pickup lines if technically, I've already picked you up?" I say, wrapping my arms around her waist, hoisting her off the ground. "See, so much magic, you're levitating."

Ren's giggles ride the breeze like a surfer catching a swell. I cannot live without her laugh. I let it crash down over me, swallowing me in its brilliant warmth.

"Cayden!"

I swing her back and forth, wanting to capture that sound so I can dial it back up when she's not around, replaying it in the recesses of my mind.

"Cayden, the cache is supposed to be right over there." She tries to point, her index finger trailing all over the place.

Okay. It's time. I set her down, ready for her to find the real treasure. "Where?"

She scans the GPS and nods her head. "There." Stepping

carefully over the gravelly terrain, she moves toward the tree where I (or Blake and Dylen rather) hid the cache.

I follow behind her, coming to a stop in front of a massive pine tree. "Here?"

Ren surveys the area. "Nothing looks out of the ordinary." Shuffling her feet on the ground, pine needles pile up along the sides of her sneakers.

"Want a hint?" My heart thumps, ready to jump out of my chest, pull down the cache, and hand it to her itself.

She glares at me from over her shoulder. "That would be cheating, Officer."

I love the way she says 'officer' when she's annoyed with me. I love everything about her. The curls that refuse to stay off her forehead, her gentleness when someone—or me—is hurting, her boundless energy, the way she sees the world, her strength and bravery, but mostly, for showing me that family isn't just the people who share the same blood. She is my heart outside of my skin, the one person who makes my pulse quicken, my insides quake, and my blood flow.

I smile, leaning back against a tree, falling in love with her all over again. "Yes it would be."

Ren searches high and low for the cache. I glance around wondering where Blake and Dylen are hiding. I know they're close; Dylen wouldn't want to miss the big moment. Hopefully, one of them thinks ahead and snaps a picture. I want to see the look on Ren's face a hundred years from now. On our wall of memories.

"I can't find it." Ren stamps her foot and a cloud of dust shimmers in the sunlight.

"Let me see the coordinates." Ren hands over the GPS and I give it a good perusal for effect. I know exactly where the cache is. "It says it should be right here." I point to the pine tree we're staring at.

"That's what I said, but there's nothing here."

Playing it up, I step closer to the tree. Ren follows, leaning in. Pushing branches aside, I peek through the boughs. "What's this?" Reaching into the tree, I wrap my hand around a life-size plastic bird strapped to a branch.

"What is that?" Ren says in wonder.

Bringing the plastic bird down, I put it into her hands. "I think this is it." My pulse beats in my ears. My hands shake. I'm surprised she doesn't notice. I'm a ball of nerves.

Please say 'yes,' Ren.

She stares at the bird. "I've never seen a cache like this." She turns it over in her hands.

Only one other time have I found a cache that looked like it belonged in the environment. Clever camouflage. Knowing Ren and her love of birds, I knew a bird was the perfect container to hide her ring.

Flipping it upside down, Ren twists the cap and pulls it away.

I hold my breath.

Upending the cache, Ren shakes the contents onto the palm of her hand: a log sheet, a miniature glass bluebird figurine, and a golf pencil.

Before she can say anything, I pluck the bluebird from her hand. "I remember the day I saw your tattoo—the bluebird. You told me some of the legends, why you chose to ink the bluebird on your skin." Her eyes are wide and she's hanging on my every word.

Don't screw this up, Sinclair.

"You said some Navajo legends believe that the bluebird helps the sun to rise each day." She nods, confirming the story. "Here's my take on the legend…having you in my life makes the sun rise each day." I press my hand to her side, right over her tattoo, pulling her close. "You're my bluebird."

Before her, I drop to one knee, and turn the ceramic bird so she can see the ring suspended from the ribbon around the figurine's neck. "Renata Elizabeth Daniels, will you make me the happiest man on the face of this earth? Marry me, please?"

Ren claps her hands over her mouth, eyes locked on the ring dangling from the ribbon. She nods, tears welling in her eyes. "Oh, Cayden." Wiping the tears from her eyes, a half hiccup, half sob, half laugh bursts from her mouth. "Oh my goodness! Yes!"

She said, "Yes"! A blissful relief overrides my nervousness. Ren Daniels is going to be my wife. Mine, forever. My family. Standing, I take her in my arms and spin her around. "Thank you, sweetheart. Thank you."

Eager to slide the diamond and sapphire onto her left ring finger, I put her down and untie the ribbon from the bird's neck. "You're my happiness and my north, Ren. Without you, I'm lost." I slip the ring over her knuckle, and push it into place, kissing her hand. "Together, we're home."

SEE THE NEXT PAGE FOR AN
EXCERPT FROM

ACROSS THE DISTANCE

AVAILABLE NOW!

CHAPTER ONE

The tape screeched when I pulled it over the top of another box. I was down to the last one; all I had left to pack were the contents of my dresser, but that was going to have to wait. Outside, I heard my best friend, Griffin, pull into the driveway. Before he shut off the ignition, he revved the throttle of his Triumph a few times for my sister's sake. Jennifer hated his noisy motorcycle.

Griffin's effort to piss Jennifer off made me smile. I stood up and walked to the door. Heading downstairs, I slammed the bedroom door a little too hard and the glass figurine cabinet at the end of the hall shook. I froze and watched as an angel statuette teetered back and forth on its pedestal. *Shit. Please, don't break.*

"Jillian? What are you doing?" Jennifer yelled from the kitchen. "You better not break anything!"

As soon as the angel righted itself, I sighed in relief. But a small part of me wished it had broken. It would have felt good to break something that was special to her. Lord knew she'd done her best to break me. I shook off that depressing thought and raced down the steps to see Griffin.

When I opened the front door, he was walking up the sidewalk with two little boys attached to each of his legs: my twin nephews and Griffin's preschool fan club presidents, Michael and Mitchell.

Every time I saw Griffin interact with the boys, I couldn't help but smile. The boys adored him.

I watched as they continued their slow migration to the porch. Michael and Mitchell's messy, white-blond curls bounced wildly with each step, as did Griffin's coal black waves, falling across his forehead. He stood in stark contrast to the little boys dangling at his feet. Their tiny bodies seemed to shrink next to Griffin's six-foot-four muscled frame.

"I see that your adoring fans have found you." I laughed, watching Griffin walk like a giant, stomping as hard as he could, the twins giggling hysterically and hanging on for dear life.

"Hey, Jillibean, you lose your helpers?" he asked, unfazed by the ambush.

"Yeah, right," I said, walking out front to join him. I wrapped my arms around his neck and squeezed. I took a deep breath, filling my lungs with the familiar scents of leather and wind. A combination that would always be uniquely *him*. "I'm so glad you're here," I sighed, relaxing into his embrace. I felt safe, like nothing could hurt me when I was in his arms.

Griffin's arms circled my waist. "That bad, huh?"

I slackened my grip and stepped back, giving him and the

squirming boys at his feet more room. "My sister's been especially vile today."

"When isn't she?" Griffin replied.

"Giddy up, Giff-in," Mitchell wailed, bouncing up and down.

"You about ready?" Griffin asked me, trying to remain upright while the boys pulled and tugged his legs in opposite directions.

"Not really. I've got one more box to pack and a bunch to load into my car. They're up in my room."

"Hear that, boys? Aunt Jillian needs help loading her boxes. Are you men ready to help?" he asked.

"Yeah!" they shouted in unison.

"Hang on tight!" Griffin yelled and started running the rest of the way up the sidewalk and onto the porch. "All right guys, this is where the ride ends. Time to get to work." Griffin shook Michael off of his left leg before he started shaking Mitchell off of his right. The boys rolled around on the porch and Griffin playfully stepped on their bellies with his ginormous boots. The boys were laughing so hard I wouldn't have been surprised to see their faces turning blue from oxygen deprivation.

Following them to the porch, I shook my head and smiled. Griffin held his hand out and I laced my fingers through his, thankful he was here.

"I'll get the trailer hitched up to your car and the stuff you have ready, I'll put in the backseat. You finish up that last box; we've got a long trip ahead of us." Griffin leaned in close and whispered the last part in my ear. "Plus, it'll be nice to say 'adios' to the Queen Bitch," he said, referring to my sister.

"Sounds like a plan." I winked. "Come on boys," I held the door open and waved them inside. "If you're outside without a grown-up, your mom will kill me." They both shot up from the porch and ran inside.

"Giff-in," Michael said, coming to a stop in the doorway. "Can we still help?"

Griffin tousled his hair. "You bet, little man. Let's go find those boxes." Griffin winked back at me and the three of them ran up the stairs.

I trailed behind the boys, knowing that I couldn't put off packing that "last box" any longer. When I got to my room, Griffin held a box in his hands, but it was low enough so that the boys thought they were helping to bear some of its weight. "Hey, slacker," I said to Griffin, bumping his shoulder with my fist. "You letting a couple of three-year-olds show you up?"

"These are not normal three-year-olds," Griffin said in a deep commercial-announcer voice. "These boys are the Amazing Barrett Brothers, able to lift boxes equal to their own body weight with the help of the Amazing Griffin."

I rolled my eyes at his ridiculousness, and smiled. "You better watch it there, 'Amazing Griffin', or I'll have to butter the doorway to get your ego to fit through."

Still speaking in a cheesy commercial voice, Griffin continued, "As swift as lightning, we will transport this box to the vehicle waiting downstairs. Do not fear, kind lady, the Amazing Barrett Brothers and the Amazing Griffin are here to help."

"Oh, Lord. I'm in trouble," I mumbled. And as swift as lightning (but really not), Griffin shuffled the boys out of the room and down the stairs.

I grabbed my last empty box and walked across the room to my dresser. I pulled open a drawer and removed a folded stack of yoga pants, tees, and dozens of clothing projects I'd made over the years. Shuffling on my knees from one drawer to the next, I emptied each of them until I came to the drawer I'd been dreading. The one on the top right-hand side.

The contents of this drawer had remained buried in darkness for almost five years. I was scared to open it, to shed light on the objects that reminded me of my past. I stared at the unassuming rectangular compartment, knowing what I had to do. I said a silent prayer for courage and pulled open the drawer.

Inside, the 5x7 picture frame still lay upside down on top of several other snapshots. I reached for the stack. The second my fingers touched the dusty frame I winced, as if expecting it to burst into flames and reduce me to a heap of ashes. Biting my lip, I grabbed the frame and forced myself to look.

There we were. Mom, Dad, and a miniature version of me. Tears burned my eyes. My lungs clenched in my chest and I forced myself to breathe as I threw the frame into the box with my yoga pants. I pulled out the rest of the photos and tossed them in before they had a chance to stab me through the heart as well.

Downstairs, I could hear the boys coming back inside and then footsteps on the stairs. Quickly, I folded the flaps of the box and pulled the packing tape off the dresser. With another screech, I sealed away all the bad memories of my childhood.

"Well, my help dumped me," Griffin said, coming back into my room alone. "Apparently, I'm not as cool as a toy car."

Before he could see my tears, I wiped my wet eyes with the back of my hand, sniffled, and plastered on a brave smile, then turned around. "There. Done," I proclaimed, standing up and kicking the box over to where the others sat.

"You okay?" Griffin asked, knowing me all too well.

"Yeah." I dusted my hands off on my jeans shorts. "Let's get this show on the road." I bent down to pick up a box, standing back up with a huge smile on my face. "I'm ready to get to college."

* * *

Griffin took the last box from my hand and shoved it into the backseat of my car. "I'll get my bike on the trailer, and then we'll be ready to hit the road." He wiped his upper arm across his sweaty forehead.

I looked into his dark eyes and smiled. "Thanks," I sighed.

"For what?" With a toss of his head, he pushed a few errant curls out of his eyes.

"For putting up with me." He could have easily gotten a plane ticket home, but he knew how much I hated airplanes. The thought of him getting on a plane made me physically ill.

He swung his arm around my neck, squeezing me with his strong arm. "Put up with you? I'd like to see you try and get rid of me."

With my head trapped in his viselike grip and my face pressed to his chest, I couldn't escape his intoxicating scent. Even though it was too hot for his beloved leather riding jacket, the faint smell still clung to him. That, coupled with the heady musk clinging to his sweat-dampened t-shirt, made my head swim with thoughts that were well beyond the realm of friendship.

I needed to refocus my thoughts, and I couldn't do that pressed up against him. I shivered and pulled away. Taking a step back, I cleared my throat. "I'm going to tell Jennifer we're leaving." I thumbed toward the house.

He scrutinized my face for a minute, then smirked. "Enjoy that. You've earned it."

I turned on my heel and let out a deep breath, trying desperately to rein in my inappropriate fantasies.

Months ago, our easygoing friendship had morphed into an awkward dance of fleeting glances, lingering touches, and an unspeakable amount of tension. I thought he'd felt it, too. The night of my high school graduation party, I went out on a limb and kissed him. When our lips met, every nerve ending in my body fired at once. Embers of lust burned deep inside me. I'd never felt anything like that before. The thought of being intimate with someone made me want to run to the nearest convent. But not with Griffin. When our bodies connected, I felt whole and alive in a way I'd never felt before.

Then he'd done what I'd least expected…he'd pushed me away. I'd searched his face for an explanation. He, more than anyone, knew what it had taken for me to put myself out there, and he'd pushed me away. Touting some bullshit about our timing being all wrong, that a long distance relationship wouldn't work, he insisted that I was nothing more than his friend. His rejection hurt worse than any of the cuts I'd inflicted upon myself in past years. But, he was my best friend;

I needed him far too much to have our relationship end badly and lose him forever. Regardless of his excuses, in retrospect, I was glad I wouldn't fall victim to his usual love-'em-and-leave-'em pattern. Griffin was never with one girl for more than a couple of months; then he was on to the next. That would have killed me. So I picked up what was left of my pride, buried my feelings, and vowed not to blur the lines of our friendship again.

Climbing the steps to the porch, I looked back at him before going into the house. Griffin had gone to work wheeling his bike onto the trailer. His biceps strained beneath the plain white tee he wore. I bit my bottom lip and cursed. "Damn it, Jillian. Stop torturing yourself." Groaning, I reached for the doorknob.

"Hey, Jennifer, we're leaving," I said, grabbing my car keys from the island in the middle of the kitchen. She sat at the kitchen table poring over cookbooks that helped her sneak vegetables into the twins' meals. Poor boys, they didn't stand a chance. Jennifer fought dirty…she always had.

"It's about time." She turned the page of her cookbook, not even bothering to lift her eyes from the page.

"What? No good-bye? This is it, the day you've been waiting for since I moved in. I thought you'd be at the door cheering."

Usually I was more reserved with my comments, but today I felt brave. Maybe moving to Rhode Island and going to design school gave me the extra backbone I'd lacked for the last twelve years. Or maybe it was just the fact that I didn't have to face her any longer. By the look on Jennifer's face, my mouthy comments surprised her as well. She stood up from the table, tucked a piece of her shoulder-length blond hair behind her ear, and took a small step in my direction. Her mannerisms and the way she carried herself sparked a memory of my mother. As Jennifer got older, that happened more often, and a pang of sadness clenched my heart. Where I'd gotten Dad's lighter hair and pale complexion, Jennifer had Mom's coloring: dark blond hair, olive skin. But neither of us had got Mom's gorgeous blue eyes. The twins ended up with those.

Beyond the couple of features Jennifer shared with Mom, though, their similarities ended. When mom smiled, it was kind and inviting. Jennifer never smiled. She was rigid, harsh, and distant. Nothing like mom

Jennifer curled her spray-tanned arms around my back. I braced for the impact. Jennifer wasn't affectionate, especially with me, so I knew something hurtful was in store. I held perfectly still as she drew me close to her chest. The sweet, fruity scent of sweet pea blossoms—Jennifer's favorite perfume—invaded my senses. For such a light, cheery fragrance, it always managed to weigh heavy, giving me a headache.

Jennifer pressed her lips to my ear and whispered, "Such a shame Mom and Dad aren't here to see you off. I'm sure *they* would have told you good-bye." She slid her hands to my shoulders and placed a small kiss on my cheek.

And there it was. The dagger through my heart. Mom and Dad. She knew they were my kryptonite. For the second time in less than an hour, I felt acidic drops of guilt leaking from my heart and circulating through my body. But what burned more than the guilt was the fact that she was right. It *was* a shame they weren't here. And I had no one to blame but myself.

I held my breath while my eyes welled up with tears. *Not today, Jillian. You will not cry.* I refused to give her the satisfaction. I stood up taller, giving myself a good two inches on her, and swallowed the lump forming in my throat. She was not going to ruin this day. The day I'd worked so hard to achieve.

"Ready to go?" Griffin said, coming around the corner. "The boys are waiting by the door to say good-bye."

Jennifer stepped away from me and gave Griffin a disgusted once-over. "And yet another reason why I'm glad Jillian decided to go away to school," she said. "At least I get a respite from the white trash walking through my front door." Piercing me with an icy stare, she continued, "With the endless parade of women he flaunts in front of you, the tattoos, the music," she scowled, "I've never understood the hold he has on you, Jillian." She stifled a laugh. "Pathetic, if you ask me."

Griffin took a step in her direction. "Excuse me?" he growled, his expression darkening. I knew he wouldn't hurt her, but he was damn good at intimidating her. He wasn't the little boy who lived next door anymore. He'd grown up. With his deep voice and considerable size, he towered over her, the muscles in his arms flexing.

She shuffled backward. "Just go." With a dismissive flick of her wrist, she sat back down at the table.

"Yeah, that's what I thought, all bark and no bite." Griffin pulled on my arm. "Come on, Bean. You don't have to put up with her shit anymore."

I glanced back at Jennifer; she'd already gone back to her

broccoli-laced brownie recipe. Griffin was right; I wouldn't have to put up with her shit while I was away. But he was wrong about her bite. When he wasn't around to back her down, she relished the chance to sink her teeth into me. It hurt like hell when she latched on and wouldn't let go.

We walked down the hallway. Michael and Mitchell were waiting by the door. "I need big hugs, boys," I said, bending down and opening my arms wide. "This hug has to last me until December, so make it a good one." Both of them stepped into my embrace and I held onto them tightly. "You two be good for your mommy and daddy," I said.

"We will," they replied.

I let go and they smiled. "I love you both."

"Love you, Aunt Jillian," they said.

"Now, go find your mom. She's in the kitchen." Knowing the boys' penchant for sneaking out of the house, I wanted to be sure their mother had them corralled before Griffin and I left.

I stood back up and looked into Griffin's dark eyes. "I'm ready." I tossed him the keys.

"I'm the chauffeur, huh?" Griffin smirked, pulling his eyebrow up. He opened the door for me and I stepped out onto the porch.

"You get the first nine hours; I'll take the back side." This time he gave me a full smile. *What would I do without him?* On the porch, I froze. It finally hit me. What *would* I do without him? Sure, I wanted out of Jennifer's house, but at what expense? Couldn't I just go to the junior college like Griff and get my own apartment? Why had I made the decision to go to school eleven hundred miles away? How could I leave him—my best friend?

The lump in my throat had come back but I forced the words out anyway. "Griff…" I sounded like a damn croaking frog.

Griffin wrapped his arms around me. "Yeah?"

"Why am I doing this?"

"What do you mean? This is all you've talked about since you got the scholarship."

"I know." I sniffled. "But, I don't know if I can do this. We'll be so far apart."

"Uh-uh. Stop that right now. I am not about to let you throw away the opportunity of a lifetime just because we won't see each other as often. You're too talented for Glen Carbon, Illinois and you know it. Now go, get your ass in the car." With his hand, he popped me on the backside, just to get his point across.

I jumped, not expecting his hand on my ass. My heart skipped and my cheeks flushed. "Hey!" I swatted his hand away.

"Get in the car, Jillian."

Damn, I already miss him.

SEXUAL ASSAULT
SURVIVOR RESOURCES

According to campus sexual assault statics provided by the National Sexual Violence Resource Center, one in five women and one in sixteen men are sexually assaulted while in college, and more than ninety percent of sexual assault victims on college campuses do not report the assault.

If you are a survivor of sexual assault, or know someone who is, there is help out there. You are not alone.

RAINN (Rape, Abuse, and Incest National Network):
www.rainn.org
NSVRC (National Sexual Violence Resource Center):
www.nsvrc.org
SOAR (Speaking Out Against Rape):
www.soar99.org
National Sexual Assault Hotline: 800-656-HOPE

Acknowledgments

Writing a book isn't a solitary effort. Lots of talented people lend their hand and expertise in turning my words into beautiful books. Without them, I wouldn't make it.

Huge thank-yous to my awesome agent and her amazing team. Louise Fury and Lioness, without the two of you, I'd be so lost. I can't do this without you. Endless thanks!

My editor, Megha Parekh, and the Forever Yours team. I'm blessed to have such a wonderful editor. Thank you, Megha, for believing in my stories. Also, a special thank-you to Lexi Smail, for the early guidance on this story.

Amanda and Meredith. Thanks for letting me vent when I need to and for being just a text message away. I love you both. Drinks. Soon. Please.

Always, the biggest thanks to my Darlings. Guess what? I love you! I'm another book closer to being able to stay home with you. Thanks for letting Mom write, and being so patient when I have to put birthday presents on hold. I promise I'll paint your room when I'm done with this next book, Nenna!

Thank you to my Lord and Savior, Jesus Christ. Through Him, all things are possible.

And lastly, a heartfelt thank-you to all my readers. I love sharing stories with people and it means so much that you picked up my book to read. It's because of YOU that I have this gig! So thank you, thank you, thank you!

About the Author

Marie Meyer is a teacher who spends her days in the classroom and her nights writing heartfelt romances. She is a proud mommy and enjoys helping her oldest daughter train for the Special Olympics, making up silly stories with her youngest daughter, and bingeing on weeks of DVR'd television with her husband.

Learn more at:
MarieMeyerBook.com
Twitter @MarieMwrites
Facebook.com/MarieMeyerBooks
Instagram @MarieMWrites
Subscribe to Marie's Newsletter:
http://ow.ly/EB5T307b4sW

www.ingramcontent.com/pod-product-compliance
Ingram Content Group UK Ltd.
Pitfield, Milton Keynes, MK11 3LW, UK
UKHW022258280225
455674UK00001B/86